A *Hope* FOR HANNAH

JERRY S. EICHER

HARVEST HOUSE PUBLISHERS

EUGENE, OREGON

All Scripture quotations are taken from the King James Version of the Bible.

Cover by Garborg Design Works, Savage, Minnesota

Cover photo © Garborg Design Works

A HOPE FOR HANNAH
Copyright © 2010 by Jerry S. Eicher
Published by Harvest House Publishers
Eugene, Oregon 97402
www.harvesthousepublishers.com

Library of Congress Cataloging-in-Publication Data

Eicher, Jerry S.
    A hope for Hannah / Jerry Eicher.
        p. cm.
    ISBN 978-0-7369-3044-4 (pbk.)
    ISBN 978-0-7369-3969-0 (eBook)
    1. Married people—Fiction. 2. Amish—Montana—Fiction. I. Title.
PS3605.I34H365 2010
813'.6—dc22

2009047456

Printed in the United States of America

One

Hannah Byler awoke with a start. She sat up in bed and listened. The wind outside the small cabin stirred in the pine trees. The moon, already high in the sky when she and Jake went to bed, shone brightly through the log cabin window.

Beside her she heard Jake's deep, even breathing. She had grown accustomed to the comforting sound in the few short months since they'd been married. She lay back down on the pillow. Perhaps it was just her imagination. There was no sound—nothing to indicate something might be wrong.

But her heart beat faster—and fearfully. Something *was* wrong—but *what?*

"Jake," she whispered, her hand gently shaking his shoulder. "Jake, *vagh uff.*"

"What is it?" he asked groggily. He spoke louder than she wished he would at the moment.

"I don't know," she whispered again and hoped he would get the hint. "I think there's something outside."

Jake listened and sat up in bed with his arms braced on the mattress.

"I don't hear anything," he said, a little quieter this time. "There are all kinds of noises in the mountains at night."

"I think something is outside," she insisted.

They both were silent a moment, waiting and listening. Hannah half expected Jake to lower his head back to his pillow, tell her the fears were a bad dream, and go back to sleep. Instead he pushed back the covers and set his feet on the floor.

Just then a loud snuff outside the log wall stopped him. They both froze. Hannah didn't recognize the sound. No animal she knew ever made such a noise.

"It sounds like a pig," Jake said, his voice low. "What are pigs doing out here at nighttime?"

"It's not a pig," Hannah whispered back. No stray pig, even in the nighttime, could create such tension. "It's something else."

"But what?" Jake asked, the sound coming again, seemingly right against the log wall.

Hannah lay rigid, filled with an overpowering sense that something large and fierce stood outside.

"I'm going to go see what's out there." Jake had made up his mind, and Hannah made no objection.

Jake felt under the bed for his flashlight and then moved toward the door. Somehow Hannah found the courage to follow but stayed close to Jake.

Their steps made the wooden floor creak, the only sound to be heard.

Jake slowly pulled open the wooden front door, his flashlight piercing the darkness as he moved it slowly left and then right.

"Nothing here," he said quietly and then stepped outside.

Hannah looked around Jake toward the edge of the porch. "It was around the corner," she whispered.

Jake walked slowly toward the corner of the house, but Hannah stayed on the porch near the front door.

Jake stopped momentarily and then stepped around the corner of the house. Hannah could only see a low glow from the flashlight. In the distance by the light of the moon, the misty line of the Cabinet Mountains accented the utter ruggedness of this country. During the day, the sight still thrilled her, but now that same view loomed dangerously.

For the first time since they'd moved into the cabin after their wedding, Hannah wondered whether this place was a little too much for the two of them. Was a remote cabin, a mile off the main road and up this dirt path into the foothills of the Cabinet Mountains, really what she wanted?

"It's a bear!" Jake's voice came from around the corner. "Come take a look—quick—before it's gone."

"Gone," she whispered.

"Come see!" Jake's urgent voice came again.

Again Hannah found courage from somewhere. She stepped around the corner of the house and let her gaze follow the beam of Jake's flashlight, which now pierced the edge of the clearing around their cabin. At the end of the beam, a furry long-haired bear—as large as the one she'd seen once at the zoo—stood looking back at them, its head raised and sniffing the air.

"It's a grizzly," Jake said, excitement in his voice. "See its hump?"

"Then why are we out here?" Hannah asked, nearly overcome with the urge to run and desperate for solid walls between her and this huge creature.

"The men at the lumberyard said there aren't many around," Jake said in her ear. "Mostly black bears down in this area."

"Shouldn't we be inside?" she asked the question another way, pulling on his arm. "It's not going away."

"It will leave sooner if we stay in sight rather than go inside," he told her, his light playing on the creature whose head was still in the air and turned in their direction.

"Well, I'm going inside," she said, her courage now wholly depleted.

"It's going," Jake announced, and so she paused. They watched, fascinated, as the great creature bobbed its head and disappeared into the woods.

"It's gone," Jake said, a bit disappointed. "That was a grizzly."

They turned back to the cabin, Hannah following Jake's lead. As they stepped onto the porch, Hannah considered their front door. Suddenly the solid slat door—so bulky before—now looked thin, an unlikely protection against the hulk that had just disappeared into the dark tree line.

"What if it comes back?" she asked.

"It won't. It's just passing through," he assured her. "They don't like humans. They're wanderers anyway. It'll probably not come this way again—ever."

Not reassured, Hannah shut the door tightly behind them and pushed the latch firmly into place.

"Bears hang around," she told him. "This one could come back."

"Then we'll deal with it. Maybe the game warden can help. I doubt it will return, though." Jake was fast losing interest and ready for his bed again.

Jake snuggled under the covers, pulling them tight up to his chin. "These are cold nights," he commented. "Winter's just around the corner. I have to get some sleep."

Hannah agreed and pulled her own covers up tight. Jake's job on the logging crew involved hard manual labor that required a good night's sleep. She didn't begrudge him his desire for sleep.

"I sure hope it doesn't come back," she said finally.

"I doubt it will," he muttered, but Hannah could tell he was already nearly asleep.

To the sounds of Jake's breathing, she lay awake and unable to stop her thoughts. Home, where she had grown up in Indiana, now seemed far away, a hazy blur against the fast pace of the past few months.

What is Mom doing? she wondered. *No doubt she's comfortably asleep in their white two-story home, secure another night just like the night before and ready to face another day just like the day before.*

Thoughts of her earlier summers in Montana—tending to Aunt Betty's riding stable—pushed into her mind. This country had seemed so glorious then, and she had dreamed of her return.

The wedding had come first. She smiled in the darkness while she remembered the special day. After a flurry of letters and Jake's visits as often as he could, Betty got her wish for a wedding in Montana. Hannah's mother realized it was for the best. Because the plans for Hannah's wedding to Sam Knepp ended in a disaster back home in Indiana, Roy and Kathy decided they couldn't have the wedding there and possibly face that embarrassment again. Even Jake was in favor of the wedding in Montana—here where they had met.

Their hearts were in Montana now—close to the land and the small Amish community in the shadow of the Cabinet Mountains. But lately Hannah asked herself if living out here in the middle of nowhere was really for their best. Then she was thankful that at least she was with Jake—better here with Jake than anywhere else without him.

But as she lay in the darkness unable to sleep, she found herself wishing for close neighbors. She wished she could get up now and walk to the front door, knowing that someone else lived within calling distance—or at least within running distance if it came to that. Now, with a bear around, a night wanderer with mischief on his mind, there was nowhere to go. She shuddered.

She wondered if she could outrun a bear and reach a neighbor's house. She pictured herself lifting her skirt for greater speed. *How fast can bears run? Can they see well at night to scout out their prey?*

Hannah shivered in the darkness and listened to Jake's even breathing, wondering how he could sleep after what they had just seen. A grizzly! Jake had been sure it was a grizzly they'd heard sniffing around their cabin just outside their bedroom wall. Why was Jake not more alarmed? He had even seemed fascinated, as if it didn't bother him at all.

She had always thought she was the courageous one, the one who wanted adventure. After all, she had come out to Montana on her own that first summer. The mountains had fascinated her, drawn her in, and given her strength. But tonight those same mountains had turned on her and given her a bear for a gift—a *grizzly*. Even the stately pine trees, with their whispers that soothed her before, now seemed to talk of dark things she knew nothing about, things too awful to say out loud.

She turned in the bed, hoping she wouldn't disturb Jake. She thought of his job on the logging crew, really a job of last resort. Yes, at first it was a blessing because they needed the income, but now it had become more and more of a burden. Jake didn't complain, but the burden was apparent in the stoop of his shoulders when he came home at night. It revealed itself in his descriptions of how he operated the cutter, navigated the steep slopes, and worked with logs that rolled down the sides of the mountains. She also heard it in his descriptions of Mr. Wesley, his boss. She had met Mr. Wesley once when he had stopped by the house to interview Jake for the job. He operated the largest timber company in Libby, and his huge, burly form matched his position, nearly filling their cabin door that day. She had been too glad Jake had gotten the job to worry much about Mr. Wesley, but after he left she was glad she wouldn't see him every day.

Hannah shivered again, feeling the sharp chill that seeped into the log house—the same one that seemed so wonderful in summer. Winter would come soon to this strange land, and neither she nor Jake had ever been through one here.

Hannah willed herself to stop thinking. Now she knew for certain. There had been something she wanted to tell Jake but had wanted to wait until she was sure. Now on this night—the night the bear came— she was certain. The strangeness puzzled her. How could a bear's unexpected visit and this wonderful news have anything to do with each other?

Two

Hannah woke only a few hours later, just before dawn. She expected to be groggy after the night's events and was surprised at how clearheaded she was.

Quietly she slid out of bed to avoid waking Jake. He could have his last few minutes of sleep uninterrupted. Hannah walked out to the large front window of the cabin, its metal frame outlined by the last of the moon. She stood in front of the window and looked toward the east where the sun would soon come up.

Jake had said windows were a problem in log cabins. He was surprised one this size hadn't broken as the logs settled over the years. It was a blessing of the Lord—a sign perhaps—she had thought. It was one of the things that had persuaded her to accept Jake's decision to buy this remote cabin.

The loneliness of the area had excited her at the time. But this morning it felt empty, a void needing to be filled. She looked for signs of the first sun ray above the Cabinet Mountains but found only stars, their brightness still undimmed.

As beautiful as it was here, for some reason a wave of homesickness for Indiana swept over her. *Indiana*. Home. There her mother would be up at this time, perhaps even earlier. She would be making soft noises in the kitchen as she prepared breakfast. There, Hannah too would be awakened, not do the waking as she soon would for Jake.

The responsibilities of the day pressed in on her. Jake's breakfast needed to be made and later the last of the garden needed tending.

Was this how life was or would be? A simple life with its demands, settled down to spurts of joy with Jake and the danger of bears lurking in the night?

One other bright thought hung on the horizon, not unlike that vigorous twinkling star above the highest peak of the mountain range. Her mother and father were coming to visit before communion Sunday. They would see aunt Betty, her mother's sister, but Hannah knew the real reason they would be coming all those miles. They were coming to see her. Perhaps that was the cause of her sudden homesickness.

Maybe so, she decided, and if that was the case, her homesickness would soon go away. As for the grizzly's visit last night, no doubt it was as Jake said—an experience that wouldn't be repeated.

Hannah returned to the bedroom and gently shook Jake's shoulder. "Time to get up," she whispered.

He slowly opened his eyes. "You're up already? A little early, isn't it?"

"I just woke up. I couldn't sleep any longer. Probably the bear last night," she suggested as an explanation.

"Yeah, maybe," he agreed, sitting up. "There was a bear last night, wasn't there?"

"Yes, there certainly was."

"It was just passing through. Bears don't hang around for very long in this area," he said, apparently feeling the need to repeat his prediction from last night. "Is it looking like rain?"

"Not that I could tell," Hannah said.

"Mr. Wesley thought we might be in for a storm. Hopefully not. I really can't lose the wages."

"Are we short on money?" Hannah asked, a little surprised by the comment. The last time she had checked their bank account, it seemed fine.

"It's fine now," Jake said, "but winter's coming soon enough. There won't be as much work for me then, and the mortgage payment is a burden."

"Then you better get to work," Hannah said. "I'll get breakfast started." She impulsively reached out and ran her hand through Jake's hair. He was cute in the morning even when he talked about bothersome things like bears and his concerns about the money.

Jake smiled sheepishly, and Hannah kissed his forehead and turned to the kitchen. With a glance around, Hannah saw she needed to make a quick trip outside to the little springhouse, which stood about fifty feet from the cabin and served as their refrigerator. Jake had repaired the ramshackle little building soon after they moved in after the wedding.

With quick steps in the cool air, Hannah unlatched the door and took a handful of eggs from the wooden pine shelves. On her return she felt the chill of the morning air sink in deeper and wondered why she hadn't noticed the cold earlier. It was never this cold quite so soon back in Indiana.

Hannah thought about Jake's fear over the growing scarcity of work. Her dad had always taken care of money problems when she was growing up. Her mom had rarely spoken of money. Now she realized part of being married was dealing with money. She would have to do her part and help Jake out when she could. As hard as he worked for what seemed like meager wages, he deserved that much out of her.

Yet, wouldn't God take care of them no matter what happened? Jake would find work somehow, and if there wasn't work, they could skimp on the money they had. She had canned vegetables from the garden last summer, and there were still some potatoes and carrots in the ground, ready to be harvested. That would all help. And they could always save more, couldn't they? Most important of all, they loved each other. Surely that would see them through anything.

Hannah bent over her woodstove and lifted the lid to start the fire. Back home in Indiana, they had gas that lit the oven and burners at the turn of a knob. They were not, of course, like the electric ones the *Englishers* used, but they were certainly better than what she had here. Yet she was happy. Jake had purchased the old woodstove secondhand in Libby at a price they could afford. Gas would be more expensive. "Wood was cheap," Jake had said, and she agreed.

Jake kept a box of kindling wood in the corner of the kitchen. Hannah took a few pieces and assembled them just so in the stove—something she had learned by trial and error. She was now able to get a flame lit rather quickly. By the time Jake came into the kitchen minutes later, Hannah had the frying pan warmed and ready to cook.

"I'll take three eggs this morning," Jake said.

"Hungry are we?" Hannah asked, taking notice of the departure from his usual two.

"It's the bear's fault," he said, grinning.

Sometimes Hannah made him oatmeal, but Jake preferred his store-bought cornflakes. Hannah winced at the price when she made the purchase at the IGA in Libby but said nothing to Jake. If he wanted corn flakes, he should have them. The few times Hannah had gone with her mother to make the Saturday shopping trip into Nappanee, paying the bill had not been on her mind. Now things had changed.

Hannah finished the eggs and then joined Jake at the table. Together they paused in silence with bowed heads. Jake didn't pray out loud yet, which was fine with Hannah. That would come in time.

"Mom and Dad are coming the week before communion Sunday," Hannah reminded him.

He nodded, his mind apparently elsewhere. Hannah turned to look outside. The first ray of sun was sending streaks of light over the Cabinet Mountains. The glory of the sight, as the colors broke through, prompted her to abandon her plate and walk to the window.

"I'm not tired of it yet," she whispered more to herself than to Jake. Such sunrises did things for her, deep down things that drew her heart closer to God.

"It is beautiful," Jake agreed from the breakfast table. "It's even nicer when you're standing on the other side of the mountain looking east." Hannah knew he had often been able to enjoy that eastward view when he had worked as a fire spotter for the Forest Service before they were married.

Jake reached for the cornflake box.

Hannah, still in awe of the morning sight outside, knew there would be no better time than now to share her news. Without fanfare she simply said, "Jake, we're going to have a baby." Her heart beat rapidly as she watched Jake's face. He looked almost as beautiful as the sunrise, and now the news seemed to make him all the more the man she wanted to love the rest of her life.

The cornflakes box stopped in midair, a few flakes falling out and landing softly in his bowl. "You are?" He said, pausing and looking intently at her.

"Yes," she said, knowing her smile lit up her face. "*We* are."

"A *baby*," Jake said as he rose to his feet. He swept her up in his arms, and she laughed softly.

"Are you *sure?*"

"Yes," she said, "very sure."

For a moment neither of them said anything.

Finally Hannah said, "Just think, Jake, you will be a father."

"Yes," he said with a sudden soberness. "That comes with a great responsibility to raise the child right."

"But you want that responsibility, don't you? You *are* happy?" she asked.

"Oh, yes! But am I fit to be a father, that's the question."

"Yes, of course, you are. You'll make a great father." Then another thought occurred to her. "Is it the money?"

He didn't seem to flinch at the question. Rather he seemed to ponder long before he answered.

"Maybe partly. I know we don't have much, but many young parents are like that. I don't think a baby makes it worse. No," he said, shaking his head, "I worry about myself, I guess. It will be a heavy responsibility. I just didn't think it would happen this soon."

"Well, you're married," she said, her voice a tease. "What did you expect?"

He grinned. "I guess I was just thinking of you." Then another thought occurred to him. "Is there a midwife close by?"

"I'll have to ask Elizabeth. She'll know what the other women do."

"The other women," he said. He sat back down and poured milk onto his cornflakes. "Hannah, you really don't have any other women to talk to about this, do you?"

"Well, there's aunt Betty. And there are a couple of women in the church."

"But if your mother were here or—"

"Or if we were there?" Hannah finished his sentence. "Jake, have you ever thought of moving back East?" she asked, the memory of the earlier wave of homesickness returning to her. "With your work the way it is—the uncertainty and all—Dad could probably get you a job at the trailer factory pretty easily."

"I don't think so," he said, shaking his head. "I like it here."

"Well, I do too," she replied, agreeing, "but that bear last night was a little scary. Do you think we can make it here—on the logging income—with the baby coming?"

"I don't really know. This is all so new. A baby and all. But you'd want to move? You'd want to leave this community," he said, looking at her with a surprised expression, "and this country? Who wants to go back and live where it's flat?"

Hannah didn't know exactly how she felt. She loved the mountains too. But there were practical considerations to think about. And now there was the baby. True, she did miss her mother right now. "I'm just thinking that if we were to go back, it would be best to do it soon, well before the baby comes so we have time to get settled in."

Jake said nothing, but Hannah could tell he was unconvinced.

"We've never lived through a winter here either," she continued. "You could be out of work for a long time. What would we do? And the bear last night—maybe that was a sign to us."

This brought a chuckle, and Jake's spoon stopped halfway to his mouth. "Surely you've learned your lesson about believing in signs, haven't you?"

"I suppose," she said and couldn't keep from smiling too.

"A 'sign' almost got you married to that…Sam boy."

"That's a little mean. You don't have to rub it in," she said defensively. "I was just trying to find the will of God. Sure, I wasn't too good at it, but it turned out all right, didn't it?"

"Yes, it did." He looked directly into her eyes from across the table, and she reached for his hand under the table. "Plus I had my own troubles," he added, "with or without signs."

Hannah could see that it was best to say nothing more on the subject.

"You'll be happy here," Jake promised. "With the baby there will be plenty to do."

Jake was finishing his last spoonful of cereal when they heard a vehicle pull up outside.

"Someone's here," Hannah said.

"Who could be here at this time of day?" Jake asked.

Three

Jake opened the door and offered a hearty "Good morning, Mr. Brunson" to their neighbor from just up the hill.

Hannah heard the sounds of a reply but couldn't understand the words. What Mr. Brunson was doing out this early in the morning, she couldn't imagine. He lived farther up on their narrow dirt road in a small two-story home built by Mr. Brunson himself some time before Jake and Hannah moved in.

"No log cabin for me," he had told her once with a chuckle when she commented on how much she loved their little cabin. "I like Eastern living too well." Why Mr. Brunson liked that kind of living while he stayed in Montana, Hannah had wondered, but the neighbor had never offered more information. He would often drive by in his beat-up Ford pickup and wave to her if she was outside. Sometimes he'd stop in for vegetables from her garden. Though she had offered the produce for free, he had insisted on paying. He paid her generously, more than she could have gotten anywhere else had she wanted to sell the produce.

"Please come in," Jake said. "We were just finishing breakfast."

"I wouldn't want to disturb that," Mr. Brunson said, stepping inside and removing his trademark John Deere cap as he ran his hand through his thin white hair. "Just thought I'd come down and see how you folks were doing this morning."

"Fine, I guess," Jake said. "We had a visitor last night, though. A bear. I figure it was just passing through. I don't think there's any danger."

"It was a grizzly, wasn't it," Mr. Brunson said knowingly.

"I think so," Jake said. "We went outside after we heard noises. It looked like it had a hump on its back like grizzlies have."

"That's what I thought. I didn't get that good of a look, but it was big, that's for sure. One of my hogs is gone, and I'm sure the bear got it. I was just hoping it hadn't done any damage down here."

At the talk of the bear, Hannah got up to join the two men.

"Good morning," Mr. Brunson said.

"Good morning," she returned. "That bear sniffed around our bedroom wall. You don't suppose it will come back?"

"If my hog tasted good, which I'm sure it did," Mr. Brunson said with a laugh, "it wouldn't surprise me if it did. I'm going down to talk with the game warden first thing."

"Will they do something?" Jake asked. "Grizzlies usually don't come this far down. At least that's what the locals said."

"I haven't been local long enough to know." Mr. Brunson's face was grim again. "I just don't like bears walking around my backyard and picking up my pigs."

"Did you find the hog's remains?" Jake asked. "If you found the kill, the game official would have to do something about it, which would solve our problem of the bear coming back."

"I found what was left of it up in the woods, but don't count on the game warden doing anything about it," Mr. Brunson said.

"Well, enough about that bear," Hannah said with a shiver. "You haven't had breakfast yet, have you, Mr. Brunson?"

"No, I haven't had time. Too many bear troubles," Mr. Brunson said, chuckling.

"Come on in and sit down, then," Hannah said. "The stove is still warm. I'll fix you some eggs and toast."

"Oh, I couldn't be a bother. Really," Mr. Brunson was quick to say and moved toward the front door.

"We insist," Jake said. "Hannah is good at frying up eggs."

"I would guess so," Mr. Brunson said as he followed Jake to the kitchen and sat down in the chair he was offered.

Hannah stirred the fire, brought the flame to a hot burn, and placed the still warm pan back on the burner. She wondered whether she could add something else to the breakfast menu. There was sausage in the springhouse. Should she get a piece for Mr. Brunson to eat with his eggs?

Hannah decided that she should and that Jake wouldn't mind. "I'll be right back," she said, leaving Jake and Mr. Brunson talking about the best way to get the game officials to take action on the grizzly.

She took a knife and plate with her to the springhouse, found the sausage, and cut a piece off, adding it to her plate. From the boneless ham, she cut enough off for Jake's lunch sandwich.

Back in the house, Jake was up, pacing in front of the counter and busy preparing his lunch, something she usually did for him.

"I'll help you in just a bit," she told him as he looked for something in the cupboards.

"The cheese," he said.

"Third drawer down," she said, "on the left. I keep a small piece there."

The crinkle of plastic told her he had found it as she stood at the stove, browning the sausage in the hot pan. She then cracked the eggs and let them slip into the pan next to the sausage.

"I'm sorry about this," Mr. Brunson commented. "You really didn't have to fix me breakfast."

"I'm glad to. It's no problem," Hannah assured him. She kept an eye on the crackling pan while she gave Jake a hand with his ham sandwich and made sure he saw the tomato and knife she slipped into the lunch bucket. It surprised her to learn how much men could miss and never see.

"Put a slice of tomato on it before you eat it," she whispered.

He nodded and grinned. They had already had the conversation before.

"Well, I really have to go," Jake said as he snapped his lunch bucket shut and saw that Hannah's attention had returned to the breakfast pan. "My ride's due soon."

"You do get out early," Mr. Brunson commented. "You like logging, Jake?"

"It's work," Jake admitted grudgingly. "I liked my forestry job much better."

"Why aren't you doing it, then?" Mr. Brunson asked.

"For one thing, it's too far to drive every day. Plus you have to live up in the cabin, and I don't think they take married couples."

"No, I don't think they do," Mr. Brunson agreed.

"Breakfast," Hannah announced, setting the plate of eggs and sausage in front of Mr. Brunson. Moments before, she had toasted a piece of bread freehand over the fire.

Mr. Brunson didn't fail to notice the results. "Right nice bread toasting there. I'll have to learn to do that myself."

"It doesn't work very well on electric stoves," Hannah said, though she was not sure what kind of appliances Mr. Brunson had.

"I have gas," he said, grinning. "Think it would taste the same?"

"That's how we always toasted our bread at home. It tastes just the same," Hannah said, glad Mr. Brunson approved. There had been times when she had failed miserably, and the bread had turned to near cinder.

"I'm gone." Jake stood in the kitchen door with his lunch pail. "See you tonight, dear."

"Be careful," Hannah said. She would have kissed him, but Mr. Brunson was there.

"Thanks for asking me to breakfast," Mr. Brunson said, grinning broadly, his fork poised above his plate and ready to dig in.

"You're welcome," Jake said, already at the open front door. The latch fell into place behind him after he stepped outside.

Hannah sat down at the kitchen table as Mr. Brunson began to eat without prayer. Her astonishment must have shown because he stopped, took a look at her face, and said sheepishly, "I'm sorry. I guess I've been uncivilized too long."

"Oh, I didn't mean to make you uncomfortable," she said quickly, embarrassed to have been so obviously shocked. The surprise was just so sudden.

"I used to pray," Mr. Brunson said. "I just needed a reminder." He paused with bowed head, his lips moving slowly. He gave her a crooked smile when he was done.

"How long have you lived here?" Hannah asked in an attempt to put him at ease.

"Not long. A couple of years," he said.

"From the East?" she asked.

"Yep—Boston. Big city. I needed some country, I guess."

"My mom and dad are coming to visit soon," she volunteered, leading up to a question that had bothered her. "I never see any visitors at your place."

"I guess you don't," he said and ran his hand over his head. "I don't have many relatives to come out and visit me."

As he finished his eggs, Hannah noticed the sausage was already gone. She wished she had cooked him two pieces.

"I'm an old man," Mr. Brunson offered, interrupting her thoughts.

"Surely you have family," she said, her voice confident. Everyone had family. "They never come to visit?"

"One brother," he said. "He lives back East. He's about as old as I am. Doubt if he wants to travel much."

"No wife?" she asked. "Surely you married." She considered she was being too bold, but the question was out before she could take it back.

"Well," he began, keeping his eyes on the now empty breakfast plate, "my brother is married. He has two children, but they are in business. They don't have much interest in me or Montana." Mr. Brunson gave her a wry smile.

Referring to the brother's children and observing something in the faraway and pained look in his eyes, she asked, "Boy? Girl?"

"Two…I mean, one each," he said. "One boy, one girl."

"Are your parents gone?" she asked as she got up and took his plate to the sink.

"I'm pretty old," Mr. Brunson said as he laughed. "They died a long time ago. I was young—still in my twenties. Mom followed a year after Dad. They were great people."

"I'm sure they were," Hannah said, touched by Mr. Brunson's emotion. "I wouldn't know what to do with both my parents gone."

"I suppose not," Mr. Brunson agreed. "Just be thankful for what you have while you have it. It could all be gone so quickly." Something in his voice made Hannah want to ask more, but she had already pried too much. She simply said, "God has been good to us. That's what Dad always says."

"He's a wise man," Mr. Brunson said. "Now, thanks for the breakfast. I must be going. Tell Jake his wife is a great cook."

"You're welcome," Hannah said, glad for the praise. Then she said, "Mr. Brunson, maybe you could come for supper some night when Mom and Dad are here."

"Oh," he said, seeming genuinely surprised, "I wouldn't want to be a bother."

"You wouldn't be," she assured him. "Dad would enjoy meeting you."

"Well," he answered, pausing slightly. With a smile he continued and said, "Maybe I will."

"I'll send Jake up, then—when I know which night. If you can't come that night, maybe some other."

Mr. Brunson found his John Deere cap by the front door and fumbled slightly as he put it on. Hannah glanced up and noticed there was the hint of moisture in his eyes as he left.

Hannah walked back to the kitchen and began to wash the breakfast plates. Out the window, the solid light of the risen sun was showcasing the slopes of the Cabinet Mountains.

Four

Hannah began the work she had planned for the day. She started with the ears of corn that needed to be harvested from the garden and carried to the front yard. She estimated how much corn she could can that day and plucked enough ears for what she hoped would do the job.

She tried to remember how her mother knew the right amount and wished she could consult her now, but that wasn't possible. There was aunt Betty, but Hannah discarded that thought quickly. It was simply not practical because of the distance involved and the time such a buggy trip would take. No, she was on her own, and she'd just have to figure it out by herself.

After adding wood to the kitchen stove, Hannah began husking the corn in the yard. She considered how difficult managing a wood stove could be compared to the gas range she was used to at home. But this was her home now, and she realized Montana was rougher than Indiana. Hannah was determined to make the best of things and knew being with Jake was worth whatever extra effort she'd have to make.

As she worked the corn, she reminded herself of how *Da Hah* had brought both her and Jake here separately just so they could meet, eventually fall in love, and marry. The memory warmed her heart greatly and filled her with relief, knowing she had been spared from marrying Sam Knepp. It was, no doubt, a relief to Sam too. She had heard that Sam had married her old friend, Annie. So it was Annie, and not Hannah, who was now comfortably settled and married in Indiana. True, Annie might be hard at work on the farm Sam's father had given him, but she was safe from bears. Hannah smiled. And Annie, no doubt had a gas range.

She and Jake had been invited to Sam's wedding. After some serious deliberating about how it would look, they went to the wedding, and nothing was said to anyone. It was almost as if that horrible day had already become ancient history to the people she knew. And that was good. Good for her and good for Sam and Annie. Everything had worked out so well. Annie had looked radiant that day, and Sam was all shiny in his new black suit with his hair slicked down over his forehead. Sam had blushed as the bishop married them. He surely loved Annie, and for that she was glad.

But she wasn't going to think about that anymore. This was where she wanted to be and where she belonged—with Jake. And now a baby was growing inside her. For some reason she was already thinking of the baby as a boy. It seemed as natural to her as breathing. Jake needed a boy. Not that he had ever mentioned it before, but still she wanted to give him a boy. She wanted his firstborn to be the delight of his eye, the pleasure of his heart. This child would be a joy for both of them. Of that she was certain.

Hannah took a break from her husking and went in to check the fire. Although it still burned steadily, the flames seemed low and so she added another piece of wood. She then returned to her husking, but this time she sat in a chair as she pulled off the husks and threw them in a pile. Jake would carry them to the garden for mulch when he came home. Jake was like that, always willing to help her with such things even when he came in from work exhausted.

She must be careful, Hannah told herself, not to impose on Jake too much. This was especially true with the baby on the way and the extra work that needed to be done. Her mother had once mentioned something to that effect about her father, but Hannah couldn't remember the exact reasons her mother had given. She just knew she didn't want Jake to be overburdened. He already had enough to do.

When she had finished husking the corn, she left the ears lying on the ground and returned to the kitchen. She pulled her pressure cooker off the bottom shelf of the cabinet and carefully added the correct amount of water. Trying to remember what her mother had done next, Hannah tapped the pressure gauge to check it. Sure enough, the little black needle bounced in response to her taps.

She had purchased the cooker at a garage sale in Libby soon after she and Jake were married. Surprisingly, she had not received one among the wedding gifts. She remembered, with regret, receiving a cooker for her presumed wedding to Sam, but after the wedding was cancelled, Kathy had insisted they return the gifts.

She tapped the round gauge again and got another little bounce out of the needle. Surely it was fine. It had given her no problems all summer. Still, the idea of a malfunctioning gauge on a pressure cooker was not a trifle. That would be one embarrassment she could do without.

"You'll be a good boy," she told the cooker, "and do your job just right." She then laughed at herself and said aloud, "I do need a baby. I'm talking to the kitchen pots!"

Hannah left the control knob in the off position and pushed the cooker to the side of the stove. She then returned to the yard to slice the corn from the cobs. When she had enough for one sizeable batch, she went back to the kitchen and filled the jars, pleased to find there was still corn left over.

She slipped the filled jars into the cooker and moved it back onto the stove. Hopefully she could cut enough corn for a second batch before the cooker whistled. Quickly she went back to the pile of corn in the yard and sliced away, glad this job would soon be done.

When Hannah stepped back into the kitchen, she was disappointed to find that the fire was lower than it should be and the water wasn't boiling yet. After searching for the cause, she saw that the ash pan was full. She would have to remove the sliding tray, carry the pile of ashes to the edge of the woods, and dump it.

Jake, because of his fire spotting days, had frequently warned her of the danger of a fire starting from ashes. Back home in Indiana, there was no stove to make fires in and few woods to burn up. Here, though, there was great danger, and so Jake had cleared a little area by the side of the garden to dispose of ashes safely.

Usually Hannah would have dumped the ashes without much thought, but this morning everything seemed to need extra care. With the tip of the pan, she spread the pile thin because she knew that thinly spread ashes would cool faster.

When she returned to the kitchen, she found the fire burning much better. She added extra wood to keep it hot just in case.

She heard the whistle of the cooker none too soon, sounding only moments after she had packed the second batch of corn into the jars. After she checked the strength of the fire again, Hannah set the control knob on the cooker. The pressure was steady, and so she left the kitchen to check the garden and plan the rest of her day.

There were still a few tomatoes left on the vines. She walked the row to be sure of the number, counting enough to easily make another batch of canned tomatoes. That would come in handy this winter since both she and Jake enjoyed tomato soup.

She had delightful visions of the two of them—soon to be three, she reminded herself—sitting in the cabin, sipping tomato soup, and eating popcorn in the evenings while the snow piled up thick outside. When, then, should she tackle the job? Today yet? Hannah decided the task would be a little too much. She glanced up to find the clearness of the sky reassuring. With no rain in sight, the tomatoes could wait until tomorrow.

She returned to the kitchen to check on the cooker. One look at the gauge assured her all was well. Five more degrees and she could slide it off the hot part of the stove. She added another piece of wood to keep the flame steady.

Because she didn't want to go far and didn't want to wait in the kitchen, Hannah stepped into the living room where two of Jake's shirts needed mending. She had draped them over the couch yesterday. From her mother's instruction, she knew this was not a good practice and she should keep such things in the sewing room. But here she had no sewing room and little space to keep mending projects.

With her mother coming to visit, perhaps she should think of someplace else to put the mending. But her mother was sensitive, she reminded herself, and would understand how little space they had. For that Hannah was thankful.

Just as she was considering all this, the unimaginable happened. From the kitchen Hannah heard the unmistakable sound of the pressure cooker blowing. The awful sound shook through her body. Soon after she was filled with horror and shame for allowing such a thing to happen. Hannah Byler, the just lately minted Hannah Byler, had blown up her pressure cooker.

Her first thought, as she turned toward the kitchen, was, *This is not something I can hide under the proverbial rug. Everyone is going to find out about this!* The emotion of what had just happened swept over her. Few Amish women blew up their cookers, and those who did were not forgotten quickly.

Some would, no doubt, tell her to just be thankful she wasn't in the kitchen at the time, but at the moment, she wished—at least partly— she had been. The thought that a few small burns would help stir up some sympathy flashed through her mind. But no, she had come out unscathed.

Her first look into the kitchen quickly caused her to forget her lack of injury. The lid to the cooker lay mangled on the floor, and the ceiling now had a deep gash in it. Even worse, corn and pieces of glass were splattered on every wall except the one in the living room furthest from the stove. Great clouds of steam rose from the stove top where much of the spilled water had landed. If she had been in the room, she was certain the result would have been more than a few burns.

Hannah's next thought was of Jake and how he would come home that night to a wife who had blown her kitchen to pieces. It wasn't as if he didn't have enough to do already. She felt an urge to rush in and clean up—to sweep up the pieces of glass, to pull the corn off the rough logs, to wipe away the water, and to make it look as if this had never happened. Instead, she gave way to feelings of a great weariness. Her legs didn't want to work. She returned to the living room, ignored the mended shirts draped across the back of the couch, sat down, and burst into tears.

Five

Hannah spent the rest of the morning cleaning the kitchen. The immensity of the task was soon evident—not just by the corn and glass pieces stuck to the walls but by the damage from the metal fragments.

One of the upper cabinet doors was broken, and Jake would have to fix it. After she wiped the others off, she discovered that they were water-stained but seemed to be okay. She figured no one could fix the gash in the ceiling. *It will remain there forever as a reminder for all the world to see,* she thought despairingly, *of the young woman who blew up her pressure cooker.*

As she washed the corn off the walls, she noticed it left little yellow stains behind. Because of that she decided to let it dry out first and then sweep it off the walls with her broom. Hannah glared at the old stove, the handiest thing to blame other than herself. She could find no damage whatsoever to its hardy exterior.

"You'd live forever, you mean thing," she told it.

She didn't know what to do about the last batch of corn. Hannah no longer had a pressure cooker to work with. To throw the corn away was simply out of the question, and so that left only one course of action.

Too anxious to feel hunger, even though lunch time had arrived, she hitched their young driving horse, Mosey, to the buggy and left. Food was not important at the moment.

The drive to Betty's seemed to take forever. Hannah urged Mosey to move faster, but he protested by swishing his tail back and forth. She slapped the lines again. Mosey increased his speed momentarily and then lapsed back into a slow, steady gait. So this was how he got his name, she thought as she settled back in her seat.

Finally Hannah saw the sign that read "Horseback Riding," remembering it from her days when she ran her aunt's riding stable. As Hannah tied Mosey to the hitching rail, Betty came out of the kitchen door, her work apron around her waist.

"What's brought you around at this time of day? My, it's sure nice weather for this time of the year."

The sound of her aunt's voice pushed Hannah where she didn't want to go, and the tears threatened again. "I wondered if I could borrow your pressure cooker," she managed.

"Why, dear?" Betty asked as she searched Hannah's face. "You have one yourself. Now don't you tell me you're wanting to use two cookers at the same time with that old stove of yours. You're liable to blow the old thing up working it that hard. Didn't your mom ever tell you that?"

The blowing up remark brought the flood of tears. "I already blew up the cooker," Hannah replied, choking out the words.

"You blew up the cooker? Oh, my word!" Betty clucked. "Just blew it up? Why? Was the gauge stuck? Surely that's what it was. Did you check it? You weren't in the kitchen at the time, were you?"

"No, I was in the living room. I don't know what I did," Hannah said. "I tapped the gauge like usual. It's an old cooker, of course, but the needle bounced."

"Then no one can blame you. Not for a minute!" Betty said, consoling her niece.

"Now I'll be known as the girl who blew up her cooker," Hannah cried. "Mom will think I'm completely careless."

"Now, now," Betty said, still trying to comfort her, although there was now a slight chuckle in her voice.

"It's not funny," Hannah said indignantly.

"No, I suppose not," Betty agreed. "But really, you ought to be thankful. You are a girl who can blow up her cooker and yet not have a single scratch or burn. Look on the bright side of things. You're strong. You survived walking out on your own wedding. But now look at you.

Married already and well settled in. You have nothing to worry about. Everything will be just fine, but I suppose you need help cleaning up?"

"No. I'm already done." Hannah said, wiping a tear.

"So you need a cooker, and I'm canning myself." Betty got back to business.

"Oh," Hannah was quick to say, "I didn't know. I can ask Elizabeth. Maybe I can borrow hers."

"That's farther in the other direction," Betty said. "I couldn't let you do that. Now, wait a minute. I believe my old cooker is still in the basement."

"Your old one?" The horror crept into Hannah's voice.

Betty laughed again. "Don't worry. This one won't blow. It's been faithful for all these years. The only reason I got a new one was so I'd have two at the same time. Today, though, I'm only using the one."

"Are you sure?" Hannah wasn't entirely convinced.

"You can't blow two in one day," Betty assured her.

To which Hannah said, her voice sarcastic, "Ha. To me anything could happen right now. At least it feels that way. There was a grizzly at our place last night. Mr. Brunson came down this morning. The grizzly got his pig."

"My, my, you are having your troubles. Bears aren't such a big thing around here, though, especially on the main roads. They usually don't bother people, but it does happen. This is Montana, after all. You'll get used to it. If it bothers you too much, the game warden will probably have the bear moved."

"That's what Jake and Mr. Brunson want to look into."

"See there? It'll be okay. Now the cooker. Just give me a minute, and I'll dig it out of the basement."

Hannah waited by the buggy, and Betty soon came back as promised and placed the cooker behind the buggy seat.

"I'll bring the cooker back as soon as I can," Hannah said as she climbed into the buggy. Mosey wearily lifted his head to look back at her as if checking to see if he needed to move again.

"Don't worry," Betty said. "Keep it till you're done. I'll only need one for the rest of the season."

"Maybe Jake can buy me a new one."

"That might be a good idea," Betty said with a chuckle and stepped back as Hannah convinced Mosey to move with a shake of the lines.

On the way home, Hannah wondered if she should have told her aunt about the baby. But no, she couldn't bear the thought of telling Betty before she told her own mother. If it ever got back to her mother, knowing she wasn't the first to know might hurt her feelings.

Jake found Hannah in tears that evening when he came into the house swinging his lunch pail in his hand. Hannah was still at work in the kitchen, lifting the last of the canned corn from Betty's used cooker. As she told Jake about her day and showed him the damaged ceiling and cabinet doors, he expressed surprise that she had also managed to prepare a small casserole for their supper.

"You shouldn't have made supper with all that going on," he told her.

"Then what would we have eaten? You have to eat. I can't let you starve. What kind of wife would I be?"

"Still a very good one," he assured her. "Now, what needs to be done around here? It looks like you've cleaned up already. Let me take the cooker out and dump the water."

"It can go down the drain," Hannah said. "The corn husks still need to be picked up. They're in the yard, and now it's almost dark. It can wait."

"No, I can still do it," he said as he lifted the warm cooker from the stove and carefully poured the hot water down the drain.

"Do you think I'm an awful cook?" she asked hesitantly. "I just blew up my kitchen."

"Of course not," he said without even a pause. Hannah noticed and loved him for that statement. "Grandma Byler blew hers up years ago," he continued, "and got some nasty burns. We can be real thankful nothing liked that happened to you. What if you had been in the kitchen?" She was certain his eyes were full of genuine concern. "It does happen. Grandma has been a family story for years."

"That's just what I was afraid of," Hannah said with renewed cries. "That would be one way to get famous, I guess." His grin brightened her face a bit. "Maybe I'd better get those husks in the garden before dark."

When Jake came back, Hannah had the supper plates set out. The casserole and simple additions of bread, jam, butter, and corn were set in the middle of the table.

"I'm sorry there's no cake or something sweet," she said as they sat at the table. "I guess we have to live on love."

"One could live a long time on that," he said, still grinning, "but this is plenty. Let's pray before I starve."

When he had finished and Hannah had pushed the casserole in his direction, Jake said, "Well, Mr. Wesley said logging jobs this winter might be hard to come by."

"What does that mean?" she asked.

"He said that maybe we should best be looking for other jobs during the winter. If his work is cut back, so is mine," Jake said with a catch in his voice.

Hannah gasped as Jake passed the casserole back. The smell stirred her hunger, forgotten for so long in the hurry of the day. Jake's words didn't take immediate effect, as if she heard them from a great distance. Then they soaked in slowly.

"But if you lose your job, what will we do?" she asked.

"I guess we must trust God," Jake said without much confidence in his voice.

That's just what Father would say, Hannah thought, *yet it sounds so strange coming from such a young man. Is this how young married life is for all couples? Surely not! But how do we get through this?*

"I guess we must," she said with a question in her voice. Then she touched his arm and looked for some source of comfort in his eyes. They were as deep and wonderful as ever—and Hannah found her comfort. She wanted to climb inside and hide from the world in a place with Jake where all was safe and secure.

"Maybe I can find something else," Jake was saying, "although it is a rough time to be looking for work."

"Do you think it's a bad sign?" Hannah asked.

"What?" he asked.

"Me—blowing up the kitchen today. And the grizzly. Are things going to be hard for us? And what about the baby?"

Jake's face darkened momentarily, but then he collected himself. "There's always a way out. Somewhere. Hasn't God been good to us so far?" Jake gave her a thin smile. "You didn't marry Sam, remember? We have each other and now a new life coming. *Ours.* God is good and will always be."

"I didn't know it would be like this, though." Her voice was hushed. "Is it like this for everyone?"

"I don't know." He found her eyes. "I've not been here before, but God will take care of us. We have to know that."

She saw his tenderness and let her own face soften. "I guess you're right. I'm just afraid sometimes."

"I think everyone is," he assured her.

That night in bed, with the moon shining in through the window, they awakened once again to the sounds of the grizzly outside.

"Just let it be," Jake whispered in the darkness. "Maybe the game warden will do something about this now."

Hannah said nothing, but she found and held Jake's hand until it was quiet outside.

Six

The next morning Hannah saw Jake off as usual before the sun was up. She watched him walk to the blacktop road for his ride. At breakfast she had again voiced her thought that if Jake were to lose his job, they should consider a move back East.

"No," Jake said, "not yet anyway. We shouldn't make any fast decisions." After a moment he asked, "Hannah, this isn't about that bear, is it?"

"Maybe. Partly. But your job too."

Gently but firmly Jake took charge of her fears, "It'll be okay with the bear. Mr. Brunson will likely go to the game warden especially because it came back. If not, maybe I can run down and report the matter myself."

Hannah thought their problem was more complicated than that and sighed. The bear's appearance might have marked the start of their troubles—or so it seemed to her—but matters now looked bigger than just the bear.

True to Jake's hope, Mr. Brunson drove his truck up the driveway and parked it in front of the house just as the sun rose. The first rays of light flooded across the yard. To save Mr. Brunson the walk to the house, Hannah went out to meet him in the yard. He saw her approach, waved, and waited in his truck.

"Nice of you to come out," he said when she was within earshot. "Old bones hurt in the morning."

"Jake was hoping you would stop by," she said.

"Bear back?" he guessed.

Hannah nodded. "We heard it again. I don't know what it's after, though. Nothing is missing this morning. Jake was hoping you could tell the game warden about it. Maybe today? I don't think I like a bear wandering around."

"That's where I'm going now," Mr. Brunson said, his tone emphatic. "I took a picture of the eaten hog—or his remains, anyway—to prove the matter. I'm going right into town and see what can be done. Maybe we can get some action tonight. If not—" Mr. Brunson's face darkened again, and then he smiled when he saw Hannah watching him intently. "No, I suppose not. I better not shoot the thing myself. The law's kind of hard about such things."

"Don't be giving Jake any ideas," Hannah said. She could just see Jake standing in the cold night air, aiming his hunting rifle into the darkness while the enraged bear grabbed for him.

"We wouldn't want to do that," Mr. Brunson assured her. "There's a considerable fine associated with the penalty."

"That we couldn't afford," she said with certainty. "This bear could be quite a problem, it seems."

"That's what the law is for in this country—one would hope," Mr. Brunson said, his face grim. "Let me see what I can get done today. I'll try to stop by after Jake gets home. I might be able to give you both some good news."

After Mr. Brunson left, Hannah wasn't sure whether to be relieved or not. From what he said, the game warden would soon do something about the bear, and that would eliminate one of her reasons for moving back East. She was surprised at the twinge of joy she felt. Apparently she didn't want to move as intensely as she had thought. And it was true—a move back to Indiana would uproot their lives here, which had just begun to take firm hold.

And Jake so wanted to stay here. If that was what Jake wanted, then she had better support him, whatever her own inclinations might be.

"So, sweet Montana, be my sunshine," she said out loud to the heavens, glancing up at the last redness of the sunrise before she walked back into the house. Hannah smiled at her own words and then hummed them with a tune of her own, thankful no one else was around. It was enough that she enjoyed the little tune herself. "Sweet Montana, come on now. Take your bears away. Back to the mountains they must go, so we can stay. Yeah, yeah, yeah, that's what I say."

Back in the kitchen, Betty's pressure cooker still sat on the back corner of the counter, where she had left it after yesterday's corn canning. Hannah eyed the cooker warily, her nerves still raw, the memories still vivid. *Should I or should I not take on the tomatoes today?*

Jake hadn't said anything about the weather, which he usually did if a major rain was moving in. He liked to pass on the reports his boss gave him. *Perhaps he's distracted,* Hannah thought. *I've given him plenty to be distracted about by sharing the news of the baby and blowing up the kitchen.* She winced at the thought.

Hannah went back outside and took another look at the tomatoes. Judging the coming weather by the color of the sunrise, she decided they had to be done today, whatever her feelings about the cooker. Her mom had often moved up their scheduled wash day in response to a red sunrise. And this sunrise certainly qualified as red.

Hannah got her bowls from the pantry and headed for the garden. She soon abandoned her effort to calculate how much she needed for two batches of tomato juice and simply picked what was there. The ripe tomatoes were going to be wasted if she didn't.

Halfway down the row, the tomatoes suddenly ceased. Puzzled, she moved on and found a tomato here and there but not nearly as many as there should be. Her suspicions roused, she found evidence in the moistened ground right there where she stood—bear prints with the distinct claw marks in front and wider indentations on the sides and back.

A shiver ran up Hannah's back. *The bear had been right here! Its huge furry body had lumbered down this row of tomatoes, sampling them as it went.*

She gathered courage to check further down the row, all the time wondering if the bear was still around. The protection of the log cabin seemed far away. She held panic at bay, though, figuring grizzlies had enough sense not to come out in the daylight.

The tomatoes reappeared a few plants down, and Hannah finished filling the bowl. She decided she had enough to can and returned to the front yard, where she set up the strainer and began to work.

It was a messy job. The tomato juice splashed on her apron no matter how carefully she worked. Still, she continued to mash the tomatoes through the strainer, adding salt from memory to the mixture.

When the jars were filled, she carefully set them in the cooker. She tightened the lid and slid the cooker onto the hot part of the stove. With skepticism she eyed the gauge, which seemed to be working, and then stepped out of the kitchen while the cooker heated up. Glancing in every few minutes, she watched the pressure rise to eleven pounds. She then quickly slid the cooker off the hot area.

For the next fifteen minutes, she made quick trips back and forth between the kitchen door and the stove, rushing in and out to make sure the pressure stayed at eleven pounds. Finally, with a deep sigh of relief, she moved the cooker completely off the heat. The point of danger over, Hannah stayed in the kitchen. When the pressure had gone down completely, she undid the top with a gentle pop, and a small cloud of steam rose.

While the cans cooled on the kitchen table, she repeated the process and still had tomatoes left. Hannah wanted to quit now but decided instead to press on. She figured Jake would understand if they had only leftover casserole for supper.

When he got home, Jake found her happy with her accomplishments. Rows of red tomato juice jars lined the kitchen counter behind her. Every so often a jar lid would pop softly as it sealed. Soon the whole batch would be sealed and ready to store.

"Our winter stash," she told Jake as she let her joy wash away her weariness.

"You must have canned all day," he said, obviously impressed. "Why didn't you take a break from yesterday?"

"I think it might rain tomorrow. I didn't want to be searching for wet tomatoes in the mud."

"It will rain," Jake said, surprised. "The boss said so. But how did you know?"

"The sunrise was red."

"I guess it was," he said. "I didn't notice. We're not even going to work tomorrow. That's how certain Mr. Wesley is."

"So what will you do tomorrow, then?"

"Maybe I can talk to the game warden about the bear."

"Good news." Hannah gave him a smile and a quick kiss. "Mr. Brunson stopped by this morning. He was going to talk to the warden today. He took a picture of what the bear did to his hog and wanted to show it to the warden."

"That is good news," Jake said as he sat down at the kitchen table. Knowing he'd want supper soon, she gave him another kiss, pulled the wrapper off the leftover casserole, and then opened the oven door.

"Hope you're happy with leftovers."

"That's fine," he said, grinning. "A man could almost live on kisses. Did Mr. Brunson say if he'd let us know what he found out?"

"He said he'd stop by when you were home if he had news."

"Hopefully it's good news. Guess I'll wash up," Jake said and disappeared in the direction of their small bathroom, its water flow, like that of the kitchen, fed by the pressure from the spring.

Moments later Hannah heard Jake pump air into the gas lantern they used for evening light. To keep expenses down, they used gas only in the evening and only in the living room. The kerosene lamps were used otherwise. That had been Hannah's idea, but she doubted whether it actually saved that much.

Jake never complained, though. He seemed to like the routine. He came in and hung the lantern on the center ceiling nail of the living room before he sat down to read. In the kitchen, Hannah continued to set the table by the light of the kerosene lamp.

Minutes later she called out, "It's ready," and Jake came quickly to the table.

The weariness of the day swept over her again as they bowed their heads to pray.

After supper Mr. Brunson stopped in as promised.

"The game warden said he'd come by tomorrow," he reported. "I don't know what he'll do, but he looked at my pictures."

"Hopefully something will be done then," Jake said. "I'll be home tomorrow. So maybe that will help—if the game warden comes."

"He'd better, but who knows. Goodnight, then," Mr. Brunson said and turned to leave.

That night the noises from the bear outside were even more pronounced. Perhaps it was emboldened by the rain that fiercely drenched the log walls of the cabin.

Hannah lay in bed unable to ignore the troubling sounds until Jake finally got up and yelled out the front door.

"That should do it," Jake said, his voice weary as he climbed back into bed.

Apparently it did because for the rest of the night they heard nothing but silence.

Seven

The rain was still coming down when Hannah and Jake awoke the next morning. Because Jake had planned to stay home, the alarm had not been set. Unable to sleep in and after a few tosses and turns, Jake said, "I can't sleep." He propped himself up on his elbows, briefly looked around the dark room, and then got out of bed and dressed.

"Me neither," Hannah agreed but made no move to get up.

Jake left the room, and in a few moments, Hannah heard Jake light the gas lantern and the hiss of the lantern in the living room.

With a groan, Hannah halfheartedly got out of bed. Jake would be hungry and anxious for breakfast.

As she walked into the living room from the dark bedroom, Hannah squinted, unable to focus for a minute. The day was gloomy. There was no doubt about that. But with Jake home, perhaps the house would stay more cheerful. Some days Hannah felt lonely after spending all day alone in the house, but soon the little one would be here. She blinked, rubbed her eyes, and smiled at Jake, who was sitting on the couch.

"Will we have breakfast soon?" Jake asked hopefully.

"Yes," she said, squinting again from the bright light. "Do you want anything different since you're home?"

"No," he said, his nose in a magazine, "just the usual."

Hannah didn't know if all men were as unimaginative as Jake when it came to food, but she decided a rainy morning called for something special. If nothing else, it would serve to cheer herself a little.

"I'll make some bacon," she said, remembering the special breakfasts her mother prepared at home. Jake glanced up and nodded but went on reading.

"Will you bring some bacon in from the springhouse?" she asked.

"Sure," Jake said and then hesitated, seeing the rain outside. "You really think we need to have bacon?"

"Yes," Hannah said. Then she stopped by the kitchen opening as the thought occurred to her for the first time. "Jake, what if the bear got into the springhouse? Maybe that's what it's after."

"It's likely," Jake allowed. He then set aside his magazine and took his raincoat from the small closet by the front door. "It can't get in, though. I built it strong enough," Jake said more to himself than to Hannah.

"How do you know?" Hannah asked. "This is a grizzly."

"I know," he said, his face sober. "I'll check, but I really don't think it could get in."

True to his word, Jake was back in the house quickly, a grin on his face. "That's what it was after, all right. It didn't get in, but there were big claw marks on the logs."

"You think we should tell the game warden about this?"

"I suppose—if he comes out." Jake sounded skeptical. "It probably won't do any good, though."

"No, I suppose not," Hannah said, taking the bacon from him and disappearing into the kitchen. With the fire lit in the wood stove, she had breakfast soon on its way to the table.

Afterward, Jake did look pleased with his breakfast, and Hannah had to ask, "Did you like it?"

"Good as Mom's," Jake grinned.

Hannah relaxed at the compliment. "So what are you planning to do today?"

"Book work, maybe," he said.

"The checkbook is balanced," Hannah said, glad to have done it before he could get to it.

"I know," he said, nodding. "Just looking at my—" He paused briefly, caught his mistake, smiled, and then continued, "*Our* financial situation."

"We're making do," Hannah assured him, "but just barely. The bank payment on the house takes such a large chunk each month."

"How else could we have done it?"

"Rented maybe," Hannah said. "This is such a nice little cabin, though, dear and all."

"Reasonable too," Jake reminded Hannah, "for this area. It was quite a deal. Both Steve and Betty thought so."

"I know," Hannah said, "and I do like it here."

"We'll make it somehow," he said, sighing and getting up from the table, "though I don't quite know how."

Hannah cleaned the kitchen while the rain dripped heavy on the windowpane and Jake busied himself at their little desk in the living room. Jake had insisted he make the entire desk by himself. Hannah wasn't really surprised that he was so good at woodworking. Jake was good at a lot of things.

The top was a plank of a large log, sawn in half, sanded smooth, and carefully varnished. For legs, Jake used hickory wood with the cut knots showing their full glory. On the right side, two slabs of log formed the vertical frame for the drawers, which slid on wooden slides, softened by stick-on cloth gliders Jake purchased at the hardware store in Libby.

After some figuring, Jake said, "We're still making it okay."

Hannah said nothing. She wanted Jake to enjoy the moment without her input. *He deserves success*, she thought but felt a sorrow gather around her heart. She couldn't help but wonder, *Would our efforts be better spent back in Indiana where Jake would get paid for the real value of his work? Here, it seems, there is a lot of work but he gets paid less than what I know my dad makes. Practically speaking, a move might be in our best interests.* But then Hannah pushed her thoughts aside and concentrated on the kitchen.

By midmorning, the rain slacked off, and Jake was ready to venture outdoors. At that same time, Mr. Brunson drove his truck up to the front of the cabin. Along with him was a dark green, clearly marked state vehicle.

"Mr. Rogers," Mr. Brunson said, introducing the officer when Jake and Hannah stepped outside. "Mr. and Mrs. Byler."

"So I hear you've been having bear trouble," the young officer said. *He definitely looks like a game warden*, Hannah thought. His uniform was a little torn down by his ankle, but when he stepped forward and shook hands with Jake, his grip was strong, and his courtesy nod in her direction was polite.

"Every night," Jake said, "even with the heavy rain."

"Rain doesn't stop them much," the young officer replied, chuckling. "Foraging for the winter, I'd say. It won't be long before the snows start. Let's take a look around, then. There ought to be some tracks out yet."

Jake led the two men to the spot along the bedroom wall where the noises had come from. Hannah followed and watched. The officer bent close to the ground for a better look and grunted as he used his finger to draw the outline of a faint print.

"Bear all right."

"Grizzly?" Jake asked.

"You think it was a grizzly?" the officer asked.

"Yes," Jake told him.

"How could you tell?"

"It had a hump on its back—a big one."

"You saw it?"

"The first night," Jake said.

"You got a good look?"

"Sure. I saw it with my light."

"Let me see your light," the officer said.

Mr. Brunson seemed agitated at the officer. "Do you doubt his word? It was a grizzly. What will you do about it? These are nice young people. There's no reason for a grizzly to be haunting them at night, let alone eating my pig."

"Let's see the light," the officer repeated and then continued to study the ground as Jake went to get it.

"Anything else bothered around here that you know of?" he asked, this time directing his question in Hannah's direction with a turn of his head.

"The bear was in my garden," Hannah said. "I found paw prints. Then Jake found scratches on the springhouse this morning."

"Are you missing anything?" the officer asked.

"Maybe some tomatoes, but I don't know if bears eat tomatoes." She grimaced. "There's nothing missing in the springhouse. Jake built it strong."

"You keep meat in the springhouse?" the officer asked Hannah.

She nodded. "We don't have refrigeration." Then she added with a smile, "It's cheaper that way."

"I suppose so," the officer allowed. He stood up again as Jake came back with his light. "It also attracts bears."

"Now, don't you go blaming us," Mr. Brunson said. "These young folks are doing real well here. They don't need a bear messing things up. Folks ought to be able to live the way they want without the law coming and saying otherwise."

"I wasn't saying that," the officer said, answering Mr. Brunson. "I'm just saying that if the bear didn't get in this time or thinks it can't next time, it probably won't be back."

"Now, don't be saying that either," Mr. Brunson said, still sounding put off by the officer's casual attitude. "Ignoring the problem won't solve it either."

The officer ignored Mr. Brunson and reached for Jake's light. He flicked the switch and sent the beam first against the wall of the cabin and then out across the garden. Even in the day with the sun about to break through the dark clouds, the light reached underneath Hannah's tomato plants.

"Good enough," the officer said. "So it might be a grizzly."

"That's what the man said," Mr. Brunson snapped.

"A black bear isn't much of a problem," the officer said, directing his remark toward Jake and ignoring Mr. Brunson. "Problem black bears can be disposed of easily—if we have to. Grizzlies are another matter. Where this one came from, I don't know. There are some in the south Cabinet area, but they usually stay there. It might be from the Bitterroot or Bob Marshall areas. Either way, we could have it trapped and taken back, but it might not do much good. Bears are like that."

"So why not just take it out?" Mr. Brunson asked. "If you can't do it, I can."

The officer looked at Mr. Brunson skeptically. "I hope you're just joking. Grizzlies are protected around here. Unless you want to tangle with the Feds, not to mention us, you better leave this bear alone."

"That's what I thought," Mr. Brunson answered, fairly pouting, his voice low in a tone Hannah had never heard him use before. "Little use you people are. Home and property could be eaten up with no help coming from the authorities."

"Let's take a look at this springhouse of the Byler's." The officer gave another sharp glance at Mr. Brunson. "Then I'll file my report. We'll see that the problem is taken care of one way or the other."

"What about my property?" Mr. Brunson asked. He didn't sound mollified at all.

"We'll take a look at that too," the officer said, his voice restrained.

The officer walked with Jake, looked carefully at the springhouse, lifted the heavy door, and then let it swing shut.

"It's well built," he concluded. "It should be okay if you keep it shut tight. Never let it get in, though. Once it does, you'll have to tear this down. Bears would never forget such a haul. This would give them a big one."

"Sounds like you plan on this being a long-term problem," Mr. Brunson said.

"We'll do something," the officer said, assurance in his voice.

"You'd better," Mr. Brunson said.

The officer asked a few more questions of Jake and Hannah and then left. He followed Mr. Brunson farther up the dirt road to look at the site where Mr. Brunson's pig had been eaten.

At around three o'clock, the rain started again, chasing Jake from the yard to the barn where he started a new woodworking project. He had told Hannah he was going to build a log dresser for the master bedroom and a crib for the baby. The latter made Hannah feel reassured and cared for by Jake, and it was a diversion from thinking about the troublesome bear.

The rain also brought Jake's boss to the cabin just before supper. His truck rattled to a stop in front of the cabin. Jake opened the front door and greeted him with, "It's good to see you," and he stepped aside to let the burly man come in.

"I can't stay, son," he said, his eyes not meeting Jake's. "I have bad news."

"Yes," Jake said, a catch in his throat that Hannah heard all the way out in the kitchen.

"I just lost my next contract—the big one behind the Cabinet Mountains. I'm afraid I have to lay off half the crew until work picks up again, what with winter coming and all."

Jake said nothing, the silence so loud Hannah gasped.

"I'm sorry, son," the man's voice reached Hannah clearly. It carried genuine compassion, like an attempt to put salve on a wound. "It's hard for all of us. That's why I came to tell you myself."

Eight

The rest of the evening seemed to drag on forever. Jake sat in the living room under the light of the gas lantern, but he was in his own world. Hannah shed her tears in the kitchen, taking care to hide them from Jake. This was hard enough on him. Her tears would only add to the burden of everything else. She would stop by the couch, rub his shoulders, and then move on.

"Would you like some supper?" she asked, trusting her voice at the moment to not break down.

Jake shook his head, his eyes staring blankly out the front window. "We have to have money to live on," he said, his voice low.

She almost spoke the old cliché *We can live on love* but caught herself. The silliness of it almost brought the tears again.

"I'll make you supper anyway," she said. "You need it."

"I need a job," he said, his voice flat. "I need to take care of you and the baby."

She wrapped her arms around his shoulders and then simply allowed the tears to come, not caring that they dampened the top of Jake's head.

"Maybe this is a sign that we should go back to Nappanee," she whispered. She saw their condition in its starkest terms, the darkness outside driving her thoughts.

"We can't," he said, his voice still flat but determined. "We can't leave this place. I don't see how."

"But the baby's coming," she said softly. "Winter will soon be here. You heard what the officer said—they're not going to do much about that bear. It's a grizzly, and they're protected by law."

"We just can't," he said quietly, his elbows now on his knees, his face in his hands. "We belong here—both of us. We belong to this place, this country, this church. I just feel it. I've felt it since the first time we came here. It was to be you and me—together—here."

"But things change. We all dream," she said. "Sometimes it's not right, not what we think it is." She felt his shoulders stiffen under her hands.

Smiling gently, he said, "We're supposed to stay here."

"But what will we do? Lose the cabin? At least if you sold it now, you could get plenty of money for it. In the winter, who knows? There might be no buyers then."

Jake turned to face her, his young features drawn in pain. The tears stung her eyes again as he took both her hands in his.

"Yes, it might be easier," he said slowly as if the thought was still forming in his mind. "But to do what is right is always best."

Hannah was silent for a moment and then simply said, "But what will we do, then?"

"I don't know," Jakes said, "but we need to stay. I'll go look for work tomorrow. Something will turn up."

"There are plenty of jobs at home. I know Dad could get you in where he works. They pay well."

"Let's try here first," he said with a sigh, weariness filling his young face and stirring compassion in Hannah.

"You are the brave one," she said, kissing his forehead. "I always thought I was, but you are so much braver."

"No," he said, "you really are. You married me." A slight grin played on his face. "Any regrets?"

"Don't say that," she said, chiding him. "Of course not."

"Your Sam wouldn't be out of work," he said.

This made her laugh. "Me, a farmer's wife? No, I don't think so."

"Is that the only reason?" he asked.

She laughed again. "You silly, of course not!"

"Just checking." He let go of her hands. "Now, about that supper, is the offer still good? I feel a little better."

"Wait a minute," Hannah said. "You mentioned Sam, but what about that girl? Do you wish she hadn't jilted you? She was much better looking than me."

"No she wasn't." And with that, Jake stood and kissed Hannah.

When they parted, Hannah said, "I'll start our supper."

"Supper—" Jake agreed, "let's have a good one."

Hannah sent Jake out to the springhouse for ham, potatoes, and a head of lettuce. When he brought the items in, Hannah put him to work peeling the potatoes and then asked him to wash the bowls she had finished using. This kept Jake occupied until the gravy was done.

An hour later they sat down to the meal—ham with mashed potatoes and gravy, corn from her garden, salad with cut tomatoes, and cake left over from earlier in the week. Jake bowed his head for prayer and surprised her when he prayed out loud. The words sounded melodious—reverent—and they soothed Hannah's heart, seeming to catch the spirit of her feelings. The young couple was being pushed out of their youth, their innocence, and their ideals and into a world they had never been in. She could see it in Jake's face as his lips moved, forming the German words. She could feel it in her own body, which now held their child. She wept from the sheer overwhelming strangeness of this world that lay before them.

"It'll be okay," Jake said as he reached for her, his fingers finding their way to her hands and gripping them. "We'll make it."

Hannah wished she had Jake's confidence but simply nodded, pulled her handkerchief from her apron pocket, and used it until her emotions were under control.

"It's hard, I know," Jake said, "but God will help us."

Hannah took comfort in the words, but most of all she took comfort that Jake had said them. Never before had he said anything like this, in this tone of voice and with this amount of confidence. She clung to the anchor offered, not certain whether it came from Jake, his words, or the God to whom he had directed his prayer.

They finished their supper in silence by the light of the kerosene lamp. Afterward, Jake helped dry the dishes, and after the last plate was done, he returned to the living room while Hannah lingered in the kitchen, putting away the rest of the things.

She could hear the soft rustle as Jake turned the pages of whatever book he was reading. Through the window she watched the moon rise above the Cabinet Mountains. It was full, a circle of shimmering glory suspended above the tops of the last pine trees that formed the boundary between land and sky.

Here in Montana the moon stirred her in ways it never had in Indiana. She had never understood why and often wondered if it was the lack of factory lights or towns on the horizon. Perhaps the mountains themselves caused this feeling of wildness, this untamed shiver that ran down her back.

This land had always seemed to be her friend, especially on nights like this when the moon ruled the sky. Yet now she had a deep unsettled feeling that nature had a mind of its own, a mind unfriendly to the presence of humans, and that it regarded them as interlopers, much as she viewed insects in her garden. She shook her head but was unable to shake the sense of uneasiness.

Hannah finally hung up her apron and joined Jake in the living room.

"It quit raining," Jake said, trying his best to make casual conversation.

"It has," she agreed.

"I'm going into town tomorrow, to Libby."

"Oh?" She looked up in surprise, wondering what Jake would want in town. They had little money or need to spend it, with or without his joblessness.

"Bishop Nisley mentioned the hardware store might have a job. The manager had asked him about Amish labor the other week. I just thought of that."

"What do they pay?" Hannah said, wondering aloud.

"I don't know, but anything is better than what I have now."

"I would hate to see you just give away your time. They can't pay much."

"We will make it," Jake said. "God will help us. It starts, though, with doing what you can do even if it doesn't pay that much."

The room settled into silence for a few minutes, and then Jake asked, "Has the *Family Life* come this month?"

"Yesterday. It's in the bedroom."

Jake left the room, returned a minute later, and settled back in his chair, scanning the table of contents and then flipping quickly to a specific page.

Curious, Hannah leaned over to read the title of the article, "Learning to Make Home Businesses Profitable."

"Interesting," Jake mumbled, his eyes on the page.

"What's interesting?"

For an answer he read out loud, "The larger Amish communities have long prospered in the area of small business, many of them having ready and willing buyers available in the pool of tourists who visit their areas. This has produced cottage industries of furniture makers, vegetable growers, goat farmers, and a number of others specific to the area.

"Now, though, the need for small businesses is growing, especially in our smaller communities without readily available factory jobs. They also provide options for younger families in communities where farmland now sells at exorbitant prices."

Jake stopped and then said, "The article goes on with some good ideas on how to start and what one might do."

"You're thinking of starting your own business?" Hannah asked.

Jake shrugged, his eyes returning to the article. "I don't know. Maybe I could."

"What would you do?"

"I don't know yet."

Hannah felt like probing deeper but decided against it. It had been enough for one day.

Not long after, the two headed for bed.

"Do you think the bear will return tonight?" Hannah asked.

Jake glanced out the window, pondering the bright night sky. "I don't think so. It didn't find much here last night. Maybe it's done."

"I hope so," Hannah said.

She fell asleep easily, listening to Jake's steady breathing beside her. She woke only once, late in the night with the moon still full and bright in their bedroom window. She listened for strange sounds that might be the bear and, hearing none, slipped back into sleep.

Nine

The next morning Jake prepared to drive to Libby and begin his job hunt right after breakfast.

"The hardware store will be open by the time I get into town," he told Hannah as he left for the barn to harness their driving horse.

Moments later Hannah watched him steer the buggy toward the main road and felt forsaken, even though she was used to his absence each day. Perhaps it was the uncertainty of what he would find once he got to town she reasoned as she stepped outside to look at the Cabinet Mountains.

Morning was when she especially enjoyed being outside. The ever-sharp freshness of this country invigorated her. Today, though, the mountains looked forbidding with their clouds still hanging heavy on the peaks.

Well, she told herself, *it's just the weather. Jake will know what to do.* But still the uneasiness wouldn't leave.

After Hannah started the breakfast dishes, she heard a truck approaching and knew at once it had to be Mr. Brunson. She went out to the driveway to meet him.

He rolled down his window as she called, "Good morning! I hope you have some good news about the grizzly."

Mr. Brunson shook his head. "Sorry. The state isn't going to be of much help."

Hannah's face fell as she envisioned many more nights with the bear outside the cabin walls.

"He said that with winter coming soon, the bear will hibernate. All bears do. He thinks its pattern might change in the spring."

"I guess we'll have to live with it, then," Hannah said, hopelessness in her voice.

"Sorry. I'd shoot the thing, but you know how that would go."

Hannah nodded. She didn't want to encourage breaking the law. Then she blurted out their news, the desire to share with someone else having become too great. "Jake lost his job last night. His boss stopped in after you left."

"I'm sorry to hear that, and with winter coming." Mr. Brunson looked concerned. "Any prospects?"

"He's in town looking right now. He hopes the hardware store has an opening."

"Well, I hope he finds something. Jake's a good man," Mr. Brunson said as he put his gear shift in reverse.

"Don't forget about supper," Hannah said. "Mom and Dad will be here in a few Sundays. They're staying a whole week."

"To a good supper, then," Mr. Brunson said. "I'll look forward to that. It will be nice to meet your folks." Then he backed out of the driveway and gave her a final wave as he drove toward the main road.

Hannah felt the aloneness creep in again and wished it were Sunday already. She would see Betty or Bishop John's wife then. There were others too, but Hannah was looking forward to the comforting hug Betty would give her when she told her aunt about Jake losing his job.

While Hannah grew up, Betty had always seemed much older, almost ancient from a little girl's perspective. Even during the summers when Hannah helped with the riding stable, she thought of Betty's age that way. Of late, though, the distance between them had become much smaller. How that could be, Hannah wasn't certain.

Being ancient herself was not an attractive answer, but she began to think that maybe that was what was happening. *I do feel kind of ancient all of a sudden—with the bear, the baby, and now Jake's job loss.*

The baby. For the first time that morning, joy filled her. A child, her and Jake's child, and she had not told her mother yet. Should she? This life inside of her. This new beginning. This great unknown. *Is this the way all expectant mothers feel? I suppose so, but this feels very much like I am the very first woman to ever feel this way. What joy!*

How strange, she thought. *I don't even know whether this child is a boy or a girl, yet it doesn't seem to matter. Is this how Mom felt—not knowing, yet feeling the capacity to love regardless?*

How will this child turn out? Will it look like Jake or me? When it lies in the crib, so small and newborn, will Betty say she can tell exactly where this child comes from? Likely so, Hannah thought and smiled at the vision of Betty bending over the side rail and discerning the distant lineage of this newcomer.

Her mother needed to be told. She could write, but that didn't seem to be the thing to do. Already she could feel the words form in her mind, in letters on the page. Yet, she paused. Her mom was coming soon, so why not wait and tell her in person?

Yes, she quickly decided she would wait. It would be more fun. It would make her feel closer. She felt tears form. How wonderful it would be to tell her mother while she was sitting in the living room, surrounded by the walls of her cabin—Jake's and her cabin. This would make it so much more real.

Still, communion Sunday seemed a long way off. Her parents would stay in the spare bedroom during their visit, and that needed preparation or at least a good cleaning. But not yet. If she cleaned it now, the room would just get dirty again before her mother arrived.

No, it would require a last-minute rush to prepare, making everything as spotless as it could be in a log cabin. The dust and dirt were downsides to living in a log cabin, but she hoped her mother would see the plus side too. "Romantic" was not a word her mother would use, of course, but it was the word that occurred to Hannah.

Then she remembered where Jake had gone this morning. So quickly had she forgotten and forgotten also why she wanted to move back East. But did she really? Like Jake, she loved it here. It was the very opposite of what she grew up with, but she dearly hoped it wouldn't be taken away from them.

This was no doubt what Jake felt and why he was less shaken by the present than she was. If you knew where you belonged, it made the staying easier and the leaving harder. If only she could be as certain as Jake. If only she had his faith that it would all work out okay.

Hannah returned to the kitchen. Her dishes were done for the morning, and she turned her attention to other matters—mending, weeding, and the many small chores that presented themselves afresh every morning.

Just before noon she heard the clatter of Jake's buggy on the gravel and hurried out to the porch. One look at his face told her everything.

"I'm sorry," she said even before he stepped onto the porch.

He looked as if his shoulders carried a great burden. She was struck by how out of place it looked on someone so young.

"Nothing," he said simply. "Mr. Howard said in a few weeks maybe, when the snow season starts but not now."

"What are we going to do?" she asked.

"I don't know. I think I might have to start some business on my own."

"Like you were reading about in *Family Life?*"

Jake nodded.

Hannah wasn't sure what to think. "You'll need money for that."

"I know," Jake agreed.

"But from where?"

He shook his head.

"My parents are coming soon. Maybe you could ask them," she offered.

Jake shook his head again. "Not your parents. We're not asking them for money. I'm not taking the chance of losing it."

Not sure whether Jake was being stubborn or strong, she studied his face.

"I'm not asking," he repeated, seemingly reading her thoughts.

"But the baby—" she said.

"I know. Something will be done," he replied, and he lapsed into silence.

"I'll have lunch ready soon," Hannah said after a few moments, hoping that would somehow provide a little comfort to his obviously bruised feelings. She wished she could do more, but what?

"I'll put the horse away," Jake said and returned to the hitching post where Mosey waited patiently to be let out of the buggy traces.

Hannah had sandwiches ready when he came in. Jake sat down at the kitchen table. Outside the early clouds still hung around, having grown darker now.

"Do you think it's going to rain?" she asked in an attempt to make conversation.

"It could." Jake didn't offer anything more.

"Do you think your logging job might be available in the spring?" she asked.

"I doubt it," he said quietly but didn't elaborate.

"Why?" she asked.

"There's something about the business," Jake offered. "I don't think it's prospering very well. Logging's not the thing to be involved in right now."

She trusted Jake's instincts in the matter and laid her hand on his arm.

"Hannah, you still think we should move back East, don't you?" he asked.

Surprised that it was occurring to him now, she hesitated. "I think we need to do what's best for all of us, including our baby."

"So do I," Jake said, "but I really do think we should stick it out a little longer."

"I don't doubt you," she whispered even though her courage was weak.

"If God wants us here, we should stay," Jake said, apparently in an argument with himself, "no matter what."

Not sure how to take that—as if God came down and told people where to live—Hannah puzzled over how to answer. "I have feelings both ways," she ventured. "Today I wanted to stay, but then I think of the money and the baby."

"I know," Jake said, "me too."

They finished their sandwiches in silence—not an uncomfortable silence, just a troubled one. She wished it wasn't so, but the fact that Jake would be around for the rest of the day turned out to be more of a disturbance than she had expected. He sat and read while she cleaned, and then he went out to the barn.

She had supper ready at the regular time, but Jake ate little, silently pushing the food around on his plate.

Later, they read by the light of the lantern, its hiss quickly drew Hannah into sleepiness and away from her troubles. She glanced at Jake and guessed he felt the same way. At her suggestion they went to bed early, and Hannah hoped the extra sleep would do them good.

In the morning Jake got up first. While Hannah was still asleep, he quietly came back into the bedroom to tell her that a light dusting of snow had fallen in the night. He stayed by the bedroom window until Hannah joined him. Together they looked out at the snow—and the marks of the grizzly's night visit.

"I didn't know those tracks were there," Jake said as if he was sorry he roused her. "I didn't hear anything in the night. Did you?"

Hannah shook her head.

"That might be the last of it," Jake said and sounded as if he knew something about the habits of bears. Hannah had forgotten to tell him the news Mr. Brunson brought. At this moment she hoped both the game warden and Jake were right about the matter.

Ten

The snow quickly disappeared once the sun came out. Hannah, not yet ready for winter, was glad to see it melt. The thought of a howling whiteout surrounded by mountains intimidated her.

As they drove to church the next morning, she asked Jake, "Winter's coming early this year, isn't it?"

He shrugged. "Maybe. I don't know the country well enough to tell for sure."

She didn't press the subject because Jake was not in his best mood. With many of the odd jobs around the house finished, he sat around with nothing much to do most of yesterday. Thankfully, today they had someplace to go.

Church was being held in the house, but because the other buggies had already gathered in the yard, Jake couldn't get close enough to the walks to let Hannah out. So Jake brought Mosey to a stop in front of the barn.

"This is as close as I can get," he said apologetically.

"It's all right," she said. A quick walk in to the house wasn't something she found disagreeable. The knowledge she would soon see Betty quickened her step.

Her aunt was already in the kitchen when Hannah walked in. She made her way around the circle of women, greeting each in turn. When she reached Betty, she felt the urge to whisper news of their troubles but decided not to. It might be considered disrespectful to talk too long even with a relative since other women were in line behind her.

Betty seemed to sense Hannah's thoughts and squeezed her hand before she let go. There would be time to talk after church during Sunday lunch. Hannah was surprised when the line of women began to move almost immediately toward the living room. She hadn't realized they'd arrived that late. Young couples without children had no reason to be late for church.

She caught sight of the clock on the wall—it revealed the time to be five till nine. Somewhere she and Jake must have misjudged the time. As the line moved forward, she took her place near the end, almost the last one before the young unmarried girls started.

Only Sylvia Stoll was behind her. She had married Ben Stoll a month after Hannah married Jake. She had met Ben during her summer stays with Betty, when she thought of him as the scarred logger. His obvious interest in Hannah hadn't gone anywhere. A few months later, Ben had found Sylvia in Iowa, and they were married. It looked to Hannah as if they were a well-matched couple, both were a rugged type and well-suited for this country. *Not like Jake and me,* she thought with a shiver. *Maybe we're out of place in this wild country.* She stilled her thoughts as she sat down, shifting her weight on the hard bench.

Beside her Sylvia sat without any motion. Hannah wondered if Sylvia also had a secret pregnancy, but she, of course, couldn't ask such a thing. That she and Jake had a baby coming was joy enough.

The song leader announced his selection in a loud baritone, his voice reaching throughout the house. It was strange how the babies upstairs didn't wake up from the pronouncement, or perhaps they just quickly got used to it. Her child too would get used to it, their life, and also their ways. She smiled but only inwardly. This was, after all, church.

Hannah wasn't surprised when Jake led out in the next song. He was such a good singer that he got his turn on a regular basis.

She listened to his voice with admiration—such depth of emotion as he sang. He held the notes to their proper length and swung them up and down as expertly as she had ever heard anyone do. This was her man and half the source of the life growing within her. Thrilled at the thought, she hoped Sylvia couldn't read the joy on her face.

Here in church, surrounded by these people, she had forgotten the storm clouds that gathered at home. Even now as she remembered the thoughts, they didn't sting quite as much. Jake, if he could sing like that, would find some way to keep things going. If not, then maybe he would decide they should move back East. It was an option they both understood, Hannah was sure.

Yet, the thought of a move brought a pang of regret, more so than it had at home. But she must face reality. She was sure even Betty would agree.

The two ministers, led by Bishop Nisley, came down the stairs soon after Jake finished and found their places on the bench up front. There was nothing unusual about the sermons and nothing to indicate anything out of the ordinary.

After testimonies, Bishop Nisley got to his feet, his eyes intense, and said, "Will the members please stay. The rest are dismissed." There was nothing unusual in that either because this was pre-communion church. The surprise was yet to come.

All the nonmembers filed out, mostly children and some young people, followed by several women who would prepare lunch. For the next hour, Bishop proceeded to go through the written and unwritten rules of the *Ordnung* briefs. Some of the session was just lecture, some of it a reminder of broken rules, and some of it a question of whether new rules should be added.

Bishop said there was a question raised over how long newly purchased homes could keep their electric power. A reasonable amount of time was allowed now—two years—Bishop thought, and he received nodded agreement from several of the men. This allowance was intended to reduce the financial hardship caused by the transfer, especially for young couples.

But some believed the two years allowance was too lax. Should this rule be amended to one year? The extra time might simply promote complacency and unwanted accommodation to English ways. Several of the men nodded their heads, but several others didn't look too happy with that idea either.

In the questions and vote that followed, the proposed change raised enough objections that Bishop cancelled the move. He stated that the time allowed would remain two years. Hannah felt relief. Though she and Jake had no electricity left at their place, she didn't know what the future held, and their own financial hardships made her sensitive to others, such as young Sylvia beside her. Sylvia and Ben's place still had full electric power, which included lights, and might well be the reason the rule change was brought up. The ministers could be nervous, she thought, when time went on and young couples made no attempt to start the changeover. Yet she didn't want to prejudge. There might be good reasons Sylvia and Ben hadn't switched.

Bishop continued with his last remarks. He noted that communion service would be held in two weeks and Bishop Amos Yoder from one of the Nappanee, Indiana, districts would travel here to participate. Afterwards a new minister would be ordained. That was, of course, if there was no objection from the congregation, which there wasn't. A quick vote confirmed the matter.

The announcement of an ordination was the surprise. Bishop dropped the news just like that—no warning, no preparation, just the cold hard facts. Several of the men shifted on their seats, and a few women suddenly became very interested in their children. The new minister could be anyone from among them, provided he was male, preferably married, and in good standing as a member.

Hannah felt a chill because Jake qualified. But surely he was a long shot at best. He was simply too young for such a position. Although he could sing very well, that didn't translate into minister material. As for exactly what did translate into minister material, she didn't know. Nobody did for that matter. There was no set pattern, no guideline, and no attention paid to speaking ability, elegance in bearing, or commanding presence. The only requirements were those read from the Scriptures. Those, of course, fit most of the men in church.

The tension subsided as church dismissed. If any of the men felt like the executioner's ax was poised over their necks, the feelings got lost in creamy peanut butter sandwiches, hard cheese, and the crunch of sweet dill pickles.

Betty found Hannah after the first table setting was through. "Did you like our snowfall?" she asked in a teasing voice.

"I do if it somehow scared away our bear," Hannah whispered. She didn't want the news to spread too far.

"It should," Betty said. "Did you get the pressure cooker to work?" Betty whispered now, obviously trying to keep the accident a secret between them. "I did write to your mother about it."

"Yes," Hannah said with a grimace. "I finally got enough nerve to go back into the kitchen."

"I imagine that took courage," Betty said, "but it could happen to anyone."

"I suppose so," Hannah allowed and then got to the news she really wanted to share. "Jake lost his job."

"You don't say!" Betty was all sympathy. "Has he found anything else?"

"Not yet. He went to the hardware store on Friday. They're not hiring until the snowy weather settles in."

"More snow brings in the skiers," Betty said. "What are you doing till then?"

"Jake will think of something," Hannah said, more confidence in her voice than in her thoughts.

"I hope so. Let us know if it gets too rough."

"I will," Hannah said and meant it but wondered if she would actually have the courage to ask for help. To beg was an embarrassment, no matter the reason.

"Will your parents be staying with you?" Betty asked.

Hannah knew why she had asked. Betty wanted her to share Kathy. But Hannah wanted her mother with her the whole week and said, "Yes. They'll be with us the whole week."

"Well, how about supper at least?" Betty asked. "I'll have to steal them a little. You'll come over for supper one of those nights, won't you?"

"Of course," Hannah agreed quickly, delighted at the invitation.

"What do you think of the minister thing?" Betty whispered.

"Surprising," Hannah said because it was true and because the answer seemed safe to say. Any discussion of the subject wasn't considered good form, and she hoped Betty wouldn't go any further.

"There's Steve now," Betty said. "I'd better get ready to go."

"Will you be at the singing?" Hannah asked, thinking she and Jake might go. If nothing else, it would get them out of the house. If Betty and Steve went, Jake might be easier to persuade.

"I don't think so," Betty said, already moving toward the kitchen to pick up her wrap.

Ten minutes later Hannah saw Jake hitch the horse and joined him at the buggy.

They drove home in silence. Jake made no mention of the day's events, seemingly lost in his own thoughts.

"Do you want to go to the singing?" she asked.

Jake shook his head just as Hannah expected.

Eleven

During the first two days of the week, Jake made some repairs to the springhouse to make it even more secure from the bear. On Wednesday, he headed back into Libby to look for work. How Jake expected to find work as an Amish man in the *Englisher* world, Hannah wasn't certain. It seemed to her an impulse-driven move, born of desperation, but she admired him for his persistence. At least he wasn't sitting around the house moping.

When Betty dropped by that afternoon, she brought with her the first good news Hannah had heard in a long time. She said Bishop Nisley could use some help with barn repairs. Nothing was said about pay, and Hannah didn't raise the issue. She knew it was being offered as charity work even though Bishop's barn probably really did need the repairs. But with winter still ahead, he just as easily could have waited until spring.

Mr. Brunson stopped by just as Jake was pulling in, returning from his trip to Libby. By the time Hannah noticed and stepped out to the porch, Mr. Brunson had left, heading back toward his place.

"He was just checking on the bear," Jake said to Hannah's unspoken question.

"Did you find any work?" Hannah asked.

"Mr. Brunson asked that too," Jake said dejectedly. "The answer is no." Jake went into the house and flopped onto the couch, his whole body language communicated discouragement.

"Betty stopped by," Hannah said. "John has a few days worth of barn work for you."

"So it's come to that?" Jake asked as he stared out the window toward the quickly falling dusk.

"It's better than doing nothing," she said.

"I suppose so," Jake allowed. "Mr. Brunson said he's seen nothing of the bear the past few days."

"Neither have we, now that I think of it," Hannah said.

"It probably moved on, what with winter on its way."

"I hope it stays away. I don't want to see it back next spring," Hannah said. "So, what do you think? Will you go to Bishop's tomorrow?"

Jake nodded.

Hannah made a good supper in hopes it would cheer Jake. He would need a good dinner because he had work tomorrow—work that, no doubt, would be difficult. When she called Jake to the table, the way he looked at the mashed potatoes, gravy, and ham made her glad she had made the extra effort. His eyes were hungry enough, but the doubt on his face still troubled her. He was probably looking at the days ahead, and the dismal view was obviously spoiling his usual enjoyment of a good dinner. Hannah resolved to do all she could for him. What that was, she wasn't certain.

After supper Jake got out his Bible and read it at length in the living room. Hannah hoped he would find some comfort there. *Perhaps I should try it myself,* she thought but wasn't certain where to start.

Jake solved the dilemma when he asked her to sit beside him. "I want you to hear this," he said.

He then read aloud, "I will lift up mine eyes unto the hills, from whence cometh my help. My help cometh from the LORD, which made heaven and earth."

Jake paused as Hannah thought of the Cabinet Mountains. Normally she would have agreed with the words about looking to the hills, but lately she wasn't sure. With the bear possibly still near, the mountains had become dangerous to her.

Jake continued, "He will not suffer thy foot to be moved. He that keepeth thee will not slumber."

"You think that's true?" she asked him.

"It's in the Bible."

"The Bible's always true, isn't it?"

"Yes."

"No moving of the foot, and God never sleeps," Hannah said, thinking on the words.

"Sounds comforting, doesn't it?" Jake said.

"Until you're out of work," she answered, lamenting.

"Well, tomorrow I'll go to Bishop Nisley's," Jake said. "Let's be thankful for that."

"Yes," Hannah agreed even as she realized the work on Bishop's barn was not enough to solve their problem.

Hannah went back to finish her work in the kitchen while Jake continued reading. She heard him leave for the bedroom soon after and followed when she was finished with her kitchen work.

Hannah dropped off to sleep easily, woke only once in the night, but heard nothing unusual.

She got up to fix Jake's breakfast when the alarm went off. Jake was already in the barn and had Mosey harnessed for the ride over to Bishop Nisley's. While Jake ate his breakfast, Hannah prepared his lunch. She packed some extra food just in case he might be extra hungry and then stood by the front window to watch him leave.

Soon after, a light snow began to fall, and it continued throughout most of the gray day. Hannah liked the snow as long as it didn't disrupt their lives too much. It wasn't quite like Indiana snow, though, and that was all right with her.

Jake returned home before dark, tired but happy at having worked.

"Supper's ready," she said and then asked, "Are you going back tomorrow?"

"Yes," Jake said, "I'm going back the rest of the week. We might get done early on Friday."

And what then? Hannah wondered.

When Sunday came around, Hannah was hoping someone from the community would have heard about their situation and might have offered Jake temporary work. It wasn't to be, though, as church dismissed and not even Betty asked about Jake's job status.

Hannah's parents, Kathy and Roy, would come on Thursday, which gave Hannah plenty to do. She enlisted Jake's help by giving him a broom and wipe cloth and setting him to clean the spare bedroom.

Somehow they made it to Thursday. Hannah had to keep her thoughts to herself more than once. She began to hope more and more that her parents might be the ones to suggest a move back to Indiana. Coming from them, it might be easier for Jake to accept. Hannah loved their home, but the presence of the baby inside her caused her to think of what was most practical. They simply couldn't continue like this. With her parents coming, it would be an excellent time to make a decision, come up with a plan, and get the support they would need for the move. If only Jake would agree to it.

Even with winter ahead, they would fare much better in Indiana than here. They could rent a place instead of buying one as they had done with the cabin. That was a decision Jake would have to make, though. With her father's help, perhaps he could get a good-paying factory job, and they might be able to afford the payment on a small place.

They had formed attachments to the cabin, the mountains, and the people, but she supposed time would heal the pain of leaving Montana. Betty would be the hardest to leave. Hannah could imagine the tears when she would have to tell Betty the news, but facts were facts, and the biggest fact right now was that they needed to do something soon. Surely Jake had realized this when he studied his checkbook. The cost of groceries must be clear to him as well, and now her mom and dad would come to visit. It all added up to extra mouths to feed, paid for by money they didn't have.

Hannah felt a little guilty when she gave Jake the list of groceries she needed and sent him into town Thursday morning. Jake studied the list long and hard, she thought, but left with Mosey without saying anything. And he came back with everything, even the maple syrup she wanted for at least one breakfast of pancakes and eggs.

It will all work out, she told herself. *Mom and Dad are part of the answer to getting us back on our feet financially. They are my parents and will surely help just as Jake's parents would if they could. I will do the same for Jake's parents, if and when they come to visit.*

Hannah sent Jake up the hill to remind Mr. Brunson of Friday night's supper invitation. Betty had already spoken for Tuesday night. The van would be returning to Indiana on Wednesday, so Tuesday would be the last night her parents would be in Montana. Hannah's heart thrilled at the thought of almost a week of family with communion Sunday stuck right in the middle.

While Hannah was sweeping the kitchen floor, Jake returned with the news that Mr. Brunson was down with the flu.

"Still, he hopes to make the Friday night date," Jake said. "If not, he'll bring word even if he isn't feeling well, so you'll know."

"Is it something serious," Hannah asked.

"Nah, just the flu," Jake said. "I think he'll come, though. He looked like he needed some company."

Hannah supposed he did, stuck up there on his mountain all by himself.

That evening the van pulled in while Hannah was fixing supper. The pies were still in the oven, and the casserole was cooling on the tabletop. Jake came out of the barn to meet the van, and Hannah rushed out to the porch to find her parents had already pulled their suitcases from the van and were making their way to the cabin, her mother in conversation with Jake.

"This is a wonderful spot," her mother gushed as Hannah approached. "I remembered the area from when I visited Betty, but it's even better in the fall. And your little cabin—what a place to live!"

Kathy looked up to see her daughter. "Oh my," she said and gathered Hannah in her arms for a long embrace. Kathy let go with a question on her face. "You're not? I mean—really?"

"Yes," Hannah said, not surprised that her mother should guess.

Jake's face was the color of beets, and he said nothing. Perhaps when the baby was actually born, it wouldn't seem such an embarrassing subject to him.

Hannah hugged her dad as he turned from talking to the van driver and then said, "Well, come in. Looks like you were the last ones dropped off."

"Yes," Roy said, "we were. The others had to get to their places first. We're just the little peas in the pod."

"Roy," Kathy said in mock horror and laughed. "He's tired from the trip."

"Hard van seats," Roy said. He then turned to say one more thing to the van driver who started to back out toward the main road.

"The driver's staying in Libby for the week," Kathy said. "I guess we're all on our own till then."

It was then that transportation crossed Hannah's mind. "Oh," she gasped, "I hadn't thought of that. We only have a single buggy."

Kathy followed the train of thought and instantly waved her hand at Roy to hold the van driver. "So when will we need to get around?" she asked Hannah.

Hannah thought frantically. "Sunday. I think only on Sunday. Betty can come get you on Tuesday."

"Roy," Kathy called and rushed up to him, "we need transportation on Sunday. They only have a single buggy."

Hannah's father nodded and waved back to the van driver before he drove off to the main road. Roy arranged for the driver to meet them there on Sunday morning for a ride to church. Hannah thought of the extra money her father would have to pay because drivers for the Amish charge by the mile. It made her realize, all the more, how far apart her and Jake's situation was from her parents'.

Perhaps, though, that could change—with a move back to Indiana. Now that her mother was here, Hannah's face lit up with delight and the prospect of a change in their circumstances.

Twelve

"A log cabin," Kathy said, looking around the kitchen and—Hannah was sure—at all the dust and maybe even a few pieces of food from the cooker explosion she had missed. Now that her mother was here, things she had never noticed before or had missed in cleaning, seemed to become evident and demand attention.

"The explosion didn't do too much damage," her mother said by way of reassurance.

"It's a log cabin. Things do get dirty quickly," Hannah muttered, figuring the obvious might as well be stated. No use pretending she had a spotless Indiana Amish house.

"I didn't notice," Kathy said. "I was just looking at the logs. They seem tight enough. It's cozy."

"We like it," Hannah said, relaxing a bit.

"I suppose you do. It fits the country and the mountains, which are almost right outside your doorstep."

"That and bears," Hannah said.

"Bears? *Really?*" Kathy said, shocked.

"Yes. It's a grizzly too." Hannah made it sound as bad as she could.

"Did you hear that, Roy?" Kathy stuck her head excitedly back into the living room. "They have a pet grizzly."

Roy chuckled, "Jake was telling me it had tried to get into the springhouse."

"What are you doing about it?" Kathy's eyes were wide. "What about when the baby comes?"

"The game warden thinks it won't be back," Hannah said. "I guess it's holed up for the winter now—or at least headed for the mountains. It got Mr. Brunson's pig too."

"Mr. Brunson?" Kathy asked.

"He's our neighbor who lives just up the road. I invited him for Friday night supper. I think he could use the company because I never see anyone visiting him."

"It will be nice to meet him, then." To Hannah's surprise, her mother asked the very question she had hoped to hear. "So when are you coming to visit us in Indiana?"

"We can't. We're too poor," Hannah said and then took her opportunity. "We might move back, though."

"*Really?*"

"Jake lost his job. Bishop Nisley gave him some work last week, but this week he's had nothing."

"Just like that—moving? I thought Jake's job was long-term?"

"We're in trouble." Hannah felt as though she should justify herself, though Jake probably wouldn't have. "We have a mortgage to pay, you know."

"Most people do," Kathy said and then glanced around the kitchen. "Are you cutting your expenses? I see all kinds of food around."

"Mom," Hannah said as explanation, "you don't come visit every day. I'm not cutting expenses while you're here."

"But you should," Kathy said. "Your dad and I understand. We know how to live without money. We had our hard times too."

"I never noticed," Hannah said.

"It was while you children were young," Kathy said, "but you should be talking about this to Jake, not me. Is he agreeing to this move?"

"No," Hannah admitted, "but I think if Dad talked to him about it, he might. Dad might even be able to find him a job."

"We'll let Jake look into that," Kathy said, disapproval in her voice. It stung a little, but Hannah felt desperate. Something simply would have to be done—and soon.

With her mother's help, supper was soon on the table. Jake, all smiles tonight, asked Roy to say the prayer. It was good to hear her father's voice again as he said the simple German words of petition to God. Not that Jake couldn't pray, but he just didn't have the gravity of tone or the years of experience in his voice.

"So," Kathy said when Roy was done, "you two are going to make us grandparents. That's a first for us. Does it make you feel old, Roy?"

"*Real* old," Roy said, pretending deep regret for his future status.

"Do your parents already have grandchildren?" Kathy asked Jake.

"A few." Jake's face wasn't quite as red as earlier. "Eight, I think, and another one on the way, courtesy of my oldest sister."

"So you've lost track already?" Roy chuckled.

"It's hard," Jake said. "I have older brothers and sisters. I can't keep up with them all"

"Just like a man," Kathy said. "Don't even try."

"You're going to enjoy being a father," Roy said.

Jake was silent for moment and then said, "I hope so. It's going to be a bit hard for a while. I don't think I've told you yet, but I lost my job."

"That's what Hannah said," Kathy said.

"She's already told you?" Jake shrugged his shoulders.

Kathy said quickly, "I guess women get concerned sooner."

That seemed to satisfy Jake. "I think the hardware store may have some work soon, now that the snow is falling. At least that's what the man said."

"Jake, have you ever thought of starting your own business?" Roy asked. Hannah's heart sank. If her father gave Jake encouragement, it might be exactly the wrong thing. A move back to Indiana seemed a much better idea to her than a risky venture into self-employment.

Jake's smile broadened. Apparently he didn't notice Hannah's sudden frown. But Kathy did, and under the table, she gave her daughter a squeeze on the arm and then smiled sympathetically at her. Hannah knew her mother well. What she was telling her in her own way was that things work best if the man leads the way. It was a lesson Hannah had grown up with, but this was different, wasn't it? Her mother's eyes said no.

"I was thinking of making furniture—" Jake said, "log cabin things and that sort of line. I think they would sell well here and maybe even across the country."

"You have talked to someone about this?" Roy asked.

"The hardware man," Jake said.

Hannah looked at Jake in surprise. This was news to her.

So were his next words. "He said he could give me a place to work from and a web presence too—maybe my own website. He said I could make the furniture—maybe on the side to start with—and then full-time if things took off. I'd pay him part of my profits, of course."

"How much money would you need to start up?" Roy asked.

"None, I think." Jake seemed to be running the thought through his head. "Mr. Howard, from the hardware store, would supply the working space. Supplies shouldn't be that expensive. We'd just start out slow, selling the things after I make them."

Hannah's shock must have shown plain enough for even Jake to notice.

"I'm sorry," Jake managed. "I guess I never told you."

"I guess you didn't," Kathy said, for which Hannah was deeply grateful. At least someone other than Hannah was feeling a little irritated.

"They were just thoughts and bits of conversations," Jake said, waving his hands around. "Nothing for sure. I was waiting until I knew more about it. I didn't want to get anyone's hopes up." He looked at Hannah.

"That's understandable," Roy said in obvious support of Jake.

"Is this Mr. Howard serious about this offer?" Kathy asked.

"I think so," Jake said. "Mr. Howard has high hopes, but he's still thinking about it."

This also was news to Hannah, but she kept her composure. There would be time later to speak with Jake.

"The factories are hiring in Indiana," Roy said, unknowing of Hannah's desire to move East. "The economy is pretty good for that line of work."

Jake showed no interest, his attention now on the casserole in front of him.

"So, Dad, do you think Jake might be able to get a job?" Hannah said, trying to turn the conversation in that direction.

"Hannah," Kathy said, her voice mild in the rebuke.

"Oh, I know Hannah wants to move East," Jake volunteered and didn't seem upset. "We've talked about it. Sometimes I don't know what to do."

"Oh, really," Roy said. "So you're thinking of moving. I know it can be a toss-up at times—when you're young, that is. Move here or move there. This job or that job. When you're old like us, grandparents almost, it gets a little harder to think about moving."

"We have to do something," Hannah spoke up again. "I just think moving back East now, before the baby is born, is the smart thing. You might even help us find a place. You probably know of a house for rent right now."

Her father nodded but said, "Simple choices can have long consequences. You'll have to think about it."

"Mary and Laverne are getting married this fall," Kathy announced.

Hannah supposed her mother wanted to change the subject. The move was obviously something for her and Jake to discuss again later in private.

"Well it's about time," Hannah said, following her mother's lead. "They've been sweet on each other since school."

"Sometimes those take longer." Kathy grinned. "I don't know why."

"They *all* take time," Roy agreed. "Some just take longer than others."

"I'm sure Mary would have asked you to be one of her bridesmaids. You're married, of course, now," Kathy said. "She'll probably use her cousins."

"Do you think so?" Hannah felt honored even at the thought she might have been included. "I guess Mary and I were close."

"Who are Mary and Laverne?" Jake asked.

"School friends," Hannah said.

Jake nodded and then turned toward the front window, hearing a buggy in the driveway.

"It's Betty," Hannah said, excited and thrilled that her aunt and uncle would come over unannounced.

"My, my," Kathy said, rising from the table. "I wonder if they've had supper."

"Now, Mom, don't you worry," Hannah said quickly. "This is supposed to be my worry."

"I suppose so," Kathy said and sat back down, plainly still worried.

Jake opened the front door as Steve and Betty came in and exchanged warm greetings all around. Kathy and Betty got a little emotional as they gave each other a hug. They all found seats in the living room and launched into a conversation with Jake about the weather.

"Have you had supper?" Hannah asked as soon she could get a word in edgewise.

"Of course," Betty assured her, wiping a stray tear off her cheek. "We just had to come over tonight. It gets lonely out here. It's sure good to see family."

"It's good to see you too," Kathy said quickly.

The evening passed much too quickly for Hannah. With Betty helping, the kitchen was cleaned up in no time, and the women rejoined the men in the living room. There were moments when she forgot the log walls of the cabin or the mountains outside with its grizzly threat. They were all just family again, *Indiana* family, safe and secure as they laughed and reveled in each other's company.

This was the way it's meant to be, she told herself, glancing over at Jake more than once. He seemed to join in with no reservations, which thrilled her heart and fired her dreams. Jake was such a nice fit for her— and for her family. This was why they should all be together in Indiana. Of this she was certain.

Finally Steve insisted that Betty and he must leave so he could get some sleep for work tomorrow. As they drove away, Roy and Kathy showed signs of tiredness, and Hannah was ready for bed too. She wondered if there was something more she could say about her desire to move but decided that perhaps enough had been said already. Surely Jake could see for himself how things would work out best.

Besides, Hannah didn't feel comfortable putting pressure on Jake. The matter was simply too important.

Thirteen

Hannah could tell Jake was irritated when the alarm went off earlier than normal, but she ignored him. She wanted to get up and into the kitchen before her mother awoke.

Kathy could easily be awake already, with the strange country and all. If Hannah were to come into her own kitchen to find her mother already up, the coffee pot on, or some such thing, it would be just too much to bear.

The kitchen was dark, though, as she stumbled around in her attempts to light the kerosene lamp. The flame flickered, casting its shadows on the rough log walls. Somehow everything seemed less lonesome this morning with her mother and father in the house. Hannah sighed deeply and let the delicious feeling soak in.

Such feelings were childish, she told herself. *I am no longer a little girl. I am a woman now. Yes, a woman.* She thought of Jake asleep back in the bedroom and was reminded of how it felt when he would snuggle up and put his arms around her. Oh, how it made her feel! Yes, she was grown now.

"Good morning," her mother said behind her.

When Hannah jumped, Kathy laughed. "I'm sorry. I just couldn't sleep any longer. It must be the higher altitude or the time change or something."

"Oh, I don't know," Hannah said. "I think you'd be up anyway. Do you want some coffee? I was just thinking of heating the water."

"That would be great," Kathy said, yawning and wrapping her housecoat tighter around herself. "It's chilly up here too."

"Yes, I know. I think winter's coming early," Hannah said with wariness in her voice. The season had lost much of its friendliness. Indiana winters might also seem like a threat, but with a factory job for Jake and its steady income, snow would be more like a friend again.

"You sound sad," Kathy said. "Did you and Jake talk about moving last night?"

"No," Hannah said without further explanation.

"It's just as well. Maybe God wants you here."

"Maybe," Hannah allowed, not really wanting to discuss the subject. "What do you want to do today?"

"I don't know," Kathy said. "Maybe we could see your mountains up close. Can we go for a walk? I see your dirt road goes farther back."

"That's where Mr. Brunson lives," Hannah said. "We could walk up to his place, and I could introduce you." Since he was coming for supper, an early introduction would be just the thing. A walk and a meeting of Mr. Brunson could be managed at the same time. "That's what we'll do," Hannah decided.

"What is that?"

"Go for a walk up the road, see the mountains, and then you can meet Mr. Brunson before he comes for supper."

"That sounds fine," Kathy said.

Hannah started the fire in the stove as her mother moved on to another subject. "Sam and Annie are expecting too. But they also found a growth when she went to the doctor the first time."

"Oh no!" Hannah exclaimed.

"It wasn't breast cancer. Benign, they said. Still—" Kathy said and turned her face toward Hannah in the flickering light, "quite a scare for a young couple."

"Will she be okay, then?" Hannah asked, thinking how awful it would be to face something like that while carrying your first baby.

"Doctors performed the surgery a few days later. The family's trying to keep it secret now that it's not cancerous. But that kind of news just gets out anyway."

Kathy got up to look for the coffee can and found it in the second cabinet she checked. Hannah wondered why she hadn't simply asked, but then that was her mother. She was always so efficient, even in a strange kitchen.

"So where is this Mr. Brunson from?" Kathy asked.

"I don't know," Hannah confessed. "He was living there when we bought the place."

"Never has family visiting?"

"Not that I've seen."

"Isn't that strange?"

"I don't know. He's an *Englisher*." Hannah gave her most logical explanation. "That's one reason I invited him for supper."

"Once that water's hot, I'd like to see the outside with the sun coming up," Kathy said.

"The mountains block the view sometimes," Hannah said. "It depends how cloudy it is."

"Is it cloudy this morning?"

Hannah glanced out the kitchen window. "No, I don't think so. We can step out and look."

"That kettle will take a while anyway," Kathy said. "Let's see what the sunrise is like."

They stepped outside with their coats on and looked toward the Cabinet Mountains. The air was brisk but not cold enough to spoil their enjoyment of the early morning. The first rays of sunlight reached for the sky over the tops of the mountains. A line of clouds that hadn't been visible from the kitchen window hung low on the horizon.

"Let's get our coffee and come back," Kathy said, her voice excited. "I've never seen the sun rise over the mountains before."

Hannah followed Kathy back inside and placed another stick of wood on the fire to hurry things along. With the extra heat, the kettle soon whistled merrily.

"Sounds of home," Kathy said as they waited.

They measured coffee into the filter and let the steaming water run through and drip into their cups. Hannah gave her mother the sugar and spoon first and waited until she was done to stir her own.

Back outside, the colors of the sunrise slowly grew. Hannah had watched sunrises in Montana before, but this one seemed to work extra hard to put on its best display. With the low clouds as the backdrop, the red, yellow, and orange streaks reached upward. Greens and blues soon appeared, each vying for dominance and producing new shades of brilliance every few seconds.

Kathy reached out her arm for Hannah and pulled her close as they stood shoulder to shoulder. Never in her growing up years had Hannah felt this close to her mother. Was it because she was becoming more like her now that she was with child? Had they found a new common ground they could share?

"I'm so glad you're my mother," Hannah whispered as the colors of the sunrise deepened even further above them.

Kathy just pulled her tighter and said nothing.

"For putting up with me," Hannah's voice caught.

"You were always a joy." Kathy's voice came softly. "You're a good daughter, and you have a good husband."

Hannah didn't trust her voice at the moment. There was no sense in bawling like a little girl even though she felt like one.

They stood there for long moments until the colors began to fade above them and the sunlight grew stronger.

"We'd better go inside before you catch a cold," Kathy finally said.

Ever the mother, Hannah thought. She wanted very much to tell her mother how she wanted her to stay here forever and never leave again, but that was silly. Such moments could be cherished, but they could not last forever. Life moves on.

In the kitchen again, the two women made the pancakes and placed them in the oven so they'd stay warm until the men got up. When eight o'clock came around with no signs or noises from the bedroom, they made eggs for themselves and ate together.

Hannah smiled at her mom's boldness. "The men can eat when they get around to it, I suppose."

"It's *our* morning," Kathy said.

When her dad got up around nine, he found a seat in the living room and began a sleepy morning tease.

"Why am I so neglected in my daughter's house? No one cares one bit if an old man starves. I'll soon be nothing but skin and bone."

Hannah smiled as her mom played along.

"You have to fix your own breakfast today. We already ate ours."

"Ha. That's what I thought," Roy said in mock bitterness. "Women become useless in Montana, it seems."

"That's an awful thing to say," Kathy said, teasing him back. "You're talking to your daughter, you know."

"I was talking about *you*," Roy said.

"That's even worse," Kathy retorted.

Jake then emerged from the bedroom, rubbing sleep from his eyes.

"No food services this morning," Roy announced in his direction. "We men are on our own. It's make do or starve."

Jake was up to the humor. "When we hunger, they too hunger sooner or later," he said in warning.

"That's a man," Roy said, chuckling. "You tell 'em!"

"Oh, all right," Kathy said, rolling her eyes but smiling. "The pancakes are made. Now we'll fix your eggs. The rest you have to do yourself. Hannah and I have eaten already."

"They don't like us. Just like that, we're cast aside," Roy said with a straight face, "after all these years."

Jake had to grin as he followed Roy into the kitchen. With the eggs ready in minutes, Kathy and Hannah left the rest of the breakfast items on the table and the men alone to put things together for themselves. The two women retreated to the living room.

"They don't love us no more," Roy said, his voice mournful as he piled pancakes on his plate. "At least the syrup is still sweet. But hey, maybe that too gets bitter in Montana."

"Watch yourself!" Kathy hollered from the living room. "I heard that."

All her life Hannah had enjoyed listening to her parents gently tease each other. It only made her all the more glad they were here now—and all the more wishful that it could be permanent. If she and Jake moved back to Indiana, they would have more times—lots more times—like this. She glanced at her mother who read her daughter's look unmistakably. "We must cherish the time God gives us," Kathy said. "It goes by soon enough."

The men finished breakfast and Kathy told them about the plan to walk to Mr. Brunson's and then on up the mountain a ways.

"Well, Jake," Roy said, "they not only make us eat by ourselves, now we have to walk up the mountain too."

"Well, it *is* a nice walk," Jake said.

"Jake, don't you know we men are supposed to stick together?" Roy looked hard at him. Jake only grinned and got his coat from the closet, apparently as ready as the women to get out of the house.

Fourteen

Hannah and Kathy led the way as they walked toward the mountains and Mr. Brunson's house. Jake and Roy seemed to be deep into some discussion. From the snatches of conversation Hannah heard over her shoulder, it sounded like they were talking about Mr. Howard's furniture-making offer. Her father sounded enthusiastic, which Hannah wasn't sure she liked.

Kathy kept gushing over the sight of the mountains, all the more so the closer they got.

"I know I've seen them before," her mother said. "Maybe it's the view from here."

"It's even better farther up," Hannah said. "I've been there once with Jake after we purchased the cabin. I would imagine you can see them even better behind Mr. Brunson's cabin. I've never been that far."

A thirty-minute walk up the slight grade brought them in sight of the man's cabin, two stories high and made of little more than boards nailed upright with mismatched tin on the roof. Some of the edges even stood higher than the others.

Behind the cabin and farther up the slight slope was the barn, its structure in even worse shape than the house.

"For all its looks, the house is well-insulated," Jake said because obviously something needed to be said in Mr. Brunson's favor.

"And clean," Hannah added, remembering her brief look inside the house.

"He's a real nice gentleman," Jake said as he led the party up to the front door and knocked. Mr. Brunson, clean shaven as usual and with a smile on his face, opened the door almost at once.

"Well, what have we here?" he asked, obviously pleased to see them.

"Hannah's parents," Jake said. "Roy and Kathy Miller, this is Mr. Brunson."

"Glad to meet you," Mr. Brunson said, extending his hand.

Roy stepped right up and shook Mr. Brunson's hand readily, but Kathy stepped forward a little more cautiously, smiling and politely nodding her greeting.

"The women have us out walking," Roy said in a teasing voice. "They just won't let a man on vacation take it easy!"

"Now, that's not true," Kathy retorted. "You slept real late. You can't spend your whole vacation in bed."

"And they wouldn't feed us either," Roy continued. "Why, they turned us right out on our own."

"Sounds like you have some tough women there," Mr. Brunson said.

Jake laughed. "He likes to stretch things a little."

"Well, you want to come on inside?" Mr. Brunson said as he held the door open.

"Oh, we were just out walking," Kathy told him quickly. "Thanks anyway. Hannah says you're coming for supper tonight."

"She was kind enough to invite me," Mr. Brunson said. "I hope I'm not a bother."

"Certainly not," Kathy assured him. "We're just guests too."

"I'll look forward to it, then. Sure you folks don't want to come in? Don't have much, but it works for me."

"I'm sure it does," Kathy said. "We have a walk ahead of us, though. We'll be anxious to see you again this evening for supper."

"If your cooking tastes as good as your daughter's, supper will really be something," Mr. Brunson told her.

"We train them that way," Roy said with a chuckle. "That is—until they quit like this morning."

"Don't pay attention to him," Kathy said. "Does he look underfed to you?"

"Not in the least," Mr. Brunson assured her with a straight face.

"We'd like to walk farther up if that's okay with you," Jake said. "You have a good view of the mountains up there."

"Most certainly," Mr. Brunson said. "It's not that far. Of course there are better places, but those would be quite a climb."

"Thanks," Roy and Kathy said almost together.

Jake led the way higher up the slope. Hannah looked back and noticed that Mr. Brunson waited until they were on their way before he shut his door. Apparently he was in no hurry to be rid of their company, which bode well for supper that evening.

When Jake found the spot he wanted, he stopped and motioned toward the Cabinet Mountains. From here they could see the full range and even farther to the north and south. The majestic view took Hannah's breath away.

"I can see why someone would want to live here," Kathy said, her voice full of awe.

Roy nodded momentarily and then muttered, "There's always the thing of a job."

"Oh, Jake can hunt and fish in the winter," Hannah said. "That's the good part—even if you don't have work." Hannah hoped Jake appreciated that she stuck up for him even if she wanted to move back to Indiana.

"Well, I've seen enough of it," Roy pronounced. "Let's get ourselves back to the house. It's time for an old man's nap."

"And eating?" Kathy added.

"Of course," Roy replied, laughing. "That skimpy breakfast is long gone after this walk."

"Uh-huh," Kathy said sarcastically.

"Well then, we'd better get back before they die of hunger," Hannah said, matching her mother's tone. "It's been such a long journey—such heat, famine, and thirst."

Jake led the way back past Mr. Brunson's and down the slope toward the log cabin. Once they arrived, Roy ate plenty for lunch and then excused himself to the spare room for a nap. Jake too was tempted to take a nap but resisted the urge. He read the *Family Life* instead.

With her mother's help, Hannah made the full dinner she had planned—meat, potatoes, gravy, salad with the last of the fresh vegetables, and two cherry pies. For filling she cheated by using store-bought. At least it felt like cheating to her. She had always seen her mother make her pie filling from scratch with cherries from the grocery store. Kathy didn't mention the difference, and Hannah pushed the guilt aside. It was a time to enjoy family, she decided, not think about unimportant things like pie filling.

Mr. Brunson showed up well before the appointed supper time and was welcomed in. He took the seat offered him in the living room with Roy and Jake. While Kathy and Hannah worked in the kitchen, he made himself comfortable and easily joined in the men's conversation.

Hannah let Jake know when everything was ready, and Jake led the two men to the kitchen where Hannah instructed them all where to sit. Jake, of course, was at the head with Mr. Brunson and Roy on either side of him. Kathy sat beside Roy, and Hannah took the table's end across from Jake.

When she settled into her seat, Hannah gave Jake a look that signaled him to begin.

"Would you please ask the blessing?" Jake asked Roy.

Roy bowed his head immediately. The others followed, and he began to pray. Hannah stole a quick look at Mr. Brunson, who still looked quite comfortable, as if the German prayer didn't bother him at all.

"Do you have family around here?" Kathy asked Mr. Brunson as the food was passed around the table.

"No," he said, "no one."

"How long have you lived here?" Kathy asked. "Hannah said you were here when they moved in."

Mr. Brunson wrinkled his brow. "Most of nine years, now."

"So you must like living in the mountains by yourself?" Roy joined in the conversation. "Nice country, I must say."

"Oh, I have a son out East," Mr. Brunson said, and a shadow crossed his face. Hannah wondered why Mr. Brunson had never mentioned his son before. Maybe she and Jake hadn't asked the right questions.

"Does he ever visit?" Kathy asked, passing the bread.

"No," Mr. Brunson said, "never has."

"Then you must go back East to see him on Christmas and holidays?" Roy asked.

"No," Mr. Brunson said with what seemed like a sad chuckle.

Roy and Kathy fell silent, and Hannah wondered whether their questions had been a bit much. Mr. Brunson must have noticed too because he chuckled again.

"I guess we're not as big on family as you folks are. It's nice you invited me, though."

That relaxed everyone, and the conversation flowed again.

As he downed his last bite of cherry pie, Roy thumped his stomach and pronounced himself satisfied. Hannah considered that he must not have noticed the store-bought filling. *At the price of groceries, store filling ought to be as good as homemade*, she thought ruefully.

When the men were back in the living room, Hannah and Kathy did the dishes and then joined the men. After an appropriate amount of time, Mr. Brunson soon excused himself, thanking both Hannah and Jake for the invitation. He then drove away in his truck, the headlights bouncing up the lane toward the mountain.

"He's nice enough," Kathy said to no one in particular.

"Yes," Roy managed to say as he reached for *The Budget* to read now that Mr. Brunson was gone. *Just like he always does at home*, Hannah thought. She had forgotten how much she missed it all.

"You have to feel sorry for people without families," Kathy said vaguely in Hannah's direction, "whether it's by choice or not."

"I wonder if Mr. Brunson had a falling-out with his son." Hannah said, remembering the man's sad chuckle at the table.

"You never know nowadays," Kathy mused, "with the world as it is."

"What about his wife? He must have had one—and other children," Hannah said.

"Maybe he only had the one child. It's possible," Kathy said. "I'm glad you invited him, though. That was right thoughtful of you."

Hannah sighed with relief, thankful for her mother's approval.

Roy yawned soon after that and announced it was his bedtime.

"You had a nap," Kathy said

"I'm getting old," he answered back.

"Then you'll have to head on in by yourself," she said. "I don't come to Montana every day."

A few minutes later, Roy, fighting sleep, gave up and walked toward the spare bedroom with a grumble that no one took care of him anymore. Jake turned in an hour later, after he had completed his *Family Life* articles. Hannah and Kathy stayed up well past midnight.

Something about the late hour, having the chores completed, and the absence of the men loosened their hearts and their tongues. They spoke nonstop about the things women talk about, all the little subtleties and nuances of people's lives—what aunt Martha said, who was courting whose son or daughter, and who knew what about everyone.

The torrent finally came to an end as mother and daughter settled into a comfortable silence. Hannah knew their time together would never be as it once was, abundant and available, and in her own way tried to come to peace with the fact. The separation had proven more painful than she had expected, yet she found in their coming together again a new facet of their relationship quite beyond her imagination. They had never been so separate and yet so close.

"Do you really think you and Jake might move to Indiana?" Kathy asked wistfully.

"I don't know. Jake seems so set against it."

"Don't push it, then," Kathy said, ever the mother.

Hannah, now sleepy, simply nodded.

Fifteen

In the morning, Jake took a sudden notion to hitch up the buggy and drive into Libby with Roy. He wanted to show Roy the hardware store, talk with Mr. Howard again, and maybe pick up some things for Hannah from the grocery store. Hannah knew he made that last offer to mollify any objections she might have.

Hannah had neither objections nor need of anything from the grocery store, but she didn't think her father's presence would make any difference in Jake's conversation with Mr. Howard. Hannah was glad Jake thought well of her family, but she still hadn't warmed up to the idea of a hardware store job. Certainly a move back to Indiana would be better than that. The factories paid much better than the Libby hardware store.

When the men returned just before lunch, Roy expressed himself satisfied with Mr. Howard and the job offer Jake had received. Hannah glanced at Jake, puzzled at her dad's use of the present tense. She looked at Jake and saw him grinning.

"He wants me to start Monday, but I said I couldn't start till Wednesday, after my in-laws leave," Jake said almost gleefully.

"I told him to go right ahead and not to wait," Roy said, "but he wouldn't listen. Don't blame me if you starve out of house and home."

"He *hired* you?" Hannah asked, trying to clear things up.

"Steady work," Jake assured her. "All winter. We even spoke some more about building log furniture. He showed us the storage room out back."

"It might work out fine," Roy said. "It's a little small, but it's heated."

Hannah hoped her disappointment didn't show too much. "That's great," she managed, all the while seeing her hope for the Indiana move fly away. Thinking, *At least he has a job, and we might make it through the winter*, she said, "Does the job pay well?"

Jake was slow to answer. "Not that much—but it's work."

"It's fair," Roy said. "The real money will be in the furniture—if you can find a distributor and market it well."

Hannah and Kathy left the men to talk business and went to prepare sandwiches for lunch.

"Cheer up," Kathy told Hannah when they were in the kitchen. "It's not the end of the world."

"I don't look that disappointed, do I?" Hannah asked, hoping it was just her mother's instincts picking up on her distress.

"You can get your heart set on something. Then, that may not be God's will."

"But I wanted to move back to Indiana," Hannah whispered, "even more so since you've been here."

"Just go with the flow of things. It's better that way."

"Maybe we can move back next spring after the hardware job gives out."

Kathy spoke plainly. "It's best not to plan things like that. Spring is a long way off."

"And a cold hard winter is ahead." Hannah gave a shudder.

"But you knew about the winters before you moved here," Kathy reminded her.

"That's different from seeing one up close and personal—and a grizzly bear too!"

Kathy laughed and said, "You'll make it. We always do."

Hannah wasn't sure about that, but it was good to hear her mother cheer her on.

After the sandwiches were eaten, no one had any other ideas about what to do, and so they decided to spend the rest of the day and evening around the house. Roy took a long nap again while Jake cleaned out the horse stall. He made several trips to the garden to dump the mixture of straw and horse manure.

Mr. Brunson rattled into the driveway, interrupting Jake on his last load. Leaving the wheelbarrow in the yard, Jake walked up to the truck, chatted briefly, and turned toward the house as Mr. Brunson left.

"He wants to show his elk to Roy and me," Jake announced when he opened the door. "It sounds like a big one."

"What?" Roy asked from the recliner where he had been napping.

"Mr. Brunson wants to show us his elk," Jake repeated.

"How'd he get it?" Roy asked, rubbing his face.

"Bow and arrow," Jake said. "He's good at it."

"Interesting." Roy got to his feet and glanced at the women. "You want to come along?"

They both shook their heads. Roy shrugged and followed Jake outside.

"I guess it keeps them entertained," Kathy said when they were gone, and Hannah agreed.

The men, though, got the last laugh when they returned an hour later, toting a plastic bag full of fresh elk meat.

"What are you doing with that stuff?" Kathy asked in genuine horror as she eyed the bag of redness.

"You're making it for supper," Roy announced.

"No, I'm not. It's *elk* meat," Kathy said, her disgust obvious.

"It's the same as deer meat at home," Roy assured her.

"How do you know? It might have an awful flavor." Kathy didn't seem convinced.

Certain she had already eaten elk meat at Betty's place last summer, Hannah jumped into the conversation. "It's okay, Mom. Betty has cooked it too."

"*Betty?*" Kathy's horror seemed to only increase.

"You probably ate some when you visited her last," Hannah said as calmly as she could. She almost wanted to laugh at her mother's reluctance.

"See?" Roy said, his voice triumphant. "That settles it. We're having elk meat for supper."

"Well, I suppose I could try it," Kathy said, still eying the plastic bag of meat suspiciously.

"And Mr. Brunson is coming for supper because it's his meat," Jake said. "I invited him."

"But I hadn't planned on an extra person for dinner," Hannah protested, a thousand thoughts of cherry pies, salads, and other fixings running through her mind.

Kathy rallied first. "It won't be much, I promise you that."

"Just the meat and some gravy," Roy said, a gleam in his eye. "It has to be tender, though."

Kathy glared at him. "That may be all it will be. If it's tough, don't say you weren't warned."

When Hannah and Kathy were finished with it, the meat wasn't tough. They boiled and then fried it on the stove, using the extra wood Jake had split and hauled in that morning.

Mr. Brunson had nothing but good things to say about the hurriedly thrown-together supper, pronouncing it among the best he had ever eaten.

"You're just saying so," Kathy said. Nonetheless she enjoyed the praise.

"Certainly not," he assured her and then started to say something else but stopped abruptly, a sad look crossing his face. Hannah couldn't tell if anyone else noticed, and the conversation soon continued.

After supper the men took turns playing checkers in the living room. Mr. Brunson proved to be quite a challenge for Roy, who considered himself an expert. Jake played once in a while "to calm them down," he said for Kathy and Hannah's benefit. The real matches were between Mr. Brunson and Roy. The two battled it out, one man taking the lead and then the other. The women watched with amusement.

Mr. Brunson finally proclaimed it a draw and Roy a worthy adversary. He rose from his chair and extended his hand. "I've got to go now, old man. You do know how to play your checkers."

"Old man yourself," Roy said with a great laugh. "You are good. You sure you've got to go?" he asked with genuine regret.

"Yes, I do. Thanks for the meal again," he said in Kathy and Hannah's direction.

"Nice man," Roy said, "and can he play checkers!"

"You can be thankful to have such a good neighbor," Kathy commented. "Anyone want coffee?"

Roy did and said so with a loud, "Of course."

"Well, I knew *you* did," Kathy said. "I meant the others."

"Just get it brewing, and they'll join in," Roy said. "Why would anyone refuse coffee?"

"Maybe because they want to sleep sometime before morning," Kathy said. "You're immune to it."

"Make the poor things decaf, then," Roy said.

"She doesn't have any," Kathy said.

"I just keep regular around for visitors," Hannah explained. "We don't drink coffee."

"What a shame."

Roy was served his coffee in due course and actually got Jake to try some, "Just a splash or so in the bottom of the cup," as Jake put it. After that Hannah had to try some at her father's insistence. "Just in case," he said, "Jake can't sleep, you'll be awake together."

But neither Jake nor Hannah was affected by the caffeine, and both were sleepy before her parents were. Kathy shooed them to bed. "You don't have to wait up for us. Roy and I are quite capable of putting ourselves to bed."

After she blew out the kerosene lamp, Hannah snuggled up to Jake and decided, sleepy or not, it was time to talk about his job.

"So with this new job, we won't move this fall?" she whispered.

"Don't you think we can make it with the work from the hardware store?" he asked. "It'll get us through the winter, at least. If things still don't pick up, perhaps then we can think about a move."

"But the winter—" she whispered.

He turned toward her. "We have to experience at least one Montana winter. Wouldn't you always feel bad if you'd missed it now that you're so close?"

"I don't know about that. I used to think so."

"It's just hard for me to make such a choice," he said. "I would want to do what you want. But I have to know it's right for us."

"I know that," she said, "and I'm glad. But wouldn't it be nice to be in Indiana with a good steady job? To have Mom and Dad close?"

"Yes, it would," he said, "but we have to be sure. Maybe God wants us here."

"Why would He want that?" she asked and sat upright in the bed. Did Jake know something she didn't?

"I don't know why," Jake said. At least he sounded genuinely puzzled. "It's just a small community here. They can always use more people."

"You wouldn't stay just because of that, would you?"

"No," he said and rolled over. "I just don't know. That's all there is to it."

Jake's breathing soon evened out, and Hannah let her worries go and drifted slowly off to sleep. The distinct sound of her parent's voices rose and fell from the living room, taking her back to her girlhood memories. It was a pleasant way to fall asleep.

Sixteen

With the prior arrangement to take Roy and Kathy to church, the driver of the van showed up early, for which Hannah was thankful. To arrive late would be an embarrassment, and blaming a van driver wouldn't pass as an excuse.

She and Jake had decided they might as well go along with Roy and Kathy instead of driving their buggy.

They left at a quarter after eight and arrived at Mullet Troyer's, where church was held, about half an hour later. The driver stopped short of the barnyard, uncertain where to park. The older Troyer son stepped out from the line of men and motioned for the driver to park in a grassy spot behind the barn and away from the buggies.

The group split up at the driveway. Jake and Roy joined the men in front of the barn, and Kathy and Hannah walked to the house. Betty met them at the front door with a happy "Good morning," as she allowed her arms to linger briefly around each of their shoulders. Betty was a touchy person, and if this hadn't been church, she probably would have given them each a hug.

"It's sure a nice morning," Kathy observed.

"Yes it is—just perfect for sitting inside all day," Betty stated matter-of-factly.

That was another thing about Betty. She just said things, and usually people weren't offended. Though everyone knew the all-day church service, which today would end with communion, would be arduous, they didn't mention the subject. They wouldn't say a thing even when it was a sunny fall day and they were trapped inside with their backsides flattened for six or more hours on a hard, backless board bench. Communion Sunday was supposed to be a holy time, a time of reflection on the Scriptures, one's sins, and one's place in life.

For a moment, Hannah remembered a minister was supposed to be ordained today. The thought was quickly lost, though, as Betty led the way around the circle of women, and each greeted them in turn.

The service then began, and when the singing time had ended, the ministers came down from upstairs and the preaching started. Bishop Nisley had the first sermon. He started with Genesis and told the story up to Noah's escape from the flood in his ark. No notes, no Bible, just a quotation of facts and general plot line by memory.

A minister Hannah didn't know had the next sermon. Apparently he had come along with the van load, although neither of her parents had mentioned him. He went from Noah's entry into the new world, washed clean by the flood, up to the time of Christ's birth.

When the hands of the living room clock advanced past twelve, Bishop Nisley dismissed them for lunch.

Because the day was so nice, everyone poured into the yard for lunch, taking the short benches they could find with them. Mullet gave others chairs until there were no more. He and his family then ate inside at the kitchen table. Kathy found a spot in the yard, and Jake and Roy, quick to grab two of the short benches while they were to be had, joined her.

Hannah found Jake's boldness amusing today. She assumed it came from the fact Roy was along, and that gave Jake a sort of visitor's rights. Normally, Jake would have been the last to take a bench. He would have settled, as some had to, with one of the long, awkward benches.

They ate their lunch to the chatter of voices all around them, families kept intact by the circled benches. Only when everyone was finished did general visiting occur. Several people stopped by to speak with Roy and Kathy. Eventually Bishop Nisley made an announcement from the front door that services were to resume.

The long afternoon began. Bishop Amos Yoder made his way slowly through the Gospel accounts and worked up to the crucifixion of Christ.

The Amish believed the Scripture instructed them to tell the story of Christ's suffering each time they partook of the cup and broke the bread. Only if they started at the beginning would the story make sense—or the best sense. To them, communion was a time for the best.

Two and a half hours later, Amos arrived at the end of the story and began to pass around the bread and wine. They used one cup because that was the way Christ served it. Hannah did appreciate that Bishop Nisley used a cloth to wipe the rim after each person handed the cup back to him. Some ministers didn't. Because her back ached from the hours of sitting on a hard bench, she was glad the service had arrived at this point.

When the time came for feet washing, when normally they would be dismissed and find relief from the day-long service, Hannah noticed tension in the air. It was only then she remembered an ordination was yet to be performed. Since morning Hannah had not once thought about the ceremony, considering the matter none of her concern. There were at least ten married men in the local congregation older than Jake and several the same age as Jake. Ben and Sylvia Stoll came to mind, but she didn't consider Ben a likely candidate. A man had to receive at least three votes to be placed in the lot.

With age and experience as measuring points, Hannah decided on the spot to vote for Henry Wengerd. She and the other women would vote along with the men because, for all their traditional norms, the Amish believed in equality of the sexes in regard to voting.

As he announced the vote was soon to be taken, Bishop Amos said it was the Lord's will—not man's ability—that was to guide the voting. What that meant, Hannah wasn't certain. He then instructed them to file into the kitchen where each vote would be noted. Nothing more and nothing less, some man's life would be altered forever by these simple instructions. Amish ordination had little to do with personal calling. The voice of the church was all that was necessary. Hannah pondered this, wondering if Henry Wengerd would consider her vote—and likely that of two others—reason enough to have his life so drastically upset.

The long line of men began to move quickly. Apparently everyone had made their minds up in record time, or perhaps they just wanted to get home. The women started, and Hannah stood up when the time came for her bench to take its turn. Sylvia Stoll, who was next in line behind Hannah, waited outside the kitchen while Hannah went up to the kitchen table and whispered Henry Wengerd's name to Bishop Nisley.

Hannah was curious as to who else had received votes and wished Bishop Nisley didn't have his piece of paper so well covered up. She was glad, though, that he couldn't read her naughty thoughts. She then returned to her seat as Sylvia walked into the kitchen.

Sylvia soon joined Hannah back at their bench, and the two waited as the young girls spoke their choices to the bishop in the kitchen. Five minutes later, Bishop Amos stood up and glanced down at the paper Bishop Nisley gave him. Because there was no deacon in this young church, Bishop Nisley had brought along the books to use in the selection of the new minister. Three books were placed on the bench in preparation for the revelation of the new minister. In one of those books, a providential piece of paper had been placed. Hannah shivered at the thought.

Bishop Amos cleared his throat. "We have three names given to us by the voice of the church. Each of these brethren is to come up and choose a book. Will each man come forward in the order of these names? Henry Wengerd." Hannah felt a deep stab of guilt at her part in this. "Ben Stoll." Beside her Sylvia burst into quiet sobs. "And Jake Byler."

Hannah felt her whole body turn ice cold. *It could not be! Not Jake. He is too young. There are surely others who are more qualified.*

Hannah sat numbly as she watched the three men pass in front of her like trees. Henry went first, his step firm, and then Jake, his face as pale as the frost on their bedroom window. Ben followed, a great hulk of a figure, swaying forward as if he carried a load of logs too heavy to bear.

Without a word, Henry took the middle book, Jake took the one to the left, and Ben took what was left over. And so the fates of the three men were sealed. Amos came forward without hesitation and glanced at the clock as if he were in a hurry to get this over with. Hannah was surprised she could even breathe. *What has gotten into these church people to vote for two such young men? Has the world gone mad?*

Henry was the one most qualified. Surely God would intervene and overrule the peoples' lack of understanding in this matter. Henry was the only choice that made sense, and Hannah clung to that hope while she dug her fingernails into the palms of her hands. Jake would surely faint if his book had the piece of paper. Never had they spoken of such a thing.

Bishop Amos opened Henry's book, flipped through it, turned it upside down, and gave it a little shake. The paper was not to be found. Next, Bishop Amos took Jake's book, opened it, and then paused. Instantly Hannah knew the paper was there because of the look on Jake's face. His eyes were wild, as if he was seeing a vision too horrible to imagine.

Bishop Amos held the piece of white paper in his hand and pronounced, "We have found the will of the church and the will of God. Will you please kneel, brother?"

Jake didn't move for the longest time, and Hannah was sure Bishop Amos would have to repeat the order. Slowly Jake slid to the hardwood floor, his hands clasped in front of him.

"By the will of God and by the voice of the church," Bishop Amos said, laying his hands on Jake's hands, "you have been chosen to the high and holy office of minister. You are to serve in humility, in the power of the Holy Spirit, to rebuke, to exhort, to succor those who are ill in body and spirit, to give warning to the erring, and in all times and seasons to fulfill your calling."

Bishop Amos then gave Jake his hand and helped him to his feet. He kissed Jake as did Bishop Nisley and the other local minister, Mose Chupp.

Beside Hannah, Sylvia was quiet, her sobs abated. Even in her dulled state of awareness, Hannah was certain Sylvia had pulled away and tried to put distance between them. She, Hannah, was now a minister's wife. It happened so suddenly, so abruptly, like a shooting star falling out of heaven and onto her head. From now on, the other women would feel she was different from them, regardless of how much she wasn't. She could no longer be just Hannah Byler.

Bishop Amos dismissed the service. The space on the bench to each side of her emptied, but she stayed seated, unable to move.

Dimly she became aware of her mother and then Betty, approaching from either side. Her senses registered arms around her shoulders. Their tightness gripped her. They stayed that way—the three of them intertwined—until the dam broke and the tears flowed. They wept together as one for a life that would never be the same again.

Seventeen

As the two couples climbed into the waiting van, Hannah felt intensely out of place. She was surrounded by the yard full of Amish buggies, and today of all days, when she was now a minister's wife, they had to climb into a van to go home. Jake's buggy would at least have provided some level of comfort, of sameness. It would have supplied the feeling that she was still one of them. Instead, she felt even more alone, surrounded by black hats and shawl-wrapped women.

She still burned with the intensity of her own feelings and had yet to look at Jake's face. The driver of the van looked curiously at them as they climbed in. *Perhaps*, Hannah thought, *he is wondering if Amish communion services always produce such sober-faced men and tear-stained women.*

The driver said nothing, though, and minded his own business, whether out of good manners or simply from past experience driving Amish. It didn't matter at the moment to Hannah. She was just glad there were no questions.

The sight of Jake's shoulder beside her on the van seat brought back the memory of his frightened face when the bishop opened the book. With the memory came her first feelings of sympathy for Jake. If this was hard on her, how must this affect him? He was the one who would be doing the work required of a preacher.

Hannah slipped her hand around Jake, found his arm on the other side, and tightened her grip. Jake didn't look at her, but his face became a little less sober. She let her head lean against him, not caring how it might look to the van driver, who glanced briefly in his rearview mirror.

When they arrived home and were out of the van, Roy stayed behind to speak with the driver to arrange to be picked up Wednesday morning. Hannah and Kathy followed Jake silently into the house.

The stillness of the cabin was what struck Hannah the most. She had never thought of their home as being so silent, but it seemed so now, as if it held its breath along with them. She stood for a few moments and listened until a sudden pop of moving logs relieved her of the tension.

"Well." It was all Kathy could find to say. Jake had simply seated himself on the couch and was staring straight ahead.

"We have to get some supper," Hannah said.

"That's what I was thinking," Kathy agreed.

"I wonder if anyone will be hungry?"

"It'll be good to eat…for Jake. We haven't had anything since lunch. It's later than you think."

Hannah glanced at the clock, surprised. "The whole day seemed long," she said.

"In some ways, it's the same day as always, and yet how things change," Kathy said in a low voice.

"What are we going to do?" Hannah asked. "We're so young."

Before her eyes passed the things required of Amish ministers. They stood in front of congregations, spoke sometimes for an hour at a time, left on Sunday mornings for the upstairs council meeting, were in on all church problems, made general decisions on things great and small, had to provide counsel for any member who needed it, and brought correction and rebuke to those who disobeyed the church *Ordnung*.

Her Jake, nervous in public Jake, who had started praying out loud at home only recently, would now have to read long prayers in public, stand and speak without any help, and all in a very short time. How soon, Hannah didn't know as she had never paid attention to such things, but surely it would come quickly.

"How soon before he has to preach?" Hannah asked.

"About a month, I think," Kathy replied. "That's about how much time they give them to get ready."

"Ready…" Hannah said, more a statement than a question.

"I know," Kathy said. "It doesn't seem very long, now that you think about it."

Hannah was silent as she considered that in just four Sundays her Jake would be up there in front of the whole church. The thought made her fingers go cold.

"God will help you," Kathy said, adding, "I guess," as if she had some question about it.

"Jake is alone in the living room," Hannah said. "Maybe we ought to be with him."

"Probably," Kathy agreed. She was moving toward the door when Roy came in. She stopped, waiting for a moment.

"Maybe Dad will talk to him," Hannah whispered, "since supper needs to be made."

"Food will do him good," Kathy suggested again.

"Let's just heat up leftovers, then."

Hannah lit the stove, the flame catching with the first match, and Kathy went outside to retrieve the meat, gravy, and fruit Jell-O from the springhouse. While her mother was gone, Hannah heard her father clear his throat and then begin talking to Jake in the living room.

"I know this was unexpected, son, but such things usually are. We just never know what the Lord has in mind on these matters."

Jake must have nodded because Roy continued after a brief silence.

"It comes, though, with great honor, this office does. You are one of few who are called to lead our people. Not many receive this good burden. I know in this hour it doesn't feel so good. It feels probably the exact opposite, like your world has come to an end."

Again there was silence before Roy continued.

"Yet you must remember. Our forefathers—now over five hundred years ago—needed no special training or gift from God. The first one knelt and asked to be baptized as an adult. The others performed the baptism. That was all they had—just the truth and the support of the brethren."

"But I am one of the youngest ones," Jake finally said, his voice shaking. "There are others who are much better."

"It makes no difference," Roy said. "It is God who decides. He is the one who chose David to be king. David was younger than his brothers."

"I don't know," Jake allowed, but his voice sounded a little stronger to Hannah. Behind her the door opened as Kathy entered, her hands full of the leftovers.

"Dad's talking to Jake," Hannah whispered.

"Is he doing any good?" Kathy asked.

"I think so. Anything helps right now."

"It's good Roy is here. He almost didn't come along for the trip," Kathy said.

"Who would have thought something like this would happen?"

"Not me." Kathy set the bowls down on the kitchen table. "But you just never know."

The old stove was warm by now, and Hannah placed the meat and gravy in the oven. Kathy set the table, the silverware clinking in the silence of the kitchen. Jake's and Roy's voices had ceased in the living room.

"It'll be a few minutes yet," Hannah said, more to make conversation than anything.

"There's bread yet to slice," Kathy offered for the same reason.

"We'll wait till the food is warm," Hannah decided as an urge to be with Jake came over her. "We can sit in the living room."

"You're going to have to learn your German better," Roy said as they walked in.

Hannah glanced at Jake's face. He seemed calmer now. His eyes were weary. The sadness was still there, but the fear was gone.

"Why do you say that?" Jake asked, his voice almost a whisper, as if he were uncertain what lay behind anything.

Silent now, Roy looked like he wished he hadn't spoken. He finally managed, "When you preach, you know, it takes more German words than we normally use."

Jake absorbed the information, his face blank, and then said, "I guess I'd better start studying, then."

"Maybe I can send you a German language book when we get home," Roy said.

"Should you be telling him so much so soon?" Kathy spoke up. "Jake's got enough on his mind already."

"I know," Roy agreed, looking contrite. "I'm sorry."

"No. That's okay," Jake said quickly. "The sooner I know, the better."

Hannah was a bit relieved at how brave Jake looked, seemingly facing what lay ahead with newfound courage. But then the cloud passed over his face again.

"What's wrong?" she asked, leaning in his direction.

"In four weeks," he managed to say.

"*Da Hah* will help you," Roy said softly.

Hannah moved closer to Jake, put her arms around his neck, and pulled him tight against herself. At the moment, she didn't care what her parents might think of this display of affection. They were married, after all. She felt useless and helpless to do anything more, but she could love Jake—that much she could do. Maybe it could help.

Jake managed a slight smile but then looked uncomfortable, so she released her arms but stayed close.

"The food," Kathy said in a sudden burst. "Oh, my."

"Now you burned it," Roy said, a chuckle in his voice.

Even Jake had to laugh as Hannah jumped up.

How quickly life comes back, she thought in her rush to the stove. *It takes only a few hours to come back—life does go on.*

It was as she and Kathy placed the food on the table that Hannah realized they would surely not be moving back to Indiana now. Any doubt as to that question had been removed as completely as food from a cleaned kitchen table after a meal. A newly ordained minister did not move except for the most compelling of reasons. None of those reasons existed for Hannah and Jake. Joblessness and lack of money didn't count for much.

Hannah shoved the realization aside for the moment and waited until she and Jake were in bed to think of it again. With Jake's arms around her, she wept. She wept for Jake but also for herself, for the lost hope of a move closer to home, for the realization that Montana, cold Montana with its snows and bears, would not be parted from her.

She knew that Jake probably thought she was crying for him—and in part she was—but she also cried for herself. She would not tell him so, though. This was just something she would have to bear in silence.

"We'll make it," Jake said, stroking her hair, his strong arms tight around her.

"Yes," she said in a muffled voice. It was the right thing to say, and yet she wondered *how* they would make it.

And then, as if the day hadn't been enough already, the sound outside the bedroom wall was unmistakable.

"That wasn't the bear," Jake said, trying to sound confident but without success.

"It was just a noise," Hannah said aloud, knowing good and well it wasn't.

Eighteen

Hannah awoke late, the sun already up, its light filling the room. Jake's side of the bed was empty. Embarrassed, she dressed quickly and hurried out to discover her fears were well founded. Both of her parents were already up, and Jake was with them. Kathy and Roy had coffee cups in their hands.

Hannah was so flustered she missed the looks on their faces until Kathy said, "I guess we get to taste some of your Montana excitement."

"Like what?" Hannah asked.

"The bear was here, after all," Jake said, a little shamefaced. "It tore up the springhouse."

"It's surprising we didn't hear anything," Roy said, carefully nursing his steaming cup. "At least it left the coffee."

"You *would* say that after this mess," Kathy said.

"It is a mess," Jake added.

Hannah walked over to the living room window to see for herself. Sure enough, the springhouse was torn open, and the roof leaned toward the mountains. Jake's recent work was completely undone.

"It ate all the food," Roy said. "That's why there's no breakfast. Do you normally starve your visitors in Montana?"

"Roy," Kathy rebuked halfheartedly.

"By the way," Roy asked, "who was the last one to go to the springhouse?"

Kathy's hand flew to her mouth. "Oh, no! It was me. I got the food for supper last night."

"I wouldn't be blaming anyone," Jake spoke up.

"I'm so sorry," Kathy said. "Maybe I didn't fasten the door right."

"Could be," Roy allowed. "You're not used to such things."

"It could have gotten in anyway," Jake said. "You just never know."

"It's okay, Mom," Hannah offered. "It's a wild country in many ways."

"I'm still sorry," Kathy said.

"It could have been me," Hannah added, turning to look out the window again.

Hannah felt sick at the sight of the springhouse. This land was dangerous, and now her retreat to Indiana had been cut off with Jake's ordination. For the first time, a grudge against Jake's calling entered her heart, a bitter thought that burned through her. Why had God chosen Jake? Surely Jake could do something about it. Yet she knew there was nothing that could be done. Jake was not to blame, and that left only God or the people who voted for Jake.

Above the fallen springhouse, Hannah saw the Cabinet Mountains fill the skyline. They seemed to smirk this morning, proud of the destruction to the springhouse. They looked even taller than normal, as if they lorded over her and Jake.

"Well? What are we doing about breakfast?" Roy asked. "Should a man just blow away because the bear has been here?"

"There's a carton of eggs left," Jake said. "They're on the kitchen table. I found them against the corner of the springhouse. Some bacon too. A little bit."

"But the bear," Kathy said.

"It didn't touch it," Jake assured her.

Her mother was unconvinced, as was Hannah. At the moment, though, the thought struck her that they hadn't awakened her to let her know. Why hadn't Jake come in to tell her? Did he intend to shoulder the responsibility by himself? Didn't he care anymore what she thought about things?

Then she managed to control her thoughts. Surely Jake did care. It was just the shock of the bear's destruction and what had happened yesterday that had her emotions so torn.

"Will someone make the bacon and eggs?" Roy pleaded.

"But the bear," Kathy repeated.

"Jake and I don't care," Roy said, to which Jake nodded.

"I have some cold cereal," Hannah offered, bringing her thoughts back to what needed to be done.

Her mother was agreeable. "That's better than bear slobber, I do declare."

"You're just being dramatic," Roy said. "No matter. That leaves more for Jake and me."

Kathy ignored him and got up to follow Hannah, who was already on her way to the kitchen. Hannah opened the oven lid, arranged the kindling, and struck a match to start the fire. The smoke from the small flame curled around in the oven box and then came up the lid instead of back toward the back and the stovepipe. Irritated, she replaced the lid, and the fire promptly went out.

"Can't even start the fire," she muttered.

"It's just one of those mornings," her mother said.

Hannah lifted the lid and tried again, this time checking to make sure the damper was open. She waved with her hand at the smoke as it tried to come up the lid. Slowly the column moved sideways and then the draw started, and the flames licked hungrily on the wood. She added several larger pieces and closed the lid.

With the cold cereal on the table and the bacon and eggs fried, Kathy called into the living room that breakfast was ready. They bowed in prayer, but Jake didn't pray out loud. Perhaps he was too disturbed, Hannah reasoned but supposed it didn't matter either way. Jake would be doing plenty of praying in the future whether he wanted to or not.

Hannah felt the bitterness again and wished it wasn't there, but what was she supposed to do about it? Jake needed her now more than ever, and help she would gladly give…but why wouldn't her heart cooperate?

Kathy still refused to take any eggs or bacon, even when Roy insisted. She settled for cold cereal. "No bear for me," she proclaimed.

Hannah overcame her initial resistance and took an egg and two pieces of bacon. Jake and Roy divided the remainder between them.

They were still eating when they heard someone pull into the driveway.

"Who would that be?" Jake wondered as he got up to check.

"Mr. Brunson," Hannah guessed but stayed seated. Jake could talk to him.

"His food will get cold," Kathy, ever the mother, worried as Jake walked toward the front door.

"He'll probably be right back," Hannah guessed again.

As if to confirm her conclusions, Jake came back almost immediately and seated himself at the table.

"He's going to wait till we're done with breakfast," Jake said.

"What does he want?" Hannah asked.

"He wants us to help him," Jake replied, picking up his fork again.

When Hannah kept her eyes on him, he finally offered, "He wants help burying the bear."

"What?" Kathy exclaimed. "Is it dead?"

"Yes," Jake said. "Mr. Brunson shot it."

"Shot it?" Roy stopped in mid bite. "Shot the bear?"

"That's what he said," Jake said.

"But can you do that?" Kathy asked.

"I guess if it's bothering you," Roy said with a shrug of his shoulders.

"I don't think so," Jake said. "This was a grizzly. From what Mr. Brunson was saying, he seems to think he did something quite illegal. Might even be against federal law."

"So why are you going to help him?" Kathy asked.

"The bear tore up my springhouse," Jake answered.

"That's not a good enough reason," Kathy said.

"Seems so to me," Jake said as he continued eating. "Kind of solves the problem, doesn't it?"

Kathy was distressed, but Hannah didn't know what to say, torn between feeling glad that the bear was no more and queasy because something wasn't quite right.

"Jake shouldn't be doing this," Kathy said, addressing Roy, who wasn't saying anything.

"We'll need his help too," Jake said calmly.

"How are you digging this hole?" Roy asked.

Jake shrugged. "Mr. Brunson didn't say. He just wants to use the horse to drag the bear. I think Mosey can do it."

Kathy looked at Roy and said, "I can't believe you'd do this. They put people in jail for these things."

Roy didn't say anything.

"Maybe you shouldn't help," she continued.

"But it tore up my springhouse," Jake said, a little heatedly now. "It's going to cost a lot to build it again. You know we have to have one."

"I'll help," Roy said. "I'll even help with the cost because it might be partly our fault. We're still here for two days. Surely we can do it in that time."

"I think we can," Jake said.

"Just how illegal is this?" Roy asked.

"Why does that matter?" Kathy asked. "Illegal is illegal."

"Pretty illegal," Jake said, "if it's federal as Mr. Brunson seemed to think."

"You're a minister now," Roy said slowly, seeming to think carefully on each word. "You shouldn't be taking chances."

"It's not right anyway," Kathy said. "If it's not right, then it's not right."

"That's true," Roy agreed.

Jake's face turned as sober as it had yesterday when his name was announced. Another stab of bitterness went through Hannah. Were they to be haunted now by this responsibility? Was everything in life to be weighed by whether Jake was a minister or not?

"Maybe we should be cautious," Jake allowed.

"We'd better ask Mr. Brunson in," Roy decided, the last of his breakfast done. He pushed back his plate and stood up. Jake followed him into the living room, as did Hannah, unwilling to miss the conversation. Then Kathy followed as well.

Jake invited Mr. Brunson in, and Hannah offered him a chair.

Roy cleared his throat. "Mr. Brunson, about this bear…"

"I shot it," Mr. Brunson said. "It killed the other two of my pigs.

Enough is enough. I see it tore up your son-in-law's springhouse. I say this situation should just be handled between us."

"Was it legal, though?" Roy asked.

"Probably not," Mr. Brunson answered. "This is wild country around here. Not like Indiana. The authorities don't take lightly to having their grizzlies shot. I think it might be best to bury the thing and just have it over with."

"I can understand that," Roy said, softly enough, "but burying things doesn't always solve the problem."

Mr. Brunson seemed to think on that for a moment. "I guess that's true," he agreed, but he said the words with sorrow in his voice. It was as if the man knew this to be true from past experience and not from the bear at all.

"We really are a bit uncomfortable with this," Roy said. "With Jake's springhouse torn open and your pigs dead, maybe the authorities would be understanding."

"Don't depend on it," Mr. Brunson said, a bitter edge in his voice. "They get a lot of things wrong."

"Still…we must do what is right," Roy said. "Jake just got ordained as a minister yesterday. It might not be good to involve him. If you bury the grizzly, he will be involved."

"Ordained." Mr. Brunson paused, looking puzzled, and let the matter be. "I can't do this by myself. I'm a little old," he said ruefully.

"It might be best to let the authorities know," Roy suggested.

Mr. Brunson snorted in disgust, as if a bitter thought had just passed through his mind, but he answered kindly enough. "I suppose so. What is to be, will be. Didn't Shakespeare say something like that?" He laughed drily.

Roy didn't say anything, waiting for Mr. Brunson to arrive at his decision.

Mr. Brunson seemed to struggle with competing thoughts. He didn't wait too long, though, before he simply said, "I'll go call the game warden."

Hannah felt sympathy for the old man. Surely he wouldn't go to jail because of her father's advice. Surely not.

Nineteen

Kathy and Hannah watched with a mixture of fear and fascination as the vehicles rolled in, first the game warden's familiar truck and then a half a dozen others with all sorts of markings.

When Hannah thought there couldn't be any more—the area full of law officers—two more dark green vehicles with impressive-looking federal government seals on the front doors came up the dirt road.

"They do take this seriously," Kathy said in awe. "Do you think Mr. Brunson will have to go to jail?"

"I don't know," Hannah said. "I hope not."

Just then one officer stepped out of one of the two more recently arrived vehicles while the other remained inside, busy with paperwork. After a short conversation with a state officer, the federal officer returned to his vehicle, and the two cars continued up the road toward Mr. Brunson's.

"He probably told them where the bear was," Kathy said.

"I wonder why they didn't take him along," Hannah said.

The state officer resumed scribbling on a notepad. Beside him the other two officers seemed to do all the talking. A camera was produced, and pictures were taken of the springhouse.

After more conversation, two of the officers left as Jake came toward the cabin. Hannah met him at the front door.

Jake gave a sober look in response to the questions on Hannah's face.

"Well…tell us," Kathy said from behind her.

"It's a little scary," Jake said. "I thought for a moment they were taking Mr. Brunson off in shackles. It made me feel pretty bad about the advice we gave him. But that didn't happen."

"So what are they doing with him?" Hannah asked, her concern still not abated.

"The game warden's talking about a big fine at the least. He said there's no excuse for this kind of thing."

"Even with what happened?" Hannah felt indignation fill her.

"Grizzlies come first, I guess," Jake shrugged. "You can't shoot them unless they threaten life and limb. The game warden said he would have taken care of it."

"Mr. Brunson already spoke to him about it." Hannah felt her feelings grow stronger. "Did you tell the others that?"

"Yes," Jake said. "I said it several times. I don't think the warden wanted it said, especially in front of the other officers, but I did anyway."

"Well, maybe it helped," Kathy offered.

"Maybe," Jake allowed. "We can't help with the fine, though. It sounds big."

"How much?" Hannah wondered, thinking of their small bank account.

"Thousands of dollars from what it sounds like. I guess a judge will decide," Jake said.

Roy and Mr. Brunson were walking toward the cabin. The older man looked grim as Roy said, "I feel bad about this. It's partly our fault. You wanted to bury the bear. I wasn't expecting…this reaction. I figured they'd take it seriously but not quite this seriously."

"I'll live through it," Mr. Brunson said. "Don't worry about it."

"So how are you?" Kathy asked. "It looked bad enough from here."

"Our friendly government at work," Mr. Brunson said, but he smiled. "They think grizzlies are a big concern."

"No jail, though?" Kathy asked.

"No." Mr. Brunson laughed. "But I will have to go before the judge."

"That's too bad," Kathy offered.

"Oh, I suppose it's better this way," Mr. Brunson said, trying to put them all at ease. "It wouldn't have been good doing this my way."

"It's still hard," Kathy said.

"Yes, as I'm learning," Mr. Brunson agreed. "Yet hard is better sometimes."

Again Hannah got the distinct feeling Mr. Brunson was speaking of something more than just the decision to confess to the grizzly shooting.

"I expect these folks will stay around awhile," Mr. Brunson said, shaking his head. "What a fuss they make."

As if to accent his words, a large county dump truck rumbled past the cabin and started to climb the grade toward Mr. Brunson's place. Moments later a tractor trailer with a backhoe on it followed.

Mr. Brunson shook his head again. "They do take it seriously."

"I guess they don't have too many grizzlies," Roy said.

"I guess not," Mr. Brunson agreed. "Well…I must be going. I guess they'll let me go back to the house."

"Surely," Kathy said, sounding sorry.

"Now, don't you folks worry. I'll take care of this," he said, taking an official-looking piece of paper from his pocket.

"His citation," Roy said drily.

"Lots of money…just gone," he said with a snap of his fingers.

"Well, at least you're not going to jail," Kathy spoke up.

"Of that I'm thankful," Mr. Brunson agreed. "Enough excitement for one day, don't you think?"

"I should say so," Kathy agreed.

"Your springhouse," Mr. Brunson said, nodding toward Jake. "They are fixing it, aren't they?"

Jake nodded. "Sounds like they'll pay for it."

"Good. Let me know if they don't. Like that would do any good." Mr. Brunson chuckled at his own joke. "See you all later."

"What a morning," Kathy sighed when Mr. Brunson was out of earshot. "Poor fellow. Brave too, making the hard choice like he did."

"I'm glad we didn't help bury the bear. Especially after this," Roy said, motioning toward the mountain and the dozen or so vehicles that were still up at Mr. Brunson's.

"What was this about paying for the springhouse?" Hannah asked. "Who are *they?*"

"The state," Jake said. "The game warden said the state would pay. But we need to wait until tomorrow before we do the repairs."

"Really?" Hannah was surprised.

"But should you?" Kathy asked. "That's government money."

"I think they should," Roy said quietly. "It was their bear. It's not like Jake would be taking anything for free."

"I suppose so," Kathy said, but she didn't sound convinced.

Hannah worried about how they were to pay for the springhouse. They did need one. It was all they had to cool food items, and as her father said, they weren't taking the money for free. "The state's bear did tear it up," Hannah said out loud.

"I'm glad Indiana doesn't own any bears," Kathy said wryly.

"They probably do," Roy replied. "You just don't know it."

"At least they're not running around my front yard and climbing on my porch," Kathy said.

The reminder of Indiana struck Hannah as she remembered that tomorrow would be her parents' last day with her, and that the hope of her return to Indiana was a thing of the past.

Kathy must have noticed her face. "Did I say something?"

"Just Indiana," Hannah said, not wanting to explain further, especially in front of Jake. It would just add to his burden.

"Yes," Kathy said, "I guess Sunday did take care of that."

Hannah half expected Jake to comment, but he turned to Roy and said, "I need to get a list of materials together. If I take it to the lumberyard this afternoon, maybe they can drive the supplies out tomorrow. I can show the state the materials list then."

"I'll be glad to help," Roy said.

Jake got a piece of paper and pen from the desk, and together they walked out to the springhouse.

"I am glad Roy came along," Kathy said again. "Funny how he worried about what he would do while he was here."

Two state vehicles came back down from Mr. Brunson's, followed by the game warden's truck. When neither stopped, Kathy and Hannah went to prepare sandwiches for lunch with what little they could pull together. Even with the morning's excitement, people had to eat.

In the kitchen, Hannah felt an overwhelming urge to sneeze and quickly stepped outside. Several sneezes followed, and Jake, with pencil and paper still in hand, looked in her direction. When she smiled and gave a little wave, Jake continued to write. Back inside her mother glanced up.

"A cold?" she asked.

"Just excitement, I think," Hannah said. She felt no other signs of a cold.

"A cold might be hard with your pregnancy," Kathy said.

"But surely not serious," Hannah said.

"Well, you can't take the usual medicines, so you have to live through it."

"Oh, that's okay. I never take much anyway."

"You always were like that," Kathy agreed.

Hannah's nose tingled again but quit when she rubbed it.

"I hope that's it," she said, sure her mother had noticed the motion.

"You will see a doctor soon, though?"

"About a cold?"

"No," Kathy said, "about your pregnancy."

Hannah nodded. "Betty told me about a doctor in Libby. I'll make an appointment soon."

"That would be good," Kathy said as outside another state vehicle went by, followed by the lumbering dump truck. "There goes your bear."

"It tore up my springhouse. I'm not shedding too many tears."

"I wonder if it had a mate."

"Grizzlies aren't like us," Hannah said.

"If it would have just stayed up in the mountains, it would have been safe. Wonder why it didn't."

"And our springhouse would still be up. And Mr. Brunson's hogs would still be alive."

"Bears are awful creatures," Kathy said.

"Especially at night," Hannah shivered. She remembered the first night Jake's light had found the bear at the edge of the woods.

When the sandwiches were ready, Hannah called out to her father and Jake.

After lunch the two men hitched up Mosey and left for town. They took along the grocery list for Hannah and returned a couple of hours later with the groceries and the news that the lumber would be delivered that afternoon.

Although they were under orders not to work on the springhouse till tomorrow, Roy decided that didn't mean they couldn't clean up around the springhouse a bit. Jake wasn't so sure but gave in simply because he had an itch to get started.

Hannah worried that a government official would stop in and find Jake and her father at work and cause trouble.

At just before five o'clock, the lumber was delivered and unloaded within reach of the springhouse. By nightfall, when no one from the state had stopped by, Hannah relaxed a little.

After supper the noise of gravel under tires tensed her up again. Jake opened the door and went out onto the porch before anyone could knock.

When he let out a cheery "Good evening, Mr. Brunson," they all knew who it was.

"Would you like to come in?" Jake asked.

"No, I don't think so," Mr. Brunson said. "I just wanted to make sure everything was okay."

"Sure," Jake said. "Nobody else has stopped back by. Anything new on your end?"

No," Mr. Brunson said, sticking his head in the door for a quick hi to everyone. "Nothing new. I just have the court date in a month."

"We'll wish you the best, then," Roy said.

"Thanks," Mr. Brunson said. "When are you folks leaving?"

"Wednesday morning," Kathy said.

"A safe trip, then. Good to have met both of you." Mr. Brunson gave a quick nod in Kathy and Roy's direction.

"Thanks," Roy said. "Keep an eye on the children for us."

Mr. Brunson chuckled. "It's more like them keeping an eye on me." And with that Mr. Brunson excused himself.

"Nice fellow," Roy said when he was gone, "even if he shoots bears."

"We like him," Jake said, taking his seat on the couch again. "He's a good neighbor. I think that was partly why he shot the bear. He was trying to help us out."

"You think so?" Roy asked.

"I do," Jake said. And Hannah agreed.

Twenty

She didn't want to oversleep on her parents' last day, so Hannah had set the alarm for six in the morning. Even so, when she made her way into the kitchen, her mother was already there and attempting to light the stove.

"Why are you up so early?" Hannah asked. "Today's your last day. You should have slept in."

"I couldn't sleep," Kathy muttered. "How do you get this thing going? It's been a while since we had a wood stove."

"It has a mind of its own," Hannah said. "One day it behaves, and the next day it doesn't."

"Ah, now it's going," Kathy said as she replaced the lid, enjoying her conquest.

"It's your last day," Hannah offered again, a pang of regret surging through her.

"I know," Kathy said also with regret. "Where did the time go? At least I'm glad we came. If we hadn't, you would have gone through this all alone."

Hannah didn't want to think about that or what she and Jake might have to go through in the months ahead without her parent's help. She decided to change the subject. "Do we have to take anything to Betty's tonight?"

"Betty didn't say so, but I suppose we should," Kathy said. "We'll just make something and take it along. Do you suppose those men of ours are going to get up soon?"

"I don't know. Jake groaned when the alarm went off."

"I expect your dad will be up soon. Old people can't sleep," Kathy teased.

"I heard that," Roy said from the living room, having approached silently in his stocking feet. "So where's breakfast? Is there no service in this house?"

Kathy ignored him as he pulled out a kitchen chair.

"How's the baby?" he asked Hannah.

"Okay, I guess," she said.

"You take good care of him. Just remember that," he said, mock sternness in his voice.

"What if the baby's not a he?" she asked.

"Doesn't matter," he said with a solid smile. "Either way works. Just so he's healthy."

"What if he's not?" Hannah asked, the sudden thought producing a stab of fear.

"Oh," her father seemed unconcerned at the possibility. "They usually are. Ours all were. Your mother wouldn't have them any other way."

"Roy," Kathy said from across the table.

"But I may not be like Mom," Hannah said.

"You're my daughter," he said, meeting her eyes with a twinkle. "That's good enough for me. You just trust *Da Hah*, and everything will work out fine."

Like with Jake being chosen to become a minister? Hannah wanted to say, but said instead, "I'll try."

She knew she would indeed try, though it might be hard. Jake's ordination had temporarily shaken her confidence in the path *Da Hah* chose for people. He seemed to have a very different point of view from hers.

"Is breakfast ready?" Jake asked, entering the kitchen.

"It'll be a few more minutes," Kathy said.

"I thought we'd get an early start on the springhouse," Jake said to Roy.

"It's too cold for an early start. I haven't even had coffee yet," Roy said in mock grumpiness. "There's no service around here."

"Maybe they'd make some for me," Jake said with a grin.

"I'm sure they would," Roy said, chuckling at his own joke.

"Oh, you're both spoiled," Hannah said.

"You can say that again," Kathy quickly added.

"We could get started right now and come back in for breakfast when it's ready," Jake volunteered.

"I'm not moving without my coffee," Roy stated, pretending he was fastened to his seat.

For a moment everyone was silent, and then Jake said, "We sure are glad you came when you did. Your being here helped in ways you can't imagine."

"That's nice of you to say, Jake," Kathy said. "We want you to know we'll be thinking of you often when we're home in Indiana."

"And praying too," Roy said.

"Now, about breakfast," Kathy said. "Did you put the meat outside, Hannah?"

"Yes, it's on the shelf outside."

Kathy stepped out onto the porch and returned quickly with the bacon and eggs. Hannah started pancake batter. She knew her father would appreciate the gesture on his last morning in Montana.

"Now, if we just had some blueberries for the pancakes," Roy said while Hannah stirred the bowl.

"Talk about being spoiled," Kathy chided.

"I wasn't serious," Roy said quickly, but Hannah knew he was.

In a few minutes, the meal was ready. They all ate eagerly and enjoyed it when Roy led a short devotion afterward to start the day. Normally Hannah and Jake moved into the living room to start the day with a word of prayer, but today it was Jake who suggested they stay at the table. For some reason Hannah couldn't figure out, Jake was acting more serious than he had before. It was good, she supposed, but it *was* a change, and just now Hannah wasn't sure she wanted any more changes. The few recent ones had been quite enough. It was as though the foundations of her world were being tested.

Jake and Roy left to work on the springhouse. Roy wore an extra coat Jake had loaned him. Hannah watched them for a moment as they began work. Then she returned to the kitchen to help Kathy clean up.

Kathy suggested they make cherry pie for the supper at Betty's, but Hannah thought donuts would be better. So they made both. The donuts were more time-consuming, but Hannah wanted to stay busy. It would take her mind off her worries and the realization that in less than twenty-four hours her parents would be gone.

Around four that afternoon, a little earlier than expected, Betty arrived in the surrey buggy. The men were back in the house, relaxing, the springhouse in fresh repair. Kathy and Hannah walked out to meet Betty in the yard.

"So you believe in entertaining your visitors with drama, I hear," Betty teased before she had even stepped down from her buggy.

"What are you talking about?" Hannah asked.

"Shooting bears," Betty said. "Your parents will never come west again!"

"How did you find out about that?" Hannah asked.

"You expect news like that to stay quiet? The whole town's talking," Betty replied.

"Oh, no," Hannah groaned.

"It'll blow over," Betty assured her. "Everything does around here. It's just a little excitement to tide us over until the next little excitement. And, of course, there's the little excitement that happened Sunday too. That was sure something! Hannah, did you and Jake have any idea?"

"No, we didn't," she said. "I still don't understand how it all happened. Why Jake? He's so young."

"I've seen it like this before," Betty said. "So has your mother. A call to the ministry is often a great surprise to the person who receives it, young or not."

"You wouldn't have been wishing it was Steve?" Kathy asked skeptically.

"Oh, of course not!" Betty said emphatically. "I was a little worried about it. I shouldn't have been, I know, but I did lie awake the night before thinking about it. I could never handle such a thing."

"You could have if it was the will of *Da Hah*," Kathy said.

"Well, I suppose," Betty replied, but she didn't sound convinced. "So how are you holding up?" she asked Hannah.

Hannah shrugged, "It's a load for Jake. He took it pretty hard."

"What about you?" Betty asked.

Hannah thought for a moment whether to tell Betty and decided to plunge ahead. She might as well know. "I had been hoping we could move back to Indiana because Jake lost his job and all."

"Move!" Betty exclaimed. "Surely not."

Hannah nodded. "It seemed like the right thing to do."

"Well, I'm glad you're not," Betty said. "I mean…that you're staying here. Then about Sunday, I think God knew what He was doing. He wants you to stay."

"Apparently He does," Hannah agreed halfheartedly.

"You'll see in time," Betty told her.

Hannah wasn't so certain about that, but she was glad Betty now knew about her disappointment. Somehow it made her feel a little better, the burden lighter.

"I'll get Roy, and we'll be ready," Kathy said, moving back toward the house. "The young folks can come when they're ready."

"Hopefully not too late," Betty said.

"No," Hannah said. "We're ready. I think Jake got Mosey ready before he came in. Didn't they do a good job on the springhouse? The bear tore it up."

"Really tore it up," Kathy added.

"Maybe it was good someone shot it," Betty said. "It's the first grizzly I can remember coming down this far."

"Mr. Brunson will have to pay a big fine," Hannah said, "and all he was trying to do was help us out."

"Still he shouldn't disobey the law, I guess," Betty said as she climbed back into the buggy.

"I'll get the pies, and Roy and I will be right there," Kathy said. "Hannah can bring the donuts."

"You baked something? You didn't need to. It's my supper, after all," Betty said.

"Well, you didn't say anything, and we couldn't just sit around all day."

"Someone will eat it," Betty said. "It shouldn't be me, though."

"I'll help you carry the pies out," Hannah offered as she and Kathy walked together to the house. They loaded the pies and then half of the donuts in Betty's surrey after it became obvious there was much more room there.

Jake had Mosey hitched by the time the women were done, and the two buggies left together. As they pulled into Betty's driveway, Hannah was flooded with memories from the summer spent here before her marriage. She wondered why the memories should come tonight. Perhaps God was trying to make things a little easier for her.

That thought brought tears to her eyes, which she hoped Jake wouldn't notice. He did, but he seemed to understand and gave her a gentle smile. Again it struck her how fast he was changing. His new-found maturity at once comforted her and yet seemed strange, unsettling in a way she would never have imagined.

No one mentioned Sunday all evening, which was fine with Hannah. It was good not to think about it for a while.

They stayed later than Hannah thought they should, remembering that Jake had to drive into Libby the next morning for his new job. But the night was simply a night of family, of reveling in the company of loved ones. On the way home, Hannah felt nothing but peace. She thanked God He had comforted her for one evening at least.

Twenty-one

Hannah woke before the alarm clock went off to the sound of a van motor outside the cabin. Quickly she dressed and went out to find her parents up and the suitcases already loaded.

"We wouldn't have left without saying good-bye," Kathy whispered as she gave Hannah a tight hug. "But don't wake Jake. He has a long first day of work ahead of him. Give him our love...and a hug."

Hannah nodded. Her father took her hand and squeezed it a moment before letting go.

Hannah watched from the open cabin door as her parents disappeared into the van. The dome light blinked off, and the gravel crunched under the moving vehicle as it made its way out to the main road.

Hannah stood there as the chilly morning air poured in through the door, not wanting to turn back inside just yet. Finally she closed the door with a sigh. A glance at the living room clock told her it was no use going back to bed. She sat down on the couch and cried instead as an awful loneliness swept over her. Then she noticed Jake's Bible on the floor, the light from the kerosene lamp playing off the black cover and highlighting the gold letters. She thought about reading it—to search for comfort.

The realization that Jake had been reading his Bible the night before held her back. She knew why he had read it, the reason still oppressive. He must have been studying for his first sermon. The book before her was more her enemy than her friend. They had been thrown into a strange, unknown land, and now Jake was willing to venture forward while she was remaining behind.

Jake was walking into this new world alone, and it was up to her to follow if she wished. She felt so alone and even a bit ashamed at the same time.

For a few minutes, Hannah dozed, but she awoke to a fit of sneezing and found some tissue to blow her nose.

Just then Jake came out of the bedroom. "So they're gone," he said, placing his hand on her shoulder. "I didn't hear them leave. I should have gotten up."

"They didn't want me to wake you," Hannah said and then sneezed again. "I'm afraid the cold I was catching earlier is coming back."

"Maybe you should go back to bed. I can get my breakfast."

"No, I'll be fine. I'll get breakfast for you."

"Then I'll get Mosey harnessed," Jake said as he reached for a gas lantern in the closet. With it lit, he stepped outside and walked toward the barn, the light rising and falling with each step. Hannah took a moment to watch him go, the loneliness heavy again.

I'll get over it, she told herself resolutely. *I have Jake and will soon have the baby. And I have Betty. I'll see Mom and Dad again.* She felt a little better and started breakfast preparations.

Jake soon came back inside, and they ate in silence. Hannah was glad for Jake's good mood. It offset her own feelings of loneliness and even despair.

With breakfast done, Jake left while it was still dark. He had to be at the hardware store well before it opened. The sound of his buggy wheels soon faded, and Hannah returned to the couch to lay down. Finally her sadness gave way to sleep.

Just before ten she awoke to a wave of guilt. The dishes were still on the kitchen table, and the house was in disarray from her parents' visit. Jake had never said anything about how she kept house or how clean it was or wasn't, but she didn't want to take any chances. She often had visions of Jake growing up in a house kept spotless by the unswerving diligence of his mother. Hannah felt she should equal what he was used to.

Hannah worked as best she could, but by late afternoon she realized her sniffles and sneezes had developed into a full-blown cold. She gave in again to tiredness and was asleep on the couch when an insistent knock awoke her. Thoroughly embarrassed, she saw a buggy in the driveway and hoped it was Betty's. If it was someone else's, she didn't know how she would ever live down the shame of having been caught asleep in the middle of the afternoon. The visitor surely must have seen her through the front window.

"Hannah?" Betty's voice came clearly from the porch.

Relieved, Hannah rushed to open it, sure her embarrassment still showed on her face.

"Hannah," Betty said when she opened the door, "I have to come in."

"What?" Hannah felt alarm run through her at the expression on Betty's face. "Is something wrong?"

Betty said nothing but pushed past Hannah and sat on the couch. She motioned for Hannah to be seated beside her.

Numbly, Hannah obeyed.

"There's been a wreck," Betty said simply. "It's pretty bad, I'm afraid."

Hannah's heart seemed to stop at the news. "Mom and Dad?"

"Yes…well, the van they were in. A pickup truck came across the median."

Hannah gasped and then asked, "How bad?"

"I don't know for sure." Betty shifted on the couch, and Hannah was certain she wasn't telling her all she knew. Hannah reached out and grabbed her arm.

"You must tell me."

"Someone was killed, I believe, but the state police wouldn't release the information."

"*Who?*" Hannah knew her fingers were digging into Betty's arm.

"The state police called your cousin's house in Indiana. The Mennonites. They must have taken word down to the rest of your family."

"Did they say who was hurt…or killed?"

"No, just gave the hospital number." Betty answered the next question before Hannah asked. "I called from the neighbor's. Your cousin returned my call there and left a message. No one at the hospital would give information out, and they said neither of your parents was available. I couldn't think of who else to ask for...who else was in the van."

"There was Bishop Amos and his wife."

"Oh yes, of course," Betty said. "I should have known that."

"So what should we do?" Hannah wondered out loud. "Where is the hospital?"

"In Buffalo, Wyoming. They had been driving all day."

"We can't go there," Hannah voiced her thoughts.

"I don't know. It depends how bad it is. We may have to."

"I'll leave a note for Jake," Hannah decided, getting up, "or maybe we can catch him on the way home. He goes right past your place. If not, he can come over afterward."

"That sounds good," Betty said as she stood up.

"On top of everything else, I've got a cold," Hannah added as she grabbed a tissue.

"Why does everything come at once?" Betty asked. "They were just here with us. How can this happen?"

"I don't know," Hannah said, equally distraught.

Carefully she wrote the note to Jake, explaining what little she knew about the accident and saying she was at Betty's waiting for news.

Betty now seemed in a hurry to go, so Hannah got her coat. The crispness of the outside air caught her by surprise and provoked another bout of sneezing.

"You shouldn't be out in this," Betty said as they climbed in the buggy.

Hannah thought she shouldn't be in *any* of this—the bear trouble, the financial strain, the minister's duties, the loneliness, and now the terrible anxiety over her parents' lives—but she didn't feel she could complain about it to Betty. God was still in charge, she forcefully reminded herself, even though it didn't feel like it.

"You sure are taking this well," Betty commented as she took her seat in the buggy and handed Hannah a quilt. "Here, wrap yourself in this."

"I don't know if I'm taking it well or if I'm just numb," Hannah said.

The buggy jerked forward, and Betty drove rapidly toward her neighbor's house. Hannah used her handkerchief liberally, unable to distinguish between the tears from her cold and the tears from her fears.

"We don't bother Mrs. Emery too much," Betty said as she pulled to a stop. "Steve wants to talk with Bishop Nisley about putting a phone in the barn. Something needs to be done about our phone situation, I've been telling Steve. If Mrs. Emery isn't home, it's the phone booth in Libby. That's too far. "

"We can go into Libby if you think it's best," Hannah said. "We might be a bother here."

"Mrs. Emery won't mind. Not in an emergency," Betty assured her. She got out to tie the horse. Moments later they were at the door, but no one answered their knock. They listened but heard only silence.

"She must have gone to town," Betty concluded.

"We'd better just use the phone there," Hannah said.

"I suppose we have no choice."

With the matter decided, they drove into Libby and stopped at the grocery store on the edge of town.

"I could go on down and tell Jake," Hannah offered, "now that we're here."

"We'd better get some information first," Betty said. "Here's the phone number. Maybe you should call."

Hannah felt a quiver of fear at what might lie at the end of her phone call, but figured she might as well hear the news straight. She desperately wanted to believe the information wouldn't be too bad.

"I'll need coins," Hannah said.

"I have some." Betty reached into her coat pocket.

Hannah wasn't sure how many she would need, but the several quarters Betty produced seemed sufficient.

She dropped quarters into the slot and dialed the number on Betty's piece of paper. Her fingers trembled in the cold wind swirling around the phone booth, her nervousness only making things worse.

She dropped in more coins as directed by a digitized recording. Then a distinct voice answered, "Good afternoon. Buffalo Hospital. How may I help you?"

"My name is Hannah Byler," she said. "I am calling to talk with my mother, Kathy Miller. We had a report of an accident in which my parents were involved."

Hannah wrapped her coat tightly around her shoulders. Still the wind whipped even harder than it had on the drive into town. Bent away from the blast, she tried to use the sides of the phone booth to get a measure of shelter. There were noises on the line, and she expected the voice to tell her Kathy Miller wasn't available.

"I will page her," the voice said instead.

Silence followed for a few minutes, and then the digitized voice came back on and said, "You have fifty seconds before your time expires."

With cold fingers and a nose that was running furiously, Hannah dropped in several more quarters.

"Yes?" her mother's hesitant voice greeted.

"Mom!" Hannah forgot the wind and the cold, gladness leaping into her voice.

"Hannah," Kathy said. "How did you find us?"

"Betty," Hannah answered. She could see Betty waiting anxiously at her elbow. "The state police called Indiana. They wouldn't give us any news, though. Are you okay?" Hannah left the rest of the question unasked.

"Your dad and I are okay…but Bishop Amos didn't make it." Kathy's voice broke, coming faintly over the line through the tears.

"Amos." Hannah remembered Sunday, the ordination, and the bishop's hands on Jake's head. "He's gone?"

"Yes," Kathy said. "The accident turned the van on its side. We slid for a ways."

"But you and Dad? You're both okay?"

"Dad has a broken arm. I'm okay. I fell on him, I think, when the van turned on its side. Everybody else just has bruises."

"Should we come?" Hannah asked.

"No," Kathy said quickly, "that's not necessary. Things are being arranged. We'll get home. Word has been taken down to the family, so they know. There will be the funeral, of course, for Amos. But you won't be expected to come."

"Okay," Hannah said as the digitized voice said she had thirty more seconds. "Will you let us know when you get home?"

"Yes, I'll let you know through Betty's neighbor," Kathy agreed. "I have her number."

"All right, then. Good-bye, Mom…" Hannah said, her voice breaking.

"We'll be okay," Kathy assured her. "Please don't worry."

When Hannah hung up, Betty said, "It was Bishop Amos?"

Hannah nodded. "I need to tell Jake."

Twenty-two

Betty stayed in the buggy while Hannah went into the hardware store to tell Jake. She thought about asking for him at the front counter but decided to simply search. That would also give her a chance to see what the store looked like.

She found him on the third aisle she glanced down. He was bent over, unpacking items from a large cardboard box and placing them on the shelves.

"Jake," she whispered as she approached.

"Hannah," he said, standing up, "what are you doing here?"

"There's been an accident. The van Mom and Dad were in," she whispered, hoping the owner wouldn't see her and think she was taking up Jake's time unnecessarily.

"Your parents," he asked, "are they okay?"

She nodded quickly. "Dad's got a broken arm. It's Bishop Amos, though. He didn't make it."

"Oh, no!" Jake set the case of batteries he held on the floor. "That's unbelievable. He was just here on Sunday."

Both were silent for a second, taking it all in. Then Hannah said, "Mom doesn't know when the funeral will be."

"We can't go anyway," Jake said slowly.

"No," Hannah agreed, not certain whether Jake wanted to go or not. Would what happened Sunday give Jake reason to attend? Could it be another obligation, an expense they couldn't afford?

"Maybe some of the others will go," Jake said hopefully.

"Well, I'd better be going," she said. "Stop at Betty's house and pick me up."

"Okay," he said.

She turned to go, glancing back his way as she got to the end of the aisle. His back was already bent over the carton again. So quickly, she thought, life can change, and yet it continues on again.

When they arrived at Betty's, Hannah got out and helped unhitch the horse. As she led him into the barn, the memories flooded her again. Here she had worked that summer, dreaming about what her life would be like with Jake. Never had she dreamed it would mean being married to a minister.

She gave Betty's horse a shovel of oats and returned to the house. Betty, still concerned about Hannah's cold, settled her on the couch with a blanket and some hot tea.

"I should be doing something," Hannah soon insisted and moved to get up.

"No, you need the rest," Betty said, insisting she lie back down. "It's probably just tiredness from having your parents here all week and now this tragedy."

Hannah reluctantly settled back on the couch. She had to admit Betty's mothering did feel good. She let the cozy feeling envelope her as she felt protected for the moment from the swirling world of responsibility.

"You can't take anything for that cold—nothing stronger than tea," Betty called from the kitchen.

"I hadn't planned on it," Hannah said. "Mom already mentioned that."

"It'll be over in seven months," Betty said in an attempt to comfort her but instead made her feel even worse. *Seven months!*

Jake pulled into the driveway as dusk fell. Hannah got up quickly, wanting to catch him before he started to tie up. But as she was getting her coat, Betty popped out of the kitchen.

"Tell Jake you're staying for supper," Betty said.

"We can't," Hannah replied, though thinking how much she really wanted to stay. The loneliness of just her and Jake in the cabin weighed on her.

"Go tell him," Betty said, not taking no for an answer. "He can tie up at the barn. There's a horse blanket inside—you know where."

Hannah gave in with relief. She put her coat on and went to tell Jake. He raised no objection and seemed happy with the invitation. She got the horse blanket for him as he tied Mosey to the ring on the barn door. Behind them Steve's buggy pulled in, and Hannah left for the house as Jake waited to talk to Steve.

How Betty had prepared so much food since they had come back from town, Hannah couldn't figure out. She insisted on helping Betty set the table, though Betty wanted her to return to the couch. When Jake and Steve came in, the women joined the men in the living room, and Betty filled Steve in on the details of the day.

Later, around the table, Steve led in prayer. He thanked God for protection for those who survived the van wreck and asked for grace and comfort for Bishop Amos's family. He prayed in simple words first and then closed with a more formal prayer from the Sunday prayer book that he knew from memory.

"We still have much to be thankful for," Steve concluded, "even with Amos now gone."

"Do you think anyone from here will go to the funeral?" Betty asked. "It's a long way back East."

"Bishop Nisley might," Steve allowed and then glanced at Jake.

Hannah wondered what the look was about and didn't have to wait long.

"That makes for just one preacher here Sunday," Steve said, "except Jake."

"You don't think so!" Betty exclaimed. "Not already. It was only last Sunday he was ordained."

Steve shrugged.

"It's way too early," Betty continued. "*Way* too early."

"I was just suggesting it might happen," Steve said apologetically. "Maybe Jake could use the warning."

Jake still said nothing, but a worried look passed over his face.

"You shouldn't say things like that. It might not even happen," Betty said.

"It's okay," Jake finally said. "I'm glad Steve said something. I suppose God will give grace one way or the other."

"Yes, I'm sure He will," Steve allowed.

Hannah was surprised at what Jake had said. It sounded awfully spiritual to her. Was this what lay ahead of them—Jake becoming more and more like this while she remained just herself?

"How's the new job going?" Steve asked, changing the subject.

"Okay," Jake replied. "It will bring in some money. Not much, though. Maybe more with the log furniture business later."

"So Mr. Howard is serious about the furniture?" Steve asked.

"He seems to be," Jake said. "There's plenty of room in the back of the store. Heated and everything. He thinks with some exposure on the web, it should work. We could get orders from all over, then. We wouldn't have to rely just on the tourist trade."

"It might work," Steve allowed.

"You won't get taken advantage of," Betty asked, "working with an *Englisher* like that?"

"I'm not putting any money in," Jake said with a weary smile. "It would be his risk."

"He's a decent man," Steve said quickly. "At least he's always been with me."

"Now you kids let us know if things get too bad this winter," Betty told them. "That goes for both of you. If Jake won't say anything, Hannah can."

"God will help us," Jake said as Hannah glanced sharply at him.

"We will help you too," Betty told him. "That's what family is for—helping out."

"It's not that bad, surely," Steve said with a chuckle. "God will always help those who obey him. That's what King David said."

"King David never had to live through a Montana winter," Betty retorted.

Even Jake had to laugh at that, and it pleased Hannah to see him not quite so serious again.

Hannah expected Jake to be in a hurry to leave and was surprised when they stayed until after eight. The extra moments in Betty's house were appreciated, and Hannah drew them all in with slow breaths. When they finally stepped outside, Hannah had to pull her coat tighter around herself, her eyes watering from the sting of the wind. She hoped the weather wouldn't undo all the good effects of Betty's tea and cozy living room.

On the drive home, Jake seemed lost in his own thoughts. Hannah waited until they were in the living room with the kerosene lamp flickering before she asked, "Do you really think you'll have to preach on Sunday already?"

"It could happen," he said.

"Are you ready?"

"How does one get ready for something like that?" he asked wearily. "I've never even spoken in front of people before."

His young face was lined with worry. Hannah leaned against his shoulder, wanting to both give and receive comfort. She ran her hand through his hair, feeling as if she'd never done that before, as though her hand belonged to someone else entirely, but Jake smiled and kissed her.

"Do you think this is what is really supposed to happen?" she ventured. "Can this be the will of *Da Hah*?"

"It must be," he said, turning toward her, his face now in shadows. "We are not to question such things."

"I can't help it," she said.

"There is no choice," he said simply, "no choice at all."

"We can still move to Indiana," she said, knowing she was grasping at straws but needing to say it anyway.

"You know we can't," he said, the light of the lamp playing on his face, his eyes tender. "Even if I wanted to, this is where we belong."

"What about me?" she asked. "I don't know if I can make it. You are a preacher now. I'm not up to this. I don't know how to be a preacher's wife."

Jake turned toward Hannah and gathered her in his arms, pulling her close. "You'll do fine. Nothing has changed about us. We are still the same."

"No, we aren't," she said, allowing herself to sink into his embrace. "You are changing...and fast."

"It's for the Lord's work," he said, letting his embrace loosen. "Can't you understand that?"

"I need you," she almost cried. "I need you the way you were. It's been only a few days, and I already feel like I'm losing you. You're going to have to preach, Jake. Maybe even on Sunday, already, and in front of all those people. I wasn't made for this. What am I going to do?"

"You shouldn't talk like that," he said gently enough, but the pain didn't go away.

"I can't help it." She felt the tears come. "Our lives are so young. It's not fair. It's not fair that God asks this of us. It's not fair that the church makes such a demand on us. It's just not fair. There are others much older. Even Steve and Betty could have handled it better. Now Bishop Amos is dead. I can't stand this change, Jake. I *can't.*"

He reached out for her hands.

"We have no choice," he said simply as if he thought that was all the answer necessary. "We can't turn back. If we do, it's like forsaking God and His church. We can't do it."

That he was right, Hannah knew, but it did nothing for her pain. To turn back would destroy their lives much more certainly than going forward. Hannah leaned her head against his shoulder. Then she wept—partly from exhaustion and partly from sorrow, but mostly from the knowledge that their lives would never be the same again.

"It's all over for us," she choked.

Jake gently removed her head covering, laid the pins beside the couch, and let down her hair. He stroked her and kissed her till she quit crying.

"It will always be just the two of us," he said softly.

"The baby too," she said quickly.

"Yes," he said, "the baby too," and drew her close to him.

Twenty-three

Hannah sat on the hard bench, afraid the women around her might notice her discomfort. From how several of them had acted this Sunday morning, she knew they already felt the difference. She was now a preacher's wife, and Jake was about to leave for his first Sunday morning ministers' conference.

Hannah could see Jake sitting up front, away from his usual seat among the other men. That had been hard enough. Her first sight of him, what now seemed years ago, had been at church. He was so young and good looking, about to get picked to sing the praise song.

The thought of that moment almost brought a smile to her face, but it vanished before it could appear. She got lost in the thought that now Jake had been chosen again, only not just to sing the praise song. He had been called to preach, perhaps this very day.

Steve's prediction had come true. Bishop Nisley had left for the funeral in Indiana, leaving his only other minister besides Jake to conduct the Sunday morning service. In Amish tradition, one man never was in charge of anything if it could be helped. Perhaps if this had been the Sunday school Sunday, things might have worked out, but it wasn't. Today was the regular preaching Sunday, and two ministers must preach.

The first song started, and at the second line, Minister Chupp stood up and solemnly led the way upstairs. Jake stood and followed. In slow motion Hannah watched them leave. Jake carefully lifted his black Sunday shoes onto each step of the stairs, shoes she had freshly polished for him, hoping it wasn't vanity.

The upstairs bedroom door closed behind them, a click that shut her out, and drove home the point that Jake now went where she could never go. Around her the singing rose and swelled, and Hannah followed along. She forced her mouth to move, but inside the fear gripped her even harder.

In what seemed like forever but was really only thirty minutes, the black shoes came back down the stairs, and the singing soon stopped. Absolute silence filled the house. Who would be the first man to get up and begin speaking to the people?

It was Jake who slowly rose to his feet, his hands trembling, his gaze unsteady. Hannah tried unsuccessfully to look away. Her eyes seemed fixed on Jake's face, on every line she knew so well. His jaw muscles were tight, and his eyes focused on the floor.

Hannah wished she wasn't here, wished Jake wasn't here, wished last Sunday had never happened, wished this Sunday was not happening. But it was. Jake lifted his gaze and moved his eyes slowly around the room, but before he got to Hannah, he once again lowered his eyes.

Slowly he started to speak, haltingly at first, each word causing an ache in Hannah's heart. She had never heard him speak in public before. He quoted something that sounded like Scripture, but she wasn't sure. He then began to tell the story of the van accident, how he had received the news about Hannah's parents being involved, and about Bishop Amos's death.

Jake then spoke about Amos, how he had been a father to many, how he had been here only last Sunday, and how he had spoken to him in private after church. This Hannah didn't know, but then she realized there would likely be many things she'd never know…things she'd never find out about.

Jake said what a great encouragement this conversation had been to him, confused as he was with the sudden turn of events. Bishop Amos had said God did not call a man to a duty and not provide the strength to fulfill it.

Then Jake told the story of the shepherd who left the ninety-nine sheep safe in the sheepfold to find the one lost in the mountains. Hannah had heard the story before, but Jake told it a little differently and concluded that the task of helping the lost and hurting belonged to each one, not just to ministers. The Good Shepherd greatly cared for the lost and wanted people to care for one another.

Hannah found herself listening, even forgetting for a moment that it was Jake. Then he was done and called for prayer. Together the whole congregation knelt as Jake led in a prayer from the prayer book. From how well he read the prayer, Hannah felt certain he had read it before, but she had never seen him do so.

Minister Chupp then read the Scripture and preached the main sermon, closing as usual by asking for testimonies. Hannah tensed for a moment, thinking perhaps someone might say Jake had preached error. No one did.

After church dismissed, the tables were spread, and lunch began. In Bishop Nisley's absence, Minister Chupp announced the prayer time. Hannah realized this might be another public thing Jake would soon perform. She suddenly felt old and haggard, certain her face betrayed her emotions.

Apparently Betty noticed, took Hannah's arm, and pulled her along to sit with the older women at the first table. It only made Hannah feel worse to sit with women old enough to be her mother. But almost immediately the women put her at ease with conversation that led her to believe they thought of her as not just a minister's wife but as a person. Clara, Minister Chupp's wife, asked about her mother and father. She answered as best she could, and then Betty took over.

"Kathy called the neighbor on Friday. Roy can't work for a while because of his broken arm. I can't imagine that. Steve would have a fit too. Kathy's okay, though. Then there was the funeral yesterday, although Amos wasn't from their district. I think he's from around Shipshewana."

"When are the Nisleys coming back?" Clara asked.

"I don't know," Betty answered.

"Probably later this week," Ruth Yoder said from the end of the table. "They'll take some time to visit while they're there in the East."

"Everyone usually does," Betty agreed.

One of the younger girls brought new bowls of peanut butter and red beets, which made Hannah feel old and out of place again as she had often served the older women.

"I'm not used to sitting here," Hannah whispered to Betty.

"You'll get used to it," Betty whispered back without much sympathy.

The flow of conversation shifted, leaving Hannah to her own thoughts of Jake and his good preaching that morning. Suddenly a memory came to her from years ago. She wasn't sure of the occasion, but her father had said that preachers who preach well have extra temptations. For many of them, it goes to their heads. Some even leave for more liberal churches. "They can't stay humble enough, I guess," he had said.

Hannah remembered the words just like that, as if they had been dropped into her mind all in one piece. Would her father say that about Jake? Jake had preached well, had he not? And on his first sermon too. Who could tell where he would go with some practice?

Hannah thought of whispering a question to Betty, so strong was her distress, but someone around the table might hear, and this was not a matter for the ears of others. It might not even be something she should discuss with Betty.

Hannah wished her mother were here. She would be one safe person to go to with concerns like these.

Her thoughts were interrupted by Minister Chupp's announcement of the closing prayer. Hannah bowed her head along with the others, convinced she must talk to someone, even if it was Betty.

With the prayer done, Betty whispered as if on cue, "I need to talk to you." By the way she said it, Hannah knew that Betty intended a private conversation. She got up with a glad heart and followed Betty into the back bedroom without either of them drawing attention to themselves.

"I have something to tell you," Betty whispered once they were inside but leaving the bedroom door open.

"Yes?" Hannah waited. This would surely take just a moment, she thought. Betty would mention plans about some coming event, and then she could ask if her concerns about Jake were valid.

Betty's face became sober instead as she glanced behind her, as if to make sure no one was listening. Two sleeping babies lay on the bed, but no mothers were in sight.

Betty began, keeping her voice low, "My, can Jake preach! And his first time! I just have to tell you something. It's been bothering me for years, heavy on my heart. I have never told anyone, not even your mother, and she and I were always so close." Betty glanced behind her again.

Hannah's heart sank as she realized what Betty intended and the implications of it. *I am now the minister's wife. Even my aunt is giving me a new and unwanted respect and now intends to use me for confessions.*

A tear hung on the edge of Betty's eye. "I wish I had said something, even to Steve, but I couldn't bring myself to tell even him. We married and still I couldn't tell him. I don't think I ever can either. Today, though, for the first time, Jake gave me the courage to say it. I just have to tell you, Hannah. It hurts so inside. Keeping it here." Betty pressed her hand against her heart.

Hannah swallowed hard. There would be no sharing her own concerns with Betty today or perhaps ever. That was quite obvious. She would now be the one a woman might confess to, but she herself would not have that same freedom. Not even to her aunt.

"The other night at supper when you and Jake were there—what I said about King David and God. I shouldn't have."

Hannah felt relieved. If this was all her aunt referred to, perhaps there was nothing to fear. Betty was always one to get overworked about things. There would be time yet to ask about Jake and his possible temptations to pride.

"It's okay," Hanna said as she squeezed Betty's arm. "You didn't mean it."

"No." Betty shook her head as two tears moved down her cheeks with many more ready to follow. "It's not just that. It's the reason I say things like that. See, it's just easier to blame God sometimes, even when I know it was my own fault."

Betty clutched Hannah's arm, seemingly unaware of where she was. Hannah was deeply grateful no one else had walked in on them yet.

She doubted whether she and Betty could pass this off as a normal conversation.

"I was wild once. Your mother was too," Betty continued. "I was the bad one, though. Much worse than the others, only no one really knew. I was good at hiding things. Then too...see, Hannah..." Betty's eyes filled with pain. "I had an English boyfriend. In secret. For a long time. I thought I would die when he left me because I wouldn't go with him. Only I had wished to go! Wished it with all my heart! Oh, Hannah, I thought God would never let me love again after that. That is what I almost told Steve, so he would know. When I married him, I thought I could forget about it."

Hannah, completely overwhelmed, didn't know what to say. She had known from her mother about the *rumspringa* days of her parents' youth but not this much detail. Now she felt the burden of the confession itself and the unexpected weight it placed on her shoulders, the sorrow because she had to be the one to bear it.

"Oh, Hannah," Betty said, wiping away her tears. "I'm so glad I could tell you that. God has sent us such a good minister in Jake."

Because she didn't know what else to do, Hannah gave Betty a hug. It felt awkward, but Betty responded with a squeeze back...and then someone came in the door. They both smiled as if it were a perfectly normal Sunday morning—as if nothing had changed.

On the way home, Hannah asked Jake, "You won't ever go liberal, will you?"

"Liberal?" he asked, a puzzled look on his face.

"Nothing," she said with a shake of her head, her thoughts fuzzy. "I was just asking."

"You don't want me to, do you?" he asked with a note of horror in his voice.

"Of course not," she said.

"Good," he said, shaking Mosey's reins, urging him up the incline toward their cabin.

"You spoke well today," she said, forcing herself to acknowledge the truth, "real well."

"I don't know," he said, but Hannah was sure he liked hearing her praise.

Twenty-four

The following weekend Jake went elk hunting with Steve in the Cabinet Mountains. They took along white-tailed deer tags too, just in case there were no elk. Hannah felt certain they were driven by the joy of the hunt more than the desire for fresh meat.

Jake's anticipation of the hunt brought a smile to his face that relieved Hannah. Between his ordination and his new job at the hardware store, he had been sober long enough. The little money the job provided wasn't enough for them to live on for long, and Hannah knew how much it weighed on him.

The hunters left before dawn on Saturday morning, accompanied by two *Englishers*, friends of Steve. It was better for them not to be alone in the mountains, Steve had said. Plus the drive with the *Englishers* supplied the easiest way to reach the jump off point, where they would hike into the mountains.

The day went by fast enough for Hannah, but by four o'clock, with darkness threatening and what looked like snow clouds on the peaks of the mountains, she began to worry a bit. Everything else was going wrong for them, so why shouldn't something more happen? Maybe something worse. But no sooner had she gone out to the porch to look toward the mountains than the pickup truck pulled in.

Jake jumped from the back and waved a thanks as the two *Englishers* drove back out of the driveway. Hannah watched him expectantly, curious if he had been able to relax—and if he had shot anything.

Jake seemed happy enough as he walked toward the house after putting his gun in the barn.

"Got something, I did," he said cheerfully as he bounded up onto the porch.

"An elk?" she asked.

"No, just a deer. We need to go over to Steve's tonight. He's going to keep part of it after we butcher it. Betty will make supper for us."

"Good thing I hadn't started anything yet."

"I'll get Mosey," he said. "We need to go."

"I'll get some pans and knives," she said, walking quickly toward the kitchen.

Minutes later they were on their way, the pans and knives rattling in the back of the buggy.

By the time they arrived, Steve already had the deer strung up in the barn. Hannah, having forgotten an apron, ran into the house to see if Betty had an extra.

"What a mess!" Betty proclaimed as she opened the kitchen door. "And on a Saturday night to boot."

Hannah offered a wry smile and said, "Well, at least they enjoyed themselves. Jake did anyway. And that's worth a lot."

"Oh, Steve did too," Betty said. "There's something about men, guns, and mountains."

"Do you have an apron for me?" Hannah asked. "I forgot mine."

"Yes, I think so." Betty dug in the kitchen drawer and produced two dark blue, full-length aprons. She held them up. "Good butchering aprons. Saturday night's just not good."

"Just think fun," Hannah told her with a grin, and then she headed out to the barn. The weighty clouds seemed on the verge of dumping a white blanket of snow. The heavy air wrapped itself around her but was not about to dampen her spirits.

Jake and Steve were busy with the first deer. They had already set some of the meat out on a card table covered by clean plastic. As Hannah entered, the snow began to gently fall in thick heavy flakes to the ground.

"Looks like it's good we didn't get lost in the mountains after all," Steve said, relief in his voice.

Betty walked in and said, "You didn't get lost?"

"Not really," Jake replied quickly. "We just thought so for a moment."

"That's what I don't like about mountains," Betty declared. Hannah gave her a quick glance of agreement. Those mountains looked so innocent, so friendly, and yet they harbored dangers one would never notice at first glance.

Betty filled several bowls with water from the barn spigot, and Hannah set to work washing the meat. She separated the types of meat into different piles as best she could, and soon the table was piled half full. Betty then went even further, cutting the slabs into smaller pieces and bagging them. Two plastic tubs on the barn floor took the finished product.

A little after eight, they were done. Steve and Jake hauled the unused portions of flesh into the woods with flashlights.

"Something will take care of it," Betty muttered to Hannah.

"At least you don't have bears around," Hannah said.

"Not yet," Betty replied, not in a very good mood. "At least it's stopped snowing."

"Do you think we're in for a hard winter?" Hannah asked, dreading the answer.

"You never know." Betty shrugged, putting lids on the plastic tubs. "Snow's early enough, I guess. You think this tub's got enough meat for you?"

Hannah lifted the lid on the smallest tub, calculating briefly before her reply. "Too much," she said.

"You sure?" Betty asked.

"I'm sure. We can't use that much in the next few weeks."

"No, not without a freezer," Betty agreed, taking several bags back out. "You know how to marinate this meat? It makes a real tasty meal using the steaks."

"I don't have a recipe," Hannah said. "I'm sure you do, though."

Betty nodded. "Don't let me forget to give it to you before you go. You're staying for supper. A *late* supper."

"If it's not too much bother," Hannah said.

"There's no sense in going home to the cabin still having to fix supper. I've got plenty."

The men came back in and stamped snow from their boots.

"That's enough meat for a while," Steve said. "Now, for supper. Looks like we didn't even go too late."

Hannah followed Betty to the house and set the table while Betty heated the soup she had prepared earlier. Betty went to put her share of the meat in the propane-powered deep freezer in her basement. Hannah hoped she and Jake would have a freezer someday when they had enough money, but for now the springhouse would have to do.

Jake and Steve came in noisily after having put Jake's share of meat in the buggy. They sat down for a quick supper. Just as they were finishing and Hannah had risen to help Betty clear the table, they heard a clear, unearthly scream rent the air outside. Hannah stopped in her tracks, several bowls balanced in her hands.

"What was *that*?" Betty asked, her voice rising.

Steve and Jake jumped up from the table at the same time, two protectors ready for battle.

"It's just an animal…bobcat probably," Hannah said, remembering the bobcats she often saw at the edge of the woods near the cabin. "You did drag the deer parts into the woods, right?"

"I just knew they shouldn't have done that," Betty said from the kitchen, her voice still high pitched.

Just then they heard another scream.

"That's more than a bobcat," Steve said.

"We'd better look," Jake said.

"No you don't," Betty told them.

Steve and Jake ignored her as Steve went to retrieve his flashlight from the bedroom.

"You'd better just stay inside," Jake said to the women.

"It's just a bobcat," Hannah said, more hesitantly now that she had heard the second scream. That was an awful lot of noise for the size of creature she had seen near the cabin.

"I think it's something bigger than a bobcat," Jake said. "We'll be careful," he added in answer to her concerned look.

"I'm going with you," Hannah said, eliciting a look of astonishment on Jake's face.

"Well, I'm not!" whispered Betty, her face pale.

As the trio stepped outside, all was quiet. The snow was falling gently now. Steve's light searched the darkness with a beam of brilliant white.

"I don't see anything," Steve said as they approached the edge of the woods.

"We left the deer parts deeper in," Jake said, moving on.

"We should have buried them," Steve said with regret. "I was thinking small animals."

In answer to his words, the scream sounded again very near. Hannah grabbed Jake's arm.

"We'd better go back," she whispered.

Jake shook his head. "Whatever it is, it's too big to leave here."

"I think it's a mountain lion," Steve offered, moving deeper into the woods. Jake followed, and Hannah, who wasn't about to stay by herself, tagged close behind.

Just then a flash of eyes was caught in the beam of Steve's light. A faint outline of a long body stretched out behind those eyes.

"Hannah's right. We had better go back," Steve shouted as he bent down to search for something to throw.

The answer was another scream from the animal, its tail violently slamming against the ground.

"Maybe we'd better call the game warden," Jake suggested, hanging back as Steve advanced even closer.

"A lot of good that did with your bear," Steve replied as he lifted a good-sized branch from the ground and waved it above his head and charged toward the two eyes.

Hannah stifled her own scream as what appeared to be a large mountain lion first advanced, snarled, and then retreated slowly. Its tail thrashed wildly, and low growls rose from its throat.

"Shoo!" Steve said even louder. "Get!"

Jake seemed to gather courage and moved closer.

"Get a shovel," Steve told Jake. "We need to bury these remains. I can't have cats like this hanging around."

"Where is one?" Jake asked.

"In the barn. Hannah knows."

Hannah headed quickly to the barn with Jake following. She grabbed two shovels, handed them to Jake, and then took a hoe for herself. When they returned to where Steve had faced off with the animal, they found that Steve had successfully chased it off—for now. The two men then took turns digging several deep holes, the digging easier once they were through the frozen surface.

"That ought to do it," Steve concluded after they had pushed the last of the deer parts into the holes. Hannah used her hoe to smooth over the spot.

"That was a close call," Jake said, wiping his forehead as Steve tamped the ground with his feet.

"What if the cat digs it up?" Hannah asked.

"Then I guess we have to call the game warden," Steve said. "Something has to be done anyway. Hopefully this will work."

Back in the house, Betty looked as though she expected them to be torn to bits.

"We're alive," Steve told her, chuckling.

"Don't do things like that again," Betty said. "My heart can't stand it."

"I'll try not to," Steve said with a teasing laugh.

"We'd better get going," Jake said, moving toward the front door.

"Thanks for supper," Hannah said on the way out.

"And for help with the meat," Jake added.

When they arrived home, Hannah helped Jake stash the meat in the springhouse, making sure the door was securely fastened. One animal disturbance for the night had been enough for her.

Later Hannah took comfort in Jake's arms long after he had fallen asleep.

Twenty-five

The next day Jake didn't have any responsibilities in church because Bishop Nisley was back. The fact that he had to sit in front on the ministers' bench still bothered Hannah but less so than the previous week.

On Monday, she reminded Jake about her need for a doctor's appointment. Betty had told her Sunday about a woman doctor in Libby, Dr. Lisa, who came highly recommended. "She's not a regular obstetrician," Betty had said. "She's just a family doctor, but she's good." That was good enough for Hannah, as neither she nor Jake had a regular doctor since their move to Montana.

Hannah asked Jake to call for an appointment from the hardware store. She was a bit concerned about where they'd get the money but more concerned that their baby have a healthy entrance into the world. She was sure Jake felt the same way.

When Jake returned home, he told her the appointment was on Thursday in two weeks. Hannah raised the question about how to pay. Jake didn't say anything for a while but then simply said the money would have to come out of his paycheck. They had started building the log furniture this week, he added, and perhaps there would be more income later.

That evening, Hannah served the first of the deer burger and asked if Mr. Brunson could be invited for supper on Friday night. "I'm marinating steak," she said. "He might enjoy it."

"What about the burger?" Jake asked. "Wouldn't that be good enough?"

"You'll be good and tired of deer burger by then," Hannah assured him. "Trust me. We will be depending a lot on hunting this winter."

Jake nodded solemnly. "Then I guess I should go again before too long. The white-tailed deer licenses are easy enough to get."

"You wouldn't even have to go back to the mountains," Hannah said, hoping that would make things easier.

"I guess we're stuck with wild meat for a while," Jake said with a slight groan.

"Maybe we'll learn to like it as much as hamburger," Hannah said. She caught herself feeling more cheerful than she had in a long time, and it surprised her. *Maybe I've matured*, she thought, *faster than expected*. The thought made her laugh.

The next day a long letter full of news arrived from her mother. Her father was about to climb the walls and more than ready to get back to work. The bishop's funeral had been a sad one and large, as it often was when a tragic, sudden death occurred.

Toward the end of the letter, Kathy said the trailer factories were on a fresh hiring spree with many new openings—if one liked that type of work. Why her mother should mention this, Hannah was uncertain. It felt like salt had been poured into her still-opened wound. Did her mother think there was a chance they could move? Hannah sighed, realizing her mother meant well. Some baby news followed along with who was dating whom, as if her mother was really interested in such things. *She must be trying to satisfy my interest*, Hannah thought, *since these are the people I know.*

At the end there came a little mention—a mere drop of words on the page—that Hannah was to tell Jake the district next to theirs lacked a minister, one short of the usual number. Some minister called Benny Troyer had moved to southern Ohio.

This stirred emotions Hannah had resolved to forget. Possibilities raced through her mind until she had to calm herself down. It seemed unlikely Jake would consider this opening, and she decided not to tell him, at least for now. If an appropriate time ever came, then perhaps she might say something.

Jake came home on Wednesday night grinning with the news that Mr. Howard had set up the first tools in the shop.

"I started my first project," Jake said. "Not bad, if I have to say so myself. Mr. Howard was pleased too."

Hannah sat on the couch ready to listen, glad Jake was happy.

"I nicked my finger a little." Jake showed her the bandage.

"Surely you're not starting that!" Hannah imagined future injuries, even missing fingers.

Jake laughed at the look on her face. "I'll learn to be careful," he assured her.

"Please," she said, looking beseechingly at him, glad at least he seemed to take her concerns seriously.

"Is supper ready?" he asked.

"Yes."

"Deer burger again?"

"I have cherry pie too, though," she said, delighted when his face lit up.

"Can we afford it?" he asked.

"We had an extra can of cherries from when my parents were here. The pie is a bit skimpy. Maybe I shouldn't buy such extras for a while, though."

"Maybe," he said.

"Did you invite Mr. Brunson yet?" she asked.

"Yesterday. He said he'd come."

Just after supper, as Hannah was clearing the dishes, they heard a buggy rattle into the driveway. Jake went to the door and stepped outside onto the porch to wait. Hannah wondered who would come visiting unannounced at this time of night. Betty would, no doubt, but Hannah could think of no reason unless there was bad news. Hannah pushed the thought away and purposely stayed in the kitchen, waiting for the person to arrive.

When the door opened, Hannah could hardly believe her eyes. Bishop Nisley came in, followed by Elizabeth, his wife. Jake closed the door behind them, a concerned look on his face. Hannah instantly knew this visit could not be for social reasons.

Bishop Nisley took off his hat and held the black rim in his hands. He looked friendly enough as he took the seat on the couch Jake offered him. Hannah felt frozen to her spot in the kitchen. She saw Elizabeth glance toward her, obviously on the verge of moving in her direction even as Jake offered her a seat beside her husband.

Hannah knew she must face this, whatever it was. It might only be a church matter—perhaps this was Bishop Nisley's way of handling such things. Though, why it couldn't wait for their regular Sunday morning meeting, she couldn't imagine.

With a forced smile on her face, Hannah stepped forward to greet Elizabeth. Normally the smile would have come with no effort, as she had felt close to the bishop's wife since spending the summer at Betty's riding stable. Now, though, her smile was simply out of politeness. Was this her destiny as a minister's wife, inventing expressions while trying to feel what she ought to feel? That's what she had done when Betty confessed her youthful indiscretions, and now she did it again.

"Good evening," Elizabeth said, all smiles. "I hope we aren't interrupting your supper."

"No." Hannah forced the smile again. "We're finished."

"Can I help with the dishes?" Elizabeth glanced into the kitchen.

"I can get those later," Hannah told her quickly.

"No, I'm helping." Elizabeth obviously had made up her mind. Her help meant this visit was going to be lengthy, whatever its purpose. It seemed unlikely she would offer to help just to have a five-minute chat.

When the women were in the kitchen, Elizabeth turned the sink's hot water faucet on but succeeded in getting only cold water.

"We have to heat the water," Hannah said, motioning toward the bowl of water already warm on the stove. "We only have a spring."

"Oh, that's different," Elizabeth said. "I didn't know."

"Well..." Wild thoughts ran through Hannah's head. *Does Elizabeth think I, her new minister's wife, am completely strange for how I live? Is she disappointed in how poor we are? Does she think Jake ought to own a gas water heater?*

Elizabeth must have noticed her face. "Oh," she said, laughing softly, "I didn't mean anything. There's nothing wrong, really. We didn't always have everything just right either."

"Oh?" Hannah tried to feel normal again.

"That was in Indiana," Elizabeth recalled. "John could afford a water heater when we were married, but we did without other things."

"Oh." Hannah felt worse now, as she could well imagine the *other things* Elizabeth referred to were probably furniture—new furniture items she didn't even dream of owning. She was still stuck on a gas water heater. Shame filled her, and she wished she could disappear through the kitchen floor.

"What can I do?" Elizabeth asked, glancing around. "John probably wants us back in the living room before too long."

"I'll put some more wood on the fire," Hannah said, feeling very much like a country bumpkin who must stoke her smoky fire before she could even wash the dishes.

Perhaps it was the light from the fire as Hannah bent over the stove that gave Elizabeth a good look at her face. Hannah had made no attempt to hide her feelings.

"I'm so sorry," Elizabeth exclaimed. "Did I say something? I really didn't mean to. Here I am barging in, disrupting your evening and your kitchen."

When Hannah didn't say anything, Elizabeth gently took her arm and guided her to a chair beside the kitchen table.

"I'm sorry. This must all be so sudden. You're both so young. John thought he had to come over tonight, though I tried to tell him it wasn't that serious. He just thinks things should be taken care of before they get out of hand."

"Elizabeth," the bishop's voice called from the living room. "We shouldn't be staying too late."

Hannah was grateful she wasn't in tears yet. What had she and Jake done already? It must be something terrible. She felt frozen in place and wasn't sure she could have stood up if Elizabeth hadn't helped her.

"It's nothing serious, really," Elizabeth whispered, as if she were afraid someone might hear. "John just wants to talk to Jake."

Numbly Hannah followed Elizabeth into the living room, all attempts at fake smiles gone. She knew the bishop was looking at her, but she didn't care at the moment.

"Ah..." John cleared his throat, seeming to search for words, no preacher tone in his voice. Hannah dared glance at his face and was surprised to see it soft and tender. Jake had his head bowed, as if he already knew what was to come.

"Mose Chupp told me about the other Sunday," John said, tightly clasping his hands. "I knew you would have to preach, and that so soon."

Hannah glanced at Jake, who was still looking at the floor.

"From what he told me, you did quite well."

No one said anything.

"I know this may sound strange," the bishop continued, "but I just had a concern about that. I know it's soon, but perhaps it's best to say it now rather than having to say something more important later."

"He's just trying to help," Elizabeth spoke up. "I told him Jake meant no ill. He was trying so hard, they said."

"What did I do?" Jake managed, his eyes still focused on the floor.

"You preached pretty good," the bishop said as if that explained things. "I'm just concerned about that. So good so quickly. It can do things to a person. I don't want you spoiled, Jake. I really don't."

"He's just trying to help," Elizabeth said again. "He really is."

"So what am I supposed to do?" Jake sounded puzzled.

The bishop cleared his throat. "Apparently you are one of those to whom preaching comes naturally. You're good at this, Jake. That is a great danger. I don't want to lose you."

"How would you lose me?" Jake asked.

"I don't want to put things into your head." The bishop shrugged. "A lot of churches are looking for good preachers. Liberal churches, that is. Things get around. People hear. They make you offers. I hope you don't go down that road."

"I don't plan to," Jake said.

"Temptation is a strange thing." John spoke slowly. "It comes when we least expect it. It comes in ways we hadn't thought of. I just wanted to warn you right away. Walk humbly with God, Jake. We need you around here."

Jake nodded.

"Well, we'd better be going," the bishop said, glancing toward his wife.

"We haven't finished the kitchen," Elizabeth replied. "We were just going to start."

"I can manage," Hannah spoke up. "I really can."

The bishop waited a moment before he said, "We really should be going. Good night, then."

Jake opened the door for them, and they stepped out into the brisk night air.

Numbly Jake sat back down on the couch while Hannah went back to the kitchen. The water was boiling furiously in the bowl, and the fire had burned down to hot coals. She dipped some water out to fill the sink and added soap. Her tears soon joined the dishes in the suds. She didn't hear Jake until his arms came around her shoulders.

"I wish this had never happened. I wish we were free again. Free to…" She wondered if she should say it. "Free to move back to Indiana," she whispered.

"No." His answer came as if from far away. "God wants us to stay here."

Then she laid her head on his shoulder and wept till he gently joined his hands with hers in the kitchen sink. They washed dishes, four hands in one tub, plates sliding past their fingers, and then Jake's lips brushed her cheek.

Twenty-six

The Friday sun shone with full vigor as Hannah busied herself with preparations for the evening meal with Mr. Brunson. She had marinated the deer steak since Wednesday, using Betty's recipe plus a few added touches of her own.

Kathy had always told her a good cook must allow intuition, not just a recipe, to guide her. If something went wrong, it was just food that was wasted. *That might be true in Indiana*, Hannah thought, *but here and now, I cannot afford to be wrong.*

She had thought of inviting Steve and Betty but decided against it because Betty would wonder if her recipe had been followed to the letter. If the new formula worked, then things would be okay. If not, then Hannah would feel thoroughly embarrassed. She didn't want the pressure.

When the potatoes boiled early, Hannah let them cool by the stove while she prepared the cherry pie. The crust turned out satisfactory— not quite like her mother's but good enough. And really, could she expect to do as well as her mother? Not yet. But perhaps later in life— if she survived what she was going through now.

Waves of self-pity rushed through her, and Hannah had to remind herself that, after all, Jake loved her, and that should help her weather any storm.

She didn't understand, though, why Jake didn't want to move back to Indiana. It would make both their lives so much easier. The thought puzzled her as she peeled the steaming potatoes. He never really mentioned why. He just said God wanted them here. Was it something deeper? Some reason he wasn't telling her?

She remembered the comfort of his presence as they washed dishes last night and couldn't imagine him hiding anything from her. Yet was he? The thought wouldn't go away, and she gave up trying to figure it all out. Besides, she was too busy to be preoccupied with such impossible thoughts.

Jake arrived home at the usual time and offered to help. She told him he could set the table, which he did—not perfectly, but the dishes were in the right vicinity.

As he tugged on the tablecloth to straighten it out, he announced his good news that he had finished his first log table at the hardware store. A customer had stopped by and taken a look at the still unvarnished product and placed an order for two tables.

"Just like that," Jake said with a huge smile. There would be a bonus in his paycheck next week, Mr. Howard had said, just in time for the doctor's bill.

A few minutes later, the sound of Mr. Brunson's tires crunching on the gravel in the driveway announced his arrival. Jake lit the gas lanterns and hung one in the kitchen tonight, a little extra light for which Hannah was thankful.

When Mr. Brunson had been shown in, they sat down almost immediately to eat. They bowed their heads for prayer, but Jake didn't offer to pray out loud tonight. With the "Amen," Hannah brought out the steak from the oven. Still a bit unsure how it would taste, she set the steaming platter on the table with shaking hands. Earlier she had sampled the meat and liked what she tasted, but would the men feel the same way?

She knew men did not always agree with a woman's taste on such matters. Jake served himself gingerly while Mr. Brunson seemed to have no such qualms, piling his plate high with meat.

Jake cleared his throat and said, "You might want to go slow on that. It's Hannah's first time marinating deer meat."

Mr. Brunson laughed and turned to Hannah as he said, "I have full confidence in Hannah. She's a good cook."

"Better taste it first," Hannah said. "I might not be."

Mr. Brunson took a healthy bite while Jake put a small piece in his mouth. Both men bit down thoughtfully and for several seconds said nothing as they chewed the meat. Then they looked at each other and burst out in laughter.

"It's *awful*," Hannah cried, her hands flying to her face, a red blush rising to her cheeks. The supper was totally ruined, she was certain.

"Hannah, I've never tasted a better steak," Mr. Brunson pronounced, "not even in the best restaurants Boston has to offer."

"Agreed," Jake said, "although I've never been to the best restaurants Boston has to offer."

"You're just saying that," Hannah whispered, still unconvinced. "Is it really good?"

"Yes, it certainly is," Mr. Brunson said.

Jake just nodded.

"Have some yourself," Mr. Brunson said.

"I'll get the cherry pie first," she said, wanting to savor the moment fully.

Mr. Brunson then turned the conversation in another direction. "So how's the furniture business coming along, Jake?"

For the next several minutes, Jake eagerly brought Mr. Brunson up to date, even going into some detail about making log furniture by hand.

With dinner a success, the two men moved to the living room while Hannah cleared the table. Minutes later, Hannah joined the men for a quiet evening of conversation.

"Jake, tell me more about this ordination of yours," Mr. Brunson said.

Jake seemed not to know what to say, and for a few seconds, silence hung heavy in the room.

"I hope I'm not imposing," Mr. Brunson finally continued. "I've just wanted…for some time to talk with someone."

Hannah had an instant flashback to Betty's drawn and sober face that Sunday when she had confided in Hannah. Had people nothing but confessions to make to ministers and their wives? Was everyone hiding secrets? Was she to bear this burden all her life now?

Jake, sitting beside her on the couch, finally spoke up. "I'm still pretty new at all this, but if there's something I can do to help you…"

"It's been many years," Mr. Brunson began. "You will think me crazy, and maybe I am just a crazy old man stuck here in the mountains. Alone and crazy. Yet there is a reason for it."

Mr. Brunson took a big blue handkerchief out of his pocket and blew his nose.

Jake said nothing, just listened.

"There is the court date coming up soon," Mr. Brunson continued. "The bear thing."

Does he need help with the fine? I hope not. How on earth could we help with that? We are barely able to get along as it is.

"We would be glad to help," Jake said. Mr. Brunson, though, waved aside the suggestion.

"No son. It's not money I need. I need to confess my sins. I'm sorry to impose on you two this way." His eyes went to Hannah's face and then dropped to the cabin floor.

"Your sins?" Jake managed.

"Yes, my sins," Mr. Brunson said simply. "They are about to find me out, I think, as the Good Book says. See, I have money. That's not the problem. The fine will be big, but I can pay it. It's what will happen when I draw the money to pay the fine."

Jake looked puzzled.

"I'm not a criminal, at least not in the eyes of the law. In here I am—" Mr. Brunson placed a hand on his heart. "Let me start from the beginning…if that's okay?"

"Sure," Jake said, and Hannah nodded.

"I'm a businessman. Or I was," Mr. Brunson said, "back East, as you know. Beyond that, you *don't* know. See…" Mr. Brunson brushed away another tear. "I am also a family man. Or I was. I have a son. I had a daughter and a wife."

There followed a long silence, in which no one seemed to move.

"One night I was driving home from a social function—a business Christmas party, a busy season for the company—with my wife and daughter, whom I had hardly seen for weeks. It was raining, and there was an accident. The car slid off the road. The officer said it could have happened to anyone, but I knew—knew with certainty—that it was my fault. It would not have happened if... My wife, Bernice... Well, we were arguing. It doesn't matter about what. Some little thing. I wasn't paying attention to my driving."

"Your wife and daughter?" Jake asked.

"They were both killed," Mr. Brunson said, his face a picture of agony. "Why did I survive? I was the guilty one."

"Your son?" Jake asked.

"He doesn't know where I am. He was very bitter after the accident. He and his sister were very close. He blamed me. And he was right. So I left. I just up and left with enough money to come here to do what I wanted to do—to just forget. I planned on just staying here forever. I planned on never going back."

"Would he be looking for you?" Jake asked.

"I don't know," Mr. Brunson said. "That's the problem. I didn't want him to find a trail. That's why I left none. I made it almost impossible for him to find me here. But now what will I do? Will he try to find me? If I draw the money out of the accounts, it will be much easier for him to locate me. I just don't think I can ever face him again. The blame is too much. The way he looks at me, I just can't go back to that. It's destroyed me. Isn't it enough that I live with the guilt every day?"

"Perhaps your son has forgiven you," Jake offered. "Maybe this is God's way...of mending the past."

"Maybe in your world that seems possible. In mine, it doesn't. I wasn't the father I should have been."

"What's your son's name?" Jake asked.

"Eldon," Mr. Brunson said. "A fine boy."

"I'm sure he is," Jake said quickly. "I think if he contacts you, it would be because he wants to find you and make things right. Surely he wouldn't find you just to continue to make your life miserable."

"I guess we'll find out," Mr. Brunson said, seeming to collect himself.

"I'll surely pray that it all works out for the best," Jake said.

Jake's words—and his gentle manner with Mr. Brunson—amazed Hannah. It was a side of Jake she had never noticed.

"Well, they say that confession is good for the soul," Mr. Brunson said, his tone a bit lighter. "And I do believe just telling someone has helped a bit. You're the only folks I've ever told about this. It just seemed the right thing to do. I thank you for listening...and for praying. That would be mighty good of you."

Mr. Brunson stood to leave. "I really appreciate your time." He nodded to both Hannah and Jake. "Hannah, that was a really fine supper. The meat was the best. Thank you for inviting me."

"You're very welcome," Hannah said. "We'd love to have you come again sometime."

Jake offered his hand to Mr. Brunson, and as they shook, he said, "God has ways of seeing things are made right. I think you should consider this God's way of doing so."

"Thanks, I'll try to remember that," Mr. Brunson said as he left quietly.

Jake shut the door and came back to his seat on the couch. He silently stared at the log cabin ceiling.

"So that's what's been bothering Mr. Brunson," Hannah mused. "He often seemed sad."

"I noticed too," Jake said, offering nothing more.

"Is this why you want to stay here?" Hannah asked, the question crossing her mind suddenly.

"What do you mean?" Jake asked.

"Not move to Indiana?"

"I don't understand." Jake said.

"Is this what you mean by God wanting you here?"

"I don't know. I just believe He does," Jake said. "I can't explain it."

Hannah had no answer. She would have to trust Jake's feelings, she supposed. She leaned against Jake's shoulder, seeking shelter in this whirling world that now seemed to be her home. Outside the cabin the night settled in darker.

Twenty-seven

Although Hannah wasn't looking forward to Thursday—and her doctor's appointment—the day came soon enough. But she knew that if she was to continue having children as she hoped, doctors would have to be a part of her life.

Betty had said there was a midwife in Bonner's Ferry who preferred to be contacted after a doctor was involved. She worked with doctors not against them, Betty had emphasized.

Jake needed Mosey to get to work, so Betty was to come over to drive her into Libby for the appointment.

Hannah tried to think of what questions the doctor might ask and prepare her answers. She had developed another bruising cold during the past few days, apparently a relapse of the one she just had. It took a puzzling form with no sniffles but pain in her neck. The thought of canceling the appointment had crossed her mind, but she thought better of it. She needed to keep this appointment. Having never been pregnant before, Hannah figured she likely had as many questions for the doctor as the doctor had for her.

Betty arrived a few minutes early, which didn't surprise Hannah. She met her out by the driveway before Betty had time to tie up.

"Good morning," Betty said cheerfully. "How's the baby girl?"

"How do you know what it will be?" Hannah asked as she hopped into the buggy with a quick pull of her hands.

"I meant *you*, silly," Betty replied.

"Well, my cold came back," Hannah said.

"Do you think you should keep the appointment?" Betty questioned. "You look a bit poorly."

"Yes, I want to go," Hannah assured her. "I've got questions I want to ask."

"That's understandable." Betty shook the reins. "You won't have so many questions with the next baby. Is Jake pretty excited?"

"I think so, but he's also busy working and being a minister."

"You two do have your hands full."

"Too full! I still think we should move back to Indiana."

"You'll be okay," Betty said firmly.

The horse suddenly jerked his head into the air and shied sideways. Betty pulled sharply on the reins.

"What was that?" Hannah asked, looking back while Betty brought the horse back under control.

"Can you see anything?" Betty asked, too busy to look back herself.

"Just fence posts," Hannah said, puzzled.

"He's usually pretty good." Betty relaxed as the horse settled down to a steady pace again. "Something must have gotten into him. Good thing nothing was coming," Betty said and then turned around to look back. "One of those posts does look a little scary."

"Maybe that's what it was," Hannah agreed.

"How's Jake coming along with his job?" Betty asked, her hands firmly on the reins.

"Good, from what he says. Things are still a little tight money wise."

"I suppose so. Remember to tell us if things get too bad. We can help out."

"I don't think I'd like that," Hannah said.

"You're family." Betty gave her an admonishing look.

"Well, anyway—" Hannah left the subject there as the edge of town appeared. Her thoughts went to the doctor's office ahead of them.

Several minutes later Hannah was ushered into the examining room while Betty stayed in the waiting room. A nurse came in almost immediately and took her weight and blood pressure and then withdrew a sample of blood for the lab work. She left with a cordial "Doctor Lisa will be right in."

Hannah was pleased she didn't have to wait long. The door opened, and Dr. Lisa greeted her warmly. She was a middle-aged woman, her skin brown and weather-streaked, not at all like Hannah had expected a woman doctor to look.

"So what will it be," Dr. Lisa asked as she began her examination, "a boy or a girl?"

"It doesn't matter," Hannah said, drawing her breath sharply as the cold stethoscope touched her skin. Dr. Lisa listened intently and didn't comment for a moment.

"That's a good attitude to have," she said. "You're Amish?"

Hannah nodded.

"I thought so." Then the doctor made some small talk as she continued the exam. "I'm a doctor part-time. My husband and I have a ranch up in the mountains that keeps me busy the rest of the time."

So that explained the outdoor appearance, Hannah thought.

"I assume you're looking for a midwife?" the doctor asked.

Hannah stiffened. She hadn't anticipated this. "My aunt suggested it. Yes."

"Most of the Amish do." Dr. Lisa didn't seem offended. "I'm starting a little birthing clinic right here at the office. Why don't you let me see if I'm competitive with your midwife's fees?"

"Oh," Hannah said and let the delight show on her face. "I would like that. We can't afford much, though."

"We'll see what we can do, then." Dr. Lisa placed her hands on Hannah's neck. "What have we here? Swollen glands?"

"It's from a cold, I'm sure."

Dr. Lisa looked skeptical. "No sniffles?"

Hannah shook her head.

"Where do you live?"

"Outside of town a few miles."

"I mean—the kind of house?"

"A log cabin," Hannah said.

"Are there animals around? Any cats?" Dr. Lisa's hands went back to Hannah's neck.

"Just the driving horse."

"That's all?"

Hannah nodded, sure the grizzly didn't count.

"Have you been eating deer meat lately?" Dr. Lisa asked.

"Yes," Hannah told her, but that shouldn't be strange. It was hunting season.

"Much?"

"I suppose so. Jake and my uncle got a deer. We can't afford a lot of other meat."

"You've been cooking it well?"

"I thought so. Frying usually."

"Let me take a look at that blood test," Dr. Lisa said. "I'll be right back."

Hannah waited, fidgeting and ready to get back home and out of this place, but there was nothing she could do now but wait.

"Well," Dr. Lisa said matter-of-factly when she came back, "I don't like the looks of this."

"Is something wrong?" Hannah asked with a sudden pang of fear.

"There might be. I'll need to send the blood test to the lab in Kalispell for a confirmation."

"What do you think it is?"

"It looks suspiciously like a toxoplasmosis infection—parasites. It usually happens when the meat is not fully cooked. You have the common symptoms, and you've been eating wild meat. It doesn't happen too often and is usually not that serious. The body fights it by producing an antibody. But your pregnancy complicates things a bit."

Parasites. Hannah shivered at the thought.

"I'll know by tomorrow," Dr. Lisa said. "Can you check back then?"

"My husband can."

"I'll give you a prescription. I want you to begin taking it right away."

"Before we know for sure?"

"I'm sure enough," Dr. Lisa said. "Thankfully you're still in the early stages of your pregnancy."

"Will this affect the baby?"

"Hopefully not. He—or she—is not likely to be infected. It seems early in the infection, plus as I said, you're early yet. I'll want an ultrasound too maybe in a few weeks."

"Will that cost a lot?"

Dr. Lisa shrugged. "Maybe we can pass on the ultrasound. We'll see. It's not always conclusive anyway. I can do another type of test after you're twenty weeks along. That one we can be sure of."

"What if the baby *does* have the infection?" Hannah had to ask.

"Well, that's not good," she said simply. "There is always a chance of a miscarriage, but it doesn't happen often. Another possibility is a normal birth with the possibility of problems later."

"What kind of problems?"

"I don't want you to dwell on something that's not likely to happen. But I also want you to be informed. In some cases, there is the potential for an eventual mental disability, vision loss, possibly even seizures."

Hannah didn't take this well. The sudden news hit her hard.

Dr. Lisa put an arm on her shoulder. "But please remember, that's only in a small percentage of cases. Let's not borrow trouble."

"It's just so hard," Hannah said, referring to more than just the baby. *Why this now—on top of everything else?*

"I'm sorry, but I really do think it's best you know the possibilities as soon as possible. But remember it's not likely. It's only a possibility we have to consider."

When Hannah seemed to have calmed herself, Dr. Lisa gave her a quick hug and said, "You can get dressed now. The prescription will be at the front desk. Have it filled and start taking it right away."

"I will," Hannah said, her voice trembling.

"And don't worry," the doctor said. "We're going to assume the best."

A few minutes later, Hannah came into the waiting room, her eyes still red. She controlled herself while writing the check for the receptionist and accepting the prescription. But once outside in the buggy with Betty, she no longer held back her emotions and sobbed openly.

Betty held Hannah close, not asking any questions. The horse waited at the post.

"There, there," Betty said gently. "The Lord must really have it in for you two. Is something wrong with the baby?"

"It's not for sure," Hannah managed before she burst into fresh tears. "It's not just the baby. It's *everything*. Jake and the ordination—he's so strange now. Now I have horrible parasites."

"Parasites?" Betty asked.

"Yes," Hannah choked, "from that deer meat we've been eating. I was trying so hard to save money. Jake was too. Now we might have harmed our baby."

"You sure you know what you're talking about?"

Hannah nodded.

"Did the doctor give you any information on these parasites?"

"She told me about them, that's all, and gave me a prescription," Hannah said.

"I'll be right back," Betty said and stepped down from the buggy.

To Hannah it seemed she had been sitting there in the cold alone a long time. She was beginning to think she should go inside when Betty returned.

"They gave me this," Betty said, waving some papers around. "It doesn't look good."

Hannah sank back into the buggy seat.

"We should go tell Jake about this," Betty said.

"No," Hannah said, "he has work to do. I don't like going into that hardware store anyway."

"Maybe you're right," Betty agreed. "Let's get your medicine, then."

"That's going to cost more money," Hannah groaned. "I can't believe this."

"Believe it," Betty said. "It's part of life. Just remember the church is here to help you."

"Jake's a minister," Hannah said with no idea why she said that. The thought just pushed into her mind.

"See," Betty said as if the words made perfect sense. "All the more reason."

They drove toward the drugstore on the main street, the sound of the horse's hooves cutting like knives through Hannah's emotions. She let the tears come freely.

Twenty-eight

When Jake arrived home, he found Hannah still weeping on the couch. Clutched in her hand were the crumpled papers Betty had gotten from the doctor's office. She waved the pages weakly in Jake's direction.

Jake took them but didn't read anything. Instead he sat down and drew Hannah close. "What's wrong?" he asked. He smelled of wood shavings and winter air.

"The doctor said what I thought was a cold is really an infection caused by parasites, likely from the deer meat." Hannah sat upright. "These papers have information about them. If the baby is infected, it could mean…"

Hannah didn't finish. Jake glanced briefly at the papers, and then his eyes focused on hers again. "What about you?"

"I'll be okay," she said. "Just the baby's in danger."

"We'd better stop eating the meat, then," he said.

She shook her head. "I think the meat wasn't cooked enough. If I had cooked it longer, this might not have happened."

"So what do we do?"

"I have medicine here." She pointed toward the desk. "It cost too much."

Jake lifted the pages in his hand and scanned them for a few minutes. "We had better pray," he said softly.

Hannah felt hopelessness run through her. "I'm infected already."

"The baby isn't."

"How do you know?" She looked him in the face, searching for an answer that wasn't there. Feelings of despair and hope mingled together inside of her.

"I don't," he said. "Only God does."

"Why is all this happening to us? Does God mean for this to happen?"

"He knows our needs. He'll take care of us," Jake said.

Outside it had begun snowing, but neither of them noticed.

"I have to get supper," Hannah suddenly remembered. "But what? Can we still eat the deer meat?"

"What did the doctor say?"

"Nothing other than the infection was likely caused by the meat being undercooked."

"Steve and Betty didn't get infected, so she must have cooked it thoroughly. I wonder why I'm not sick?"

Hannah was ashamed to admit she had never even thought of Jake eating the same meat. "Maybe you just don't have the symptoms yet."

"Well, I know one thing. We can't be afraid. And it says right here that the infection, once treated, is unlikely to return. I think we'll be okay if you just make sure the meat is cooked thoroughly."

"I'll burn it black," she said half in jest.

He smiled and said, "I don't think I could eat any tonight anyway. Just do what you think best."

"I'll make soup." She made her way slowly to the kitchen. Jake picked up the *Family Life* and settled into his chair.

Hannah noticed the snow through the kitchen window. It was coming down in large flakes that drifted close to the glass pane. *So like life,* she thought, *lovely and light till you handle it. Then it leaves you cold inside. I must be cried out,* she thought as she prepared the soup.

Less than an hour later, Jake said a simple prayer as they bowed their heads before eating. He asked God to help them and give them grace for the trials of life and light from His Word to guide the way. He so tenderly asked for protection for the baby that it seemed he already held it in his arms.

When he was finished, Hannah knew there were tears still left in her after all because they rolled freely down her cheeks. Jake noticed, touched her arm from across the table, and waited until she calmed down before he dished out his soup.

"It's snowing," he said matter-of-factly.

"I know," she replied. "It looks serious."

"God will protect us," Jake said calmly. "It will soon be Christmas."

"What has that got to do with it?" She looked at him, puzzled.

"That's when the Christ child came—in the manger."

Hannah waited and wondered what Jake meant.

"The angels came close to earth that night. Maybe they come near every Christmas."

Hannah glanced sharply at him. He was changing faster than she could keep track of. If he could say things like this, it was no wonder he could preach well on Sundays. But did he mean it?

"Do you really think so?" she asked. "His angels will protect us?"

"I don't know." Jake glanced over at the window. "If they do, perhaps they will protect our child. It's not in a real manger, but it's in a sort of manger."

"It's just our baby," she said. "It's not the same as the birth of Jesus."

"Maybe to God it's enough," he said. "He has cared for little children all along, has He not?"

"You must be careful about what you say," she warned, the emotion strong in her voice.

Jake didn't seem to mind. "I know," he said, nodding slowly.

"You must be careful too with your preaching," she told him. "Remember the bishop's visit."

"Yes," he said, "it's still the will of God in everything. I know that."

"What if the baby is born with the infection?" Hannah asked. "Is that the will of God too?"

"I suppose it is...and then it is a burden we must bear." Jake sighed. "Whatever His will is, it will be what's best for us."

When they finished their soup, Hannah got up to do the dishes, and she felt a wave of exhaustion sweep over her. She managed the chore and then went to the living room where she found Jake reading his Bible.

"I'm going to bed," she said.

"I'll be along," he said. But she was fast asleep long before he closed his Bible and joined her.

When she awoke in the middle of the night, after tossing and turning with a bad dream, he was there next to her. Seeing him there was a comfort.

She had dreamed she was back home again. The house was so familiar and comforting—so strong and protecting. Each day went by normally—and yet not quite. A hidden danger seemed to follow her every move. When she hung out the wash or did the dishes, the dark cloud hovered over her. In both thunderstorms and sunshine, she felt its presence. She tried to tell her mom, but the words wouldn't come out of her mouth. She tried once to meet her father at the door when he came home from work, but no matter how fast she walked or how hard she strained, she couldn't get there in time. Even on Sunday, when she sat among all the usual people from her growing up years, she tried to scream that danger was coming, but no one could hear her.

The awfulness of it had jarred her awake. Her face was sweaty, and her arms were cold. Her only solace was that it had been a dream. It had seemed so real. Jake's even breathing was like a tonic to her. She lay back on her pillow and listened for a while.

Then the realization hit her. *I have to write to Mom,* she thought. *I should have done it yesterday. But there was no time yesterday even if I'd thought to do it.* Certain she wouldn't be able to sleep, she got out of bed, careful not to awaken Jake.

Wrapped in a blanket, she went into the living room. The snow was falling against the window. She lit the kerosene lamp, pulled the drawer open, got the paper tablet, and started writing.

> Dear Mom,
>
> It now seems like many years since you and Dad were here. I would so love to hear your voice again and see Dad sitting on the living room couch. If not here, then in Indiana,

but it seems like it will not be. Jake thinks we are to stay in Montana, and I do have to agree with him.

We seem to be having nothing but troubles. I don't understand why this should be, but I know what you would say. Trouble makes us grow up. Well...I feel like I am about as grown-up as I can stand. Things are happening so fast.

That my Jake—my good Jake—now has to stand up and preach in front of church, who would ever have imagined such a thing? I must say he did a good job the other Sunday. I wish you had been here. He was so good that it scared me.

Some here worry about him going liberal. I guess that happens. But I don't think it can happen to Jake. What do you think? Oh, Mom, you can't imagine the kind of thoughts that go through my head. There seem to be new ones everyday now.

Then the worse thing happened. I am now sick with an infection. Betty told me about a good doctor in Libby—Dr. Lisa. I went there yesterday for my first baby checkup. She found the infection. I thought it was just a normal cold, like the one I caught soon after you left.

It's not, though. I have parasites that could infect the baby too. They won't hurt me, but they might hurt the baby. Dr. Lisa is hopeful the baby will be fine. She has tests she can do later to see if the baby has been infected. But if it has been infected, there's not much she can do. And there are some conditions the baby might develop—not good ones.

I completely broke down in the buggy and cried with Betty and then here at home again. I suppose Jake wonders what to do with his wife sometimes, but he's bearing up. Did you ever have this much trouble?

One good thing, though, is Jake really likes his job. I think there will even be extra money for the doctor bills and all. I hope so. At least that's the one bright spot in our lives.

I invited Mr. Brunson for supper last Friday night. Seems he heard Jake is a preacher and shared his sad story with us. I can't tell you everything, but it might not be done yet. He seems to think his son may contact him. He was involved in an accident that killed his wife and daughter. That is why he lives out here all by himself. Now I know why he appears so sad at times.

Jake says God will surely take care of us through all this, but I'm ashamed to say I wonder sometimes. I suppose Jake does too, but he never shows it.

It's snowing outside, and I can't sleep. I had a terrible nightmare.

Well, kiss Indiana for me. I could cry about that too, but I'll have to be a big girl now. Isn't that what you would say?

With love,
Hannah

Hannah folded the paper carefully and watched the light from the kerosene lamp dance on the log cabin ceiling. What if her child was born perfect and wonderful only to be doomed to life as a cripple? She pushed the thought away.

Back in the bedroom, she carefully slipped under the covers without waking Jake and quickly fell asleep.

Twenty-nine

Jake came home the next evening with the news. His call from the hardware store to Dr. Lisa's office confirmed the diagnosis—Hannah had the toxoplasmosis infection. As if Betty knew Hannah would need her support, her buggy rattled into the driveway the next morning.

Hannah thought she might throw on a coat and meet Betty outdoors, but the chilly morning persuaded her otherwise. By the time she bundled up, Betty would already be at the door. So instead she just opened the door and waited for Betty.

Betty, not yet to the porch, called out, "You shouldn't stand there with the door open. It's too cold this morning."

"I'm glad to see you," Hannah said, making no effort to move away.

"Has there been news?" Betty asked, giving Hannah a quick sideways hug. "Let's get you inside where it's warm."

"Jake talked with the doctor yesterday. It's confirmed."

"Oh, my." Betty sounded dismayed as she sat on the couch. "Well, I guess we already knew. Have you let your mom know?"

"I wrote to her yesterday. I couldn't sleep, and so I got up during the night."

Betty shrugged. "Can't say I blame you. I've never written letters at night, but I've walked the floors aplenty."

"Mr. Brunson has his court case this week," Hannah volunteered. She felt like talking about someone else's troubles.

"That bear thing!" Betty exclaimed.

Hannah nodded and wondered if she ought to tell Betty of Mr. Brunson's family troubles but decided that wouldn't be appropriate.

"The game warden did come out and took care of the cat," Betty said. Chuckling, she went on to say, "They tracked it down right away and removed it from the area."

"Maybe they don't want another bear situation," Hannah ventured.

"I'm sure you're right. You have any coffee?" Betty started to get up from the couch, saying, "I can make some if not."

"No, let me get it," Hannah said, glad for the distraction, knowing it helped keep back the tears. "The water is already hot."

"You think there's any hope of the child not being…you know…infected?"

"We don't know any more than we did before," Hannah said.

"I think the Lord will take care of you," Betty said as Hannah left for the kitchen.

She returned with Betty's steaming cup of coffee and asked, "Why do you think so?"

"Oh, Jake—" Betty said, "preaching like he does."

Is this what Bishop Nisley is concerned about, Hannah wondered, *people who make special things out of men because they can preach well?*

"You only heard him once," Hannah said.

"I know. It's about his turn again," Betty said. "Bishop might even let him have the main part before too long."

"I don't know," Hannah said, not wanting to consider it.

"God is so kind to this church," Betty said, sipping her coffee. "Giving us a real interesting preacher, who would have thought of it? Jake Byler—I never did. He can sing, of course, but that doesn't always carry over to speaking. So young too."

"Well, the other ministers are good too," Hannah felt the need to say.

"Of course." Betty was quick to agree. "I was just saying that he's another one."

But Hannah knew what her aunt meant. Betty thought Jake was better than the others.

"I've really come to invite you for Thanksgiving." Betty said, changing the subject. "I know we're all the family you have around here. Me too, not counting Steve's side. Because his family is waiting until Saturday to get together, I thought I would take my chance and invite you both to Thanksgiving dinner."

"Thanksgiving dinner," Hannah stated more than asked.

Betty nodded. "I could ask Elizabeth and John to come too."

"Really?" Hannah asked, feeling excitement rise in her. Then she remembered the last visit with Elizabeth and John.

"Surely you would like that?" Betty asked.

"Of course," Hannah said, reminding herself that it would be okay, that Bishop Nisley had only been doing his job by warning Jake, and that Jake had received the correction well. Things were as they should be now.

"It's decided, then," Betty declared, finishing the last of her coffee. "Now I really must be going. The wash is still not done—really not even started." Betty got to her feet.

Suddenly Hannah found herself asking, "Why don't I come over for the day?"

"You would?" Betty smiled broadly, and then her face dropped. "Oh my, but I'd just work you like a hired hand if you came now. There's so much work to be done."

"All the more reason to come," Hannah declared. "I'll put some things away, and then I'll be ready to go."

"Oh, this is so good," Betty gushed. "I'm really glad I came now. I didn't think I could spare the time. Now I'm actually going to gain time!"

"Jake would say you're right. Helping others adds to ourselves," Hannah said, realizing he had never actually said it, but it sure sounded like something he would say.

"What a good preacher," Betty proclaimed.

Hannah reminded herself not to compliment Jake again, around Betty at least. Bishop Nisley apparently did have a point.

Seated beside Betty in the buggy as it rattled down the driveway, Hannah took deep breaths of the crisp air.

"Better than Indiana air," Betty said, spoiling the moment.

"I suppose so," Hannah acknowledged grudgingly. "At least Jake still has work."

"The Lord is looking out for you—both of you," Betty said firmly. "He really is. The baby too."

Hannah was about to say, *That's what Jake would say,* but caught herself. "Yes, it's in the Lord's hands," she said instead, sounding all grown up. Perhaps she had also changed right along with Jake in this land of mountains and rivers.

"Yes, it is indeed," Betty said from beside her.

As they turned right on the main road, the view of the mountains rose on both sides. The early morning fog had lifted to nearly the tops of the peaks, adding a shine of white to the wooded slopes. Sunlight poured out of the fog in sheets of blinding light.

"It's angel country," Hannah said, not able to help herself.

"But cold right now," Betty replied without taking her eyes off the road. "More to come too."

"It will be a hard winter, won't it?" Hannah asked.

"No doubt," Betty said. "Steve thinks so."

"Well, you two should know. You've lived here long enough." Hannah shifted on her seat, picturing how this road might look come January with snowbanks on either side. "Will you still be able to get around?"

"Main roads, yes," Betty assured her. "It's not that bad."

Minutes later they pulled into Betty's familiar driveway. Hannah helped unhitch and then waited while Betty took the horse into the barn.

"I'll leave the harness on," Betty shouted over her shoulder.

"Don't," Hannah said quickly, knowing to do so meant Betty would keep the visit short. "I'll put the harness back on when I leave."

"The horses are used to it. They stand all day in their harnesses at church," Betty said and opened the barn door. "You can't stay too late anyway."

"No, I guess not," Hannah agreed. She needed to be home in time to prepare supper for Jake.

"Are you still eating that deer meat?" Betty asked when she came back out.

"Jake is," Hannah said. "I just can't."

"I don't blame you," Betty replied. "If you can't eat all of it, we'll take it. That is, before you throw it away. I cook mine good and thorough. Never heard of such a thing as a parasite from deer meet."

"Jake still wants it for now," Hannah said. "He comes home pretty hungry. He works hard in the furniture shop."

"We need to see what Jake's doing sometime," Betty said as they walked toward the house. "It's probably as well done as his preaching,"

"Probably," Hannah agreed because she knew it was true. She couldn't feel bad toward Jake. He hadn't chosen to have that piece of paper put in his book. Yet he sure seemed to accept his new position—as if he kind of liked it.

"Now my work—" Betty drew in a deep breath. "My, my, here I am with the house all in a mess and so much to do."

"That's what I came for."

"Yes, I know. It just feels so…Well, wrong. Like I'm using you."

"I didn't have much to do anyway. Just the cabin to take care of," Hannah assured Betty. "I need the company anyway."

"I imagine so." Betty said. "Now, let's see. If I start the wash, maybe you can do the kitchen?"

"That would be fine," Hannah matched her words with actions and turned to the kitchen sink. A twist of the knob brought warm water and a feeling of surprise. She forgot how it was to have warm water without heating it on the stove. *I'm quickly becoming a savage and losing the advantage of a civilized lifestyle,* she told herself, *something I've known all my life.*

"Warm water," she said, just blurting out her surprise.

"I guess you don't have that," Betty said. "When's Jake going to install a water heater?"

"We seldom talk about it," Hannah said. "It costs money."

"That it does. Maybe with the furniture making you can soon afford it."

"It's not a big deal," Hannah said, shrugging. "I think Jake said the plumbing would have to be changed too if hot water was installed. The owners who built the place liked things rough, I guess."

"Well, I'll be doing the laundry," Betty said and disappeared toward the bedrooms.

Moments later the gas motor, which powered the washing machine, started up in Betty's laundry room. Hannah finished the dishes and then followed Betty outside to help her hang up the first basket of wash.

"You don't have to help here," Betty told Hannah when she saw her approach.

"Your hands are cold already," Hannah replied and blew on her own.

"Yes, they are," Betty agreed, pushing the wooden snaps onto the line to hold the first piece of clothing in place. Her hands were red from the brisk air and the cold basket.

"I hope this wash doesn't freeze," Hannah said.

"I don't think it will," Betty said, her teeth chattering. "My, it's cold, though. I don't know why it bothers me—guess I'm getting older. The sun will hit the line soon."

They continued the routine until all the wash was on the line. With Hannah's help, it went up quickly. After lunch, the sun did its job. Hannah helped bring in the baskets of clothes at about three o'clock, and then Betty insisted she drive her home.

"You have things to do at home before Jake returns, I'm sure."

Hannah agreed and went to get the horse.

The drive home was pleasant enough, though Hannah could tell it would turn cold again that night. Mr. Brunson's pickup rattled past as Betty dropped her off in front of the cabin. She wondered how he was doing and whether his son would make contact anytime soon.

"Thanks so much," Betty said without getting out of the buggy. "I have to be getting back."

"Thanks for picking me up," Hannah said. "I needed the company today."

"We all do from time to time," Betty said. She then slid the buggy door shut and drove off.

Hannah watched her leave before entering the cabin. The fire had gone out in the stove, and she had to restart it. As it flamed up, she reached for its warmth, glad to be home again.

Thirty

When Jake came home from work, Hannah met him at the door with a smile and a kiss.

"You seem to be in a pretty good mood," Jake said.

"I spent the day at Betty's," she said. "I needed it."

"We're blessed to have family close by," he said. "I have good news too."

"Oh?" More good news after the day at Betty's would be like icing on the cake.

"Mr. Howard sold our first table and set of chairs—a full set! Brought in a pretty good price, and the customer loved it. It's to be shipped back East."

"Who was it?" Hannah asked.

"I don't know. A man purchased it for his wife's dining room."

"It'll help with the doctor bills," Hannah said. "I'm glad, though, it's working out. I guess God knows we need some good news."

"There will be more good news for us—and for the baby too." Jake shut the cabin door and drew Hannah into his arms.

Hannah loved the scent of wood on Jake. His beard had lengthened since his ordination, and the hair brushed against her cheek. If he didn't trim his beard soon, it would be down past the first button on his shirt. She reached up to playfully run her hand down its length.

"You need to trim the edges," she said, laughing, "or I will."

"I guess," he said. "Just didn't get around to it."

"Supper's ready," she said, leading him to the kitchen. "Wash up."

Jake did and joined her at the table, where the soft light from the kerosene lamp darkened Jake's face, giving him an almost dangerous and exciting look. A thrill ran through Hannah, and she kissed him before she sat down.

"Still won't eat the deer meat?" Jake said as he helped himself to the meat dish she had prepared. "If you cook it through, it will be fine."

"I know," she said. "I'm just not ready yet. Maybe next time."

"Maybe I need to get you some store-bought meat," he said. "You need the strength."

"I'll do with potatoes and vegetables," she said. "Things taste funny right now anyway. Because of the baby, I guess."

"That's what Mom said—with the younger ones," he replied.

They bowed their heads together silently and gave thanks for the food in front of them. Hannah also gave thanks for Jake's work, for Betty, and for family close by. And she gave thanks for the growing baby.

As they began to eat, Hannah asked, "You miss your family, don't you?"

"I do miss Mom and Dad," he said, "more than I thought I would. We'll get a chance to visit, though, all in good time."

"Maybe around Christmas?" she suggested.

"I doubt it," Jake said. "There are too many miles to travel, and the hardware store gets busy closer to Christmas. I don't think I can get away."

"Speaking of family," Hannah said, "Betty asked us to come over for Thanksgiving. She said she might invite Elizabeth and John too. Steve's side of the family doesn't have anything planned for that day this year."

"That's good," Jake said.

"I wonder what Mr. Brunson will do for the holidays," Hannah said. "He's so alone here."

"He'll get by. He's probably used to it by now," Jake said, ladling some gravy on his potatoes. "He stopped in at the hardware store today. He looked at what we were doing and seemed quite interested, although I wasn't sure why."

"Maybe he likes log furniture."

"Maybe," Jake agreed. "He asked all kinds of questions about the business end of our arrangement and went out with Mr. Howard afterward. I don't know what that was all about. He probably was just wondering about the sales end of things."

"Maybe he could help sell more," Hannah said. "He is from back East. Maybe he knows of some ways to sell the furniture there."

"I thought of that too. He'd have to work with Mr. Howard, of course."

"Jake, why couldn't you make furniture on your own? Why do you have to go through Mr. Howard?"

"Well, there's a couple of things. First is the up-front money. It takes a lot, and I don't have it. Then there's the fact that the hardware store draws in people. If I made furniture on my own, I'd need a way for people to see it. That takes money too. I'm content with the way things are for now."

When they had finished eating, Jake asked, "You want help with the dishes?"

Hannah could see his mind was somewhere else and said, "No, I can do them."

"I'll help clear the table, at least," he said as he collected the dishes and took them to the sink.

After the table was clear, Jake left Hannah the gas lantern and took the kerosene lamp to the table by his chair in the living room. It brought tears to Hannah's eyes to realize that he had left her the best light and took the lesser one for himself.

When she was done with the dishes, Hannah brought the gas lantern with her into the living room. Its waves of light illuminated Jake as he read from the Bible. She hung the lantern on the hook and joined him on the couch. She picked up the *Family Life*, and Jake continued with his Bible.

Hannah soon discovered, though, that she couldn't keep her thoughts on the page in front of her. The black words refused to stand out from the paper. Instead, it was as if the article was written in a foreign language. Her mind kept wandering to the unrelenting push of life around her.

Where did it go? That was the question. Each day seemed to push Jake and her further along whether they wanted to go or not. *Is this how it is for everyone?*

She glanced over to Jake. His concentration on the pages in front of him was total, his lips moving slightly as he read. Outside the window was the deep night, and Hannah could almost feel the chill of the air against the logs. Jake must have noticed too because he stirred himself from his reading.

"Better add some wood to the furnace," he said and got up.

Hannah watched him as he left for the utility room to attend to their small furnace that heated the parts of the house unreached by the kitchen stove. He seemed older to her tonight, even aged already. Maybe it was just the cold, dark night that made her think so.

She had thought the same thing last Sunday as she watched him preach. Jake had taken the first sermon again—as was normal for a young preacher. No doubt Bishop Nisley wanted to prove his new minister well before he let him have the main sermon, an hour-long affair.

As Jake preached, Hannah watched his face, careful to drop her gaze to the floor when he turned in her direction. At Sunday morning church, she felt as if she had no business being part of his holy thoughts. Here at home she didn't feel that way.

Sitting beside Hannah, young Sylvia Stoll seemed to have no such problem. She readily met Jake's gaze. Hannah felt ashamed for even having the thought, but she couldn't help herself. What reason did Sylvia have to keep her eyes raised when Jake looked in her direction? Hannah asked herself if the situation were reversed and Ben was preaching, would she drop her eyes just as with Jake? She supposed not. As she realized that Ben would never be as good a preacher as Jake, she felt no better.

Jake yawned when he came back and took his seat on the couch again.

"I heard some news today," he said without looking at her.

"Yes?" She waited.

"There are to be some meetings over in Kalispell—tent meetings."

"What kind of tent meetings?" She turned to face him.

"Revival meetings. Some Mennonite group, from what I hear."

"And?" she let the question hang. Surely Jake was simply passing on information. He could have no desire to attend.

"A fellow came into the hardware store to pass out flyers. Mr. Howard let him leave some on the counter."

"You looked at them?" Hannah's eyes were wide in the soft light of the gas lantern.

Jake chuckled. "I couldn't help it. They looked interesting, and I've never been to a tent meeting."

"No," Hannah said, "surely not. You wouldn't go?"

Jake laughed this time and shook his head.

Not certain what Jake's laughter meant, Hannah sat up straighter. Did he mean, *No, he wouldn't go,* or was his laughter directed at her question?

"I could ask Bishop Nisley whether we can go," he said in a perfectly calm voice.

"You wouldn't." Hannah grabbed his arm. "Don't even think of it. Everyone would find out. They would even find out about you just asking to go."

Jake laughed again. "I'm just teasing, Hannah."

"Well, don't tease like that," she said. "It's not at all funny."

"I'm sorry," he said, glancing over at her. "I didn't mean it. It just looked interesting."

Not convinced, she studied his face for a clue.

"I was teasing," he repeated. "Really."

"Okay," she relented, drawing him toward her. "Don't scare me like that."

"Ben and Sylvia went, though," he said, dropping the words like a bomb.

"How do you know that?" she asked, frightened again.

"I'm a minister," he said simply as if that were the most obvious thing in the world. "I'm told things."

"Surely people aren't tattling to you already." She felt a new fear run through her. "I don't want to be involved with that."

Visions of her growing-up years flashed through her mind. Dennis, a distant cousin on Kathy's side, had always run to the preachers with every breach of rules he witnessed. Her parents had never liked such tattling, relative or not. Their dislike spread even further, though, reaching to the preachers who would listen to such tattletales.

"It's not like that," Jake said, seeming to understand her concern. "John mentioned it last Sunday."

So Jake had known for nearly a week already and had not shared it with her? Hannah swallowed hard, realizing that this was likely to be their future—Jake knowing things about people she didn't know or even want to know.

"I hope Ben and Sylvia aren't serious," she managed. "I'd hate to lose them."

"Me too," Jake said, reaching for his Bible again. "Bishop hopes a talk will solve the problem. He's going to see them himself."

"I hope it works," she said.

Jake nodded and turned back to the Gospel of John, the pages open before him.

A horrible thought kept Hannah frozen in place. *If Ben and Sylvia left the Amish and went liberal, my concern about Sylvia would go away.* A deep embarrassment filled Hannah. *What if Jake knows what I am thinking? I will never tell him, that's for sure.* Once again she felt the disruption of life's unexpected twists and turns.

"I'm going to bed," she said softly.

"I'll be there in a little bit," Jake said, his eyes gentle in the lantern's light.

Thirty-one

Betty extended the dining room table from wall to wall for her Thanksgiving feast. Bishop Nisley and Elizabeth had accepted the invitation, and their presence made it seem like old times to Hannah. She remembered not too long ago how she and Jake—then just a young unmarried couple—had sat at the same table with them, eyeing one another discretely across the table.

And now John and Elizabeth recalled those days with happiness and said they knew even before Jake and Hannah that they would eventually get married. Betty agreed, though Steve admitted he had been oblivious to the whole budding romance—if that was what it had been.

As they drove home, Hannah very nearly fell asleep in the buggy. They had stayed late, and the night was cold. She leaned against Jake and closed her eyes. She had needed this happy evening and was sorry it had to end.

A few days later Mr. Brunson stopped by and talked with Jake but didn't get out of his pickup. He told Jake the court appearance had gone as expected. He received a heavy fine.

The next morning, Hannah awoke to the strange feeling that

something was not right—or maybe she was feeling the baby move within her for the first time. Whatever was happening was so new to Hannah that she wanted to see Dr. Lisa as soon as possible. Today, she hoped.

When she told Jake she wanted to go to the doctor, he agreed.

"We'll go now," he said. "We'll stop by the hardware store so I can tell Mr. Howard I'll be coming in late. I want to go to the doctor with you."

Jake nervously hitched up Mosey, and Hannah climbed into the buggy. They rode to town in silence. Hannah didn't know what to say. She didn't know if what she felt was normal or cause for worry. It was all so new.

Halfway to Libby she said, "This is going to cost us money we can't spare. Maybe we should go to Betty's. She'll tell me if this is all right… or if I should see Dr. Lisa."

Jake thought a minute and then said, "No, I think we should go to the doctor's office and hope she can squeeze you in without an appointment. I don't want to waste time going to Betty's if this turns out to be serious."

Hannah just nodded and said nothing more.

When Jake stopped at the store, Mr. Howard was insistent that Jake take whatever time he needed at the doctor's office. The furniture could wait.

A few minutes later, they arrived at Dr. Lisa's office. When Hannah explained to the receptionist that she felt something might be wrong, she was shown into an examination room while Jake stayed in the waiting room.

Dr. Lisa came in a little later. After asking Hannah some questions and examining her, the doctor confirmed Hannah's worst fear.

"I'm so sorry," Dr. Lisa said, putting her hand on Hannah's arm.

"I've lost the baby," Hannah said numbly.

"Yes."

Hannah started to cry softly, almost embarrassed to show emotion to someone she barely knew.

"This happens," Dr. Lisa said gently. "It's always hard."

"It was the infection, wasn't it?" Hannah asked.

"We don't know. It would be just a guess. It could have been for other reasons."

"It was my fault."

"No, you mustn't blame yourself," Dr. Lisa said. "These things are in the hands of God. He works out what is best. Don't your people believe that?"

"That's what Jake would say, I suppose," Hannah said. "That doesn't make it any easier. I was hoping for a boy—Jake's boy."

Dr. Lisa nodded. "I understand. I'm going to write a prescription. Pick it up at the drugstore. Then I want to see you again in two weeks. If you have any concerns or other questions, please call my office."

Hannah thanked Dr. Lisa, met Jake in the waiting room, and told him the news. He put his arm around her and held her for a moment. Then as someone entered the waiting room, he pulled out his checkbook and approached the receptionist to pay for the office visit.

"No charge," the woman said. "Doctor's orders."

Jake thanked the woman but decided he would not want this to be a charity. He would wait and ask Dr. Lisa about making some furniture in trade for her services.

Outside, Jake helped Hannah into the buggy and asked, "Are you okay?"

She nodded. "We need to pick up this prescription if we can afford it. I can do without it, though, I'm sure."

"No, we're getting it anyway," Jake said firmly.

On the way home, they stopped briefly at Betty's. "She'd want to know right away," Hannah said without emotion.

When she stepped down from the buggy, Betty was standing at her open door, having heard them approach. Hannah went to her and simply began to cry. Somehow that told Betty everything she needed to know. She wrapped Hannah in an embrace and cried with her for a few minutes. Jake could not remember the last time Betty had nothing to say.

When they arrived home, Jake checked the mailbox. There was little except for what looked like a bill and a letter.

"Your mother," he said, handing it to Hannah. "It's good it came today."

"Mothers know sometimes," she said.

While Jake unhitched Mosey, Hannah sat down on the couch to read her letter.

Dear Hannah,

I know I just wrote last week, but I felt like writing today again. It seems as if time is passing so fast. I think of you often. How are you and the coming baby doing? We pray the child will be spared any ill effects of the infection.

Hannah stopped reading, the tears stinging her eyes.

Tell Jake hi for us. Indiana is still open to people moving in, but we understand about his new responsibilities. Aunt Martha was here today. I have a quilt on the frame. It's for the school Christmas sale. I've let the women know, and seems like someone stops in most every day. Last week Mary Bontrager, from the neighboring district, stayed almost all day. It was good to catch up on the news. Our two districts share the schoolhouse. That has changed since you attended. I think there were four districts sharing it then.

A bunch of couples have been called out in church recently. Dave and Esther Yoder were called out last Sunday. Seems like more and more young people are getting married these days, but why should we complain? It's a sign of a growing and prosperous church.

We hope this finds you well and in good health. May God keep both you and Jake. I think your dad wants coffee made. He's banging around in the kitchen.

Your mother

Hannah folded the letter, feeling comforted in a way. Even across the miles, her mother's love had reached her.

Jake walked in, and Hannah said, "Hi from Mom and Dad." As an afterthought, she added, "You really ought to write to your mother—especially now."

"I will tonight," Jake said.

Jake stayed home from work the rest of the day, wanting to be with Hannah. He did a few chores around the cabin but stayed close to her even when she lay down for a lengthy afternoon nap.

When she awoke, Hannah realized she needed to start supper but wondered what they were to eat. She found some leftovers and warmed them in the oven, telling Jake, "It's not much, but for tonight it'll do."

"Hannah, after this I don't want you to prepare any more of the deer meat," he said.

"We can't let it go to waste," Hannah said.

"Neither can we eat it," he said. "I'll buy hamburger for the rest of the winter. It's the principle of the thing."

"But," she protested, "think of the cost."

Jake shook his head and sat down with a sigh. "No."

"Betty said she would take what we couldn't eat," Hannah said. "She didn't want us to throw it away."

"Fine," Jake said. "I'll take it over."

Hannah felt like saying thank you, but Jake might not understand. The load of her guilt felt much lighter. Didn't he realize this was her fault?

As if reading her thoughts, Jake said "This wasn't your fault. If anything, it's mine. I shot the deer to try to save money. We shouldn't blame each other or anyone. God is still in charge, and He knows what He's doing."

Hannah nodded, thankful that Jake understood.

"God will give us children as He wishes," Jake said firmly. "Perhaps several children."

Hannah stood—unable to eat—and walked over to him and put her hand on his arm. Jake stood too and pulled her into an embrace. "God will keep us," he whispered. "Yes, God will keep us."

"It's just so hard—so very hard," Hannah said, gently crying into Jake's shoulder.

"It's harder for you…probably harder than I know." He then released the embrace but held her out at arm's length, his hands gripping her arms. She let the strength flow through her—his and hers together and perhaps even God's—she thought through her tears.

"I suppose so," she said. Before she could stop herself, she blurted out, "Jake, part of this is because you are a minister now…and…I don't know how to be a minister's wife. Everything is changing so fast—for both of us. I just don't know how I can keep up."

"You make things much easier for me," Jake whispered. "You don't know by how much."

"It's hard for you?" she asked in surprise.

"Yes," Jake said. "I never asked for this. Never dreamed of preaching. Never even thought of it. Even that very morning I never thought of it. It wasn't until I heard the bishop say my name, and even then it seemed impossible. Do you think God would work like that? I know our faith says He does, and that is how the old people believe things work. Yet why choose me?" Jake shook his head. "I prayed hard and asked God to help me. I asked for help from His Spirit. Yet, I didn't know how it would go. Getting up there the first time—you don't know how afraid I was. Now John says I preach too good. I don't know what *too good* is. I don't know what *preaching* is at all. How would I know when it's too good?"

Hannah was surprised by Jake's words. Could it be that he too was afraid of the changes that she feared? Her fingers tightened on his arms.

"Hannah, losing my job felt awful—like part of me had been torn away. How was I supposed to provide for you and the baby on the way? I tried to save money and bring in cheaper meat. Then I bring *this* upon us—the loss of our child." Jake's eyes looked weary and torn.

"No," Hannah said, moving closer to him again.

"But I have you." His face lit up. "You don't know what that means to me."

"I've wanted so much to be all you need in a wife," Hannah whispered, her hand touching Jake's head. "I've done so badly. I thought wrong thoughts. Wished wrong things."

"It's okay," Jake said. "None of that matters now. God will help us. I know He will. He already has."

"Yes," she agreed, felt a little of his faith, and drew on his strength.

"I'd better write that letter," Jake said, startling her.

"You'd better eat your dinner first," she said.

"I'm not hungry."

"Neither am I, but we had better eat," she said, taking her seat again. Though she too was still not hungry, she wanted Jake to eat.

As she cleared the dishes, he moved to the desk to write his letter.

"You'll have to let me read it," she said.

"No," he said. "I don't read the letters you write to your parents."

"That's because you never ask to," she said. "I do the dishes, you write, and then I read."

Jake grunted, but he did start the letter.

After Hannah was finished in the kitchen, she found him at the desk, still busy with his pen.

"How's it going?" she asked.

"Slowly." He held his hands over the paper.

Without saying anything, she pulled it out from under him and read out loud.

> Dear Dad and Mom,
>
> Greetings from your son in Jesus' name. If this is a terrible letter, you can blame it on Hannah. She made me do it.
>
> I hope this finds you well. We have had a great sorrow today. Hannah lost the child she was carrying through an infection, we think. We still have each other, though, and God, and so we have much to be thankful for.

"That's all I need to read," Hannah told him and kissed the top of his head.

"Give it back, then," Jake said. "I'm not done writing."

She handed it back, noticing his eyes were a little red around the edges.

"You should write more often," Hannah said. "Your mom would like that. They might even come and visit us."

"Writing and visiting have nothing to do with each other," Jake said, taking up the pen again. "Not unless you're telling them you're coming to visit, and even then one still has little to do with the other. The letter just bears the message."

Hannah noticed how his fingers wrapped around the slender pen, so firm and yet tender. She kissed the top of his head again.

"Are you preaching to me?" Hannah asked.

"Maybe," he said.

"Then I agree with Bishop Nisley," she said with another kiss. "You shouldn't do such a good job of it."

Thirty-two

The days went by, dull and uneventful, for which Hannah was grateful. She needed the quiet, and even the weather seemed to cooperate. For the most part, the winter days were mild and often included extended periods of sunshine.

Then a winter snowstorm rolled in and left a few inches of snow on the ground one night. During the next evening, more snow fell.

In the morning the snow lay a good foot deep in some places. Jake laughed when Hannah suggested he stay home from work. He told her this was typical weather for winter and the main road was open. Besides, Mr. Howard needed him at the furniture shop because sales were increasing. This was Montana, after all, and snow in the winter was normal. He then hitched Mosey to the buggy and left, the thin tires squeaking in the snow.

To add to her worries, there was to be a minister's meeting at their cabin that night. Jake had told her about it the previous Sunday during the ride home from church. Why the meeting had to be held here, she didn't know—perhaps because of who was involved.

At seven that night, Bishop Nisley and Elizabeth and Mose Chupp and his wife, Clara, would come to their cabin to talk with Ben and Sylvia Stoll.

Apparently Ben and Sylvia had gone not just to one tent meeting in Kalispell but to all of them. Something would have to be said to the couple.

"How was this done?" Hannah had asked Jake earlier, surprised that they would attend even one meeting, let alone several.

"They stayed with some friends so they wouldn't have to drive back and forth every night." Jake had said by way of explanation.

Jake arrived home that evening a little before dusk fell. It was early for him, but they wanted to be finished with supper before the others arrived. Hannah grew tenser as the time approached. She told Jake to leave the kitchen work to her, even though he had offered to help. The first buggy arrived as she was drying the dishes. Hannah made her way to the living room and waited as Jake stepped out onto the porch to welcome Minister Chupp and his wife.

Hannah could hear Jake say "Good evening" and the sound of shuffling feet as the group made its way up onto the porch. Quickly she got up, opened the door, smiled a greeting, and welcomed the guests inside. Jake stayed on the porch to wait for the others.

"I'll take your coats," Hannah said, motioning to Clara and Mose to take seats on the couch. She had chairs from the kitchen set up around the living room for the others.

"How are you making out in your cabin?" Clara asked, glancing around. Mose just smiled at her, nodded, and took his seat.

"Okay," Hannah told Clara. "I like it. It's different from what I'm used to."

"I suppose so," Clara said as she sat down. "We've been wanting to visit. This is the first chance we've had."

"We've never had church here," Hannah said. "That'll have to wait until summer when we can meet in the barn. The house is way too small."

"There's nothing wrong with the barn," Clara assured her. "I'm sure it can be arranged."

The thought caused Hannah's mind to spin. Knowing their duty to take church would come soon enough, she mentally added that job to their already large pile of church responsibilities.

"I'm sure they'll get around to it," Clara went on, "when summer comes."

Mose smiled and nodded again.

The cabin door opened behind them to admit Ben and Sylvia. Hannah heard John and Elizabeth's buggy pull in as she stood to welcome the Stolls.

"Good evening," she said, putting on her best smile.

"Good evening," Sylvia and Ben said together, their faces sober.

"I'll take your coats," Hannah said. All the while, she couldn't help wondering what would happen. Surely a reprimand of some sort was in order—and a promise from the Stolls not to attend such meetings in the future.

Elizabeth and John were inside by the time Hannah came back from the bedroom. She greeted them with a "Good evening" and took their coats as well. When she came back the third time, the conversation began in earnest as Bishop Nisley got right to the point.

"I hope Ben and Sylvia understand the reason for this meeting. We mean only good—all for Ben's and Sylvia's good. We are here to help and to inquire out of concern. I hope no hard feelings come out of this."

Jake and Mose nodded. Hannah wondered how in the world it had come to be that she and Jake were even at a meeting like this—much less hosting it in their own home—but knew she must get used to such sudden and interruptive events.

"It has reached our ears," John continued, "that you attended meetings. *Revival meetings*, I think they are called by our Mennonite friends. This is of concern to us."

"We meant no harm," Ben said. "We were invited by relatives in Kalispell. They set up a tent there, these Mennonites. It sounded interesting, so we went."

"Revival meetings?" John asked.

"Yes," Ben said.

"What do they mean by revival meetings? What is being revived?" John asked. "Do they feel their spiritual lives are dead? Have they no more commands of our Lord to fulfill? Which of God's words no longer requires obedience?"

"Don't be too hard on them," Elizabeth said, reaching over and touching his arm. "I'm sure they meant no harm."

The bishop cleared his throat. "Perhaps, but this sort of thing can lead to great error."

"We felt there was a lack in our spiritual lives," Sylvia spoke up. "I was really blessed by the preaching."

"I see," John said, settling back into the couch.

Hannah felt sure the bishop was thinking something but not wanting to say it.

"Surely you understand the need for obedience," Mose spoke up. "Have you been keeping the commandments of God?"

Ben shrugged. "We try."

"We are afraid," Sylvia said.

"That's not unusual," John said. "Many of us fear. Sometimes the fear of the Lord is a good thing."

"It's not that," Ben said. He hung his head but didn't seem ready to continue.

"See," Sylvia said, "maybe I wasn't born again—before, I mean. Now I believe I am. We…went up to the front when the preacher made the altar call. We wanted to be right with God."

Ben nodded. "He preached about repentance and getting rid of sin."

"The preacher?" Mose asked.

Ben nodded again.

"You were practicing sin?" John asked, his brow wrinkled.

Sylvia spoke up. "We just felt it—inside us. This preacher spoke of the blood of Jesus washing us."

"There's nothing wrong with that," John agreed. "But this sin you speak of. You were *sinning?*"

Ben managed a grin. "Not really. I mean, I did break a few of the church rules at times. Maybe small ones. That's all."

"I wasn't doing anything wrong, but their preaching made me feel like a sinner," Sylvia added.

"We all are sinners," John agreed. "So I still don't understand."

Hannah glanced at Jake, but he was staring at the floor. Obviously this was bishop work. She again wondered why in the world they were even here.

"I guess we felt something…for the first time…in here." Ben laid his hand on his chest. "We wanted an experience with God."

"I see," John said. "An experience."

"Yes," Sylvia nodded vigorously. "We felt washed afterward. We confessed our sins with the preacher."

"You confessed your sins?" Mose asked. "Which ones?"

"Things we had done—even as far back as our childhood. The usual sins, I suppose," Sylvia said. "Ben didn't have as many. I confessed the lie I told my mother—I'd never told anyone about it before."

"That is why we have pre-communion church," John said. "It's time then for confessions."

"We've done that," Ben said, "but this felt different."

"I can understand that. Some confessions are to be private," John said. "Have you told your mother this lie?"

Sylvia shook her head. "I felt cleansed at the meeting."

"You probably should tell your mother, though," Mose spoke up. "That would be between the two of you."

"I suppose so," Sylvia said, seemingly deep in thought.

"The other things too," John added. "Whatever you told this preacher, if they involve other people, they should be told."

Ben nodded. Sylvia still seemed to be thinking.

Hannah felt nervous for them. Her palms sweaty, she wished she were somewhere else.

"See, we are not priests," John said. "We don't stand between God and man. We don't hear others' sins. We confess our sins to God. If we sin against the church, we confess to the church. If we sin against others, we confess to them. The confessing, then, restores fellowship. It does not forgive our sins. Only God can do that."

"His blood," Ben said. "They spoke of His blood."

"That is how it is done," John agreed. "The blood of Jesus. They are right about that. Sins are only forgiven through the blood."

"So…maybe no harm has been done," Mose said and seemed to relax in his seat.

"Maybe," John allowed.

Ben cleared his throat, his eyes focused on the floor and his fingers tightly clasped.

Hannah held her breath.

"We would like to leave," Ben said.

"Leave?" John asked, stunned.

"To join the group in Kalispell," Ben said. "We feel a oneness with them. They're starting a new group with those who went to the altar."

No one said anything for a few seconds. Then John said, "Isn't this a bit sudden?"

"Maybe," Ben allowed, his eyes still looking at the floor.

"We hope this will cause no trouble with the church," Sylvia said. "God is really drawing our hearts."

"I see," John said, his face a question. "This 'drawing'? It is out into the world, then?"

"Not the world," Sylvia said quickly, "to the church of God—to other believers."

"You surely don't think—think we aren't the church of God?" Mose asked, the question lingering in his voice.

"No." Ben shook his head vigorously. "We just don't believe it's necessary to live like this to be a part of the church."

"Like this?" Mose asked.

"Buggies and such," Ben said. "The preacher said we can have God without living like this. He said some of our Amish ways might even be holding us back."

"From growing spiritually," Sylvia added.

"Yes," Ben said, "spiritually."

"You realize what's out there?" John asked. "In the world—the temptations, the evils, the trials that happen to one's faith. It's different from what you're used to."

"I suppose," Ben said. "The preacher said the grace of God would be sufficient."

"Yes," John agreed. "God might have grace even for ignorance, but in this case, I don't think you can claim ignorance."

"John," Elizabeth said, laying her hand on his arm again, "they're young."

"There is no reason to spare them the truth," John said. Then turning to the Stolls, he said, "You realize this will need to be told to the church."

"You…you won't be excommunicating us?" Ben's voice trembled.

"Will this be a Mennonite church you're going to?" John asked.

"Yes," Ben said, "I think so."

"I will see what the church and the other ministers say. Don't get a car until you join this new church—if it is a Mennonite church—and keep yourselves in the *Ordnung* till then. I know it may seem foolish to you since you are leaving anyway. You'll need all the help you can get, though. A little keeping of the rules won't hurt and might even help you. We are not the keepers of men's souls. We just watch the best we know how. Our faith has always been a voluntary one, a gathering of like hearts. If you wish to leave, I don't stand in your way."

Ben looked relieved. Sylvia even smiled.

"But if it's a wacky church, that's another matter," the bishop added. "There are some out there."

"No, it's not wacky," Sylvia said. "The preacher is a very spiritual man."

"I hope so," John said.

Hannah noticed Elizabeth had laid her hand on John's arm again.

The bishop then dismissed the meeting and said this would be discussed more among the ministry during the next preaching Sunday. He asked Ben and Sylvia if they would be willing to give this more thought. They both nodded with troubled expressions on their faces.

After everyone left, Jake stood and watched the buggy lights grow distant.

"I'm sorry to see them go," he said.

"I am too," Hannah said, surprised at how much she meant it. The young couple would be missed in the small church.

Thirty-three

Hannah sat in her usual place on the hard bench with the other women, but this Sunday, Sylvia Stoll was not beside her. Instead the line of young unmarried girls started immediately. Either Sylvia and Ben had made their final decision and already left the Amish church, or they were absent because of sickness. After the meeting the other night, Hannah couldn't help but suppose it was the former reason.

On the way to church, a cold blast swept down the mountain slopes. Last night too had been frigid. When Hannah greeted Betty in the kitchen, her aunt said that the pond they had passed on their way to church had frozen over. And now, outside the living room window of Amos Raber's place, where church was being held, the branches on the trees whipped angrily back and forth.

Hannah shivered on the bench, though the house was well heated. Amos kept his old furnace chugging along just fine. Every so often he would head for the basement to add wood to the fire. The cause of Hannah's discomfort was not the temperature but the emptiness inside of her.

Hannah hadn't expected to experience such strong feelings after losing the baby. But then she hadn't ever given a thought to the sad possibility. How could she know how to feel? And yet, for the past several days, a void seemed to have engulfed her. She had mourned more—not less—over the life that still should have been in her. She felt like weeping over a grave, but there was none.

Around her the singing rose and fell while the ministers met upstairs.

It wouldn't be long before they returned and began the preaching. Jake would be preaching this morning, she supposed. It might even be his first time doing the main sermon. Strange, she thought, how the preaching suddenly held such an interest for her.

The song ended with one last exertion, the notes rising in a joyous outburst of sound. Around the room, silence descended instantly, as if no one wanted to be the first to move. Then came a cautious shuffle of feet, and someone fumbled for his handkerchief and loudly blew his nose.

With the announcement of the next song number, the room filled with expectation, as if everyone simultaneously drew in breath for the start of the song. The sound of shoes on the hardwood steps came first, though, followed by a collapse of the room's collective readiness to sing. Hannah heard the songbooks softly close all around her. She shut her own book and laid it under the bench. Preaching hour had arrived.

Bishop Nisley delivered the first sermon, followed by the Scripture reading. Christmas was in two weeks, and Bishop mentioned the fact briefly. Jake, though, got up to deliver the main sermon as Hannah expected. He told the full story of Jesus' birth.

He stood close to the double living room windows. With his hands clasped and his young features sober, he told of the birthday of Jesus, a time to reflect on God becoming a man. Jake started with what Hannah assumed were Old Testament prophecies and spoke of the promise of a child who would be the hope of mankind. "In a world of sickness, sin, suffering, and war, God would give His answer in His own time, His solution to the world's troubles.

"The baby was born of a virgin and grew up to tread on the head of the serpent. He was bitten in the heel for His troubles and was killed. He would be called *Emmanuel*, the *Everlasting Father*, the *Prince of Peace*, and of His reign and kingdom would have no end. He would be known as the *Man of Sorrows*," Jake said. "He would weep over His people, even though they would reject Him. He would be taken as a lamb to the slaughter, to be killed like a sheep who would remain silent before its shearers. The world would never understand how God could save without an army, without a war of slaughter against His enemies, without reigning as a king from Jerusalem.

"The religious leaders of the day," Jake said, "expected something God didn't do, something He never said He would do. Their years of Scripture study had led them away from God and into their own understanding. The church leaders thought God was like them—hard, unforgiving, enforcing a harsh code of justice.

"Many of them had forgotten the beginning, when God walked in the garden with Adam and Eve and talked to them in the cool of the day. People of Jesus' day were no longer being told that God loved His people, that He created them for love, and that He could do no differently than love, as His nature demanded it.

"In the Old Testament," Jake said, "God spoke of comforting His people. He commanded the prophets to cry out to Jerusalem, to proclaim the end of her warfare, to announce her iniquities pardoned; one could receive double from the Lord for any wrongs committed."

Jake then said, "God was no longer in the garden. Sin had defiled it. Man could work all he wanted, but this earth would never be heaven. This was no longer our home. God's people were now to be pilgrims and strangers down here, never quite at home, preparing for their move to a better world where they would live forever.

"The wonder of the child's birth was not that the earth had become heaven, but that heaven had come down to earth. God became man, not to live in one place or to be at home in one country but to be at home in every man's and woman's heart, preparing them for the move to God's new world. There could never be another garden of Eden, but there could be a garden in the heart of all who believe in Jesus.

"God wants to live fully through those who believe in Him. He wants them to go into all the world, wherever sin is, and live the life of God fully—the humble, unarmed, holy life that the child brought into the manger. Such a life inevitably attracts persecution and hatred from those who don't understand.

"Our forefathers," Jake said, "never believed the earth could be made into heaven. They never sought to bring about another protected place where no scorpions crawled or wolves tore up lambs, where people could eat from the tree of life whenever they wanted to. Instead they went about their lives like sheep among wolves because that was how God had come into this world.

"It was a great mystery," Jake continued, "what God was doing. He revealed His plans slowly, throughout the pages of Scripture. He started working with one man, Abraham, and one nation, Israel. This led many religious leaders to think that where God started He was going to stop. They thought this meant God loved only Jews and worked only through war and battle.

"But God is going somewhere," Jake said as he started to walk around a little, clasping and unclasping his hands in front of him. Hannah glanced over to Bishop Nisley, afraid of what she would see. Was Jake preaching too well again—especially today with his first main sermon?

Relieved by what she saw, Hannah relaxed. A faint smile played on Bishop's face. She was certain he even nodded once. Apparently Jake wasn't straying too far from what was expected, or maybe Jake had proved himself in other ways, and Bishop now trusted him.

"Through His work with Israel, God took the best route to Christ," Jake said. "Along the way, He had allowed war, and He had allowed David to have many wives, but when Christ came, the fullness of God's will was revealed.

"The baby in the manger shows what God truly intends for His people. He shows how they are to live in a world of sin and sorrow. If God can fulfill His promise of bringing Christ into the world, if He can move past wars to the unprotected manger, then He can also fulfill His promise now.

"That promise," Jake said, "is the day coming—a day when all tears will be wiped away, all sorrow and sin removed in a new heaven and a new earth. It will be just as wrong for God's people today to think that suffering and sickness could be removed from our present earth as it would have been for the people in King David's day to think they could live without fighting wars.

"God allows imperfections because that is what is best. Somehow, in fact, God is pleased to work through the imperfections of this world."

Hannah wasn't certain, but she thought there was a glisten of tears in Jake's eyes. Then they vanished, and yet they had served to compel Hannah to listen even more closely.

"The loss of those we love, of children—even those unborn—troubles us," Jake said. "It leaves an emptiness inside, and we wonder why God would allow such loss. We go to funerals and mourn our departed loved ones. We cannot even begin to understand the suffering and sin in the world.

"Why, then, would God send us only a child in a manger as an answer to all of this? Why not just wipe out sin? Why not destroy the devil? Why not stop all the killing in the streets of our big cities? Why not raise up a righteous government in Washington that could rule without sin? Would that not seem like a better answer to us?"

Jake paused and then answered his own question. "To our understanding, perhaps so. Yet in God's design, it would be wrong. We must not think that the presence of suffering makes God unloving and uncaring."

Jake paused again to look across the gathering of men and women, many who watched him with upraised faces. "We must live," he continued, "blameless and harmless in a sinful and suffering world because that is the way God wants us to live. We should never blame God because He doesn't explain everything to us. He owes us no explanations."

Jake paused again and then decided that was all he wanted to say. He then asked for testimonies. Mose spoke and was followed by two of the older men.

Hannah sat tensely as each man spoke, fearful that someone would say Jake had erred in his sermon. But no one did. Instead they all pronounced it the Word of God and confirmed God's blessing on it.

Jake stood up again, announced prayer, and closed the service as they all knelt. The younger children made a rush to leave the room, followed more slowly by the young people. Hannah rose to help prepare the noon meal in the kitchen.

Thirty-four

"Did you notice…Sylvia and Ben aren't here?" Betty whispered to Hannah as the two women approached the kitchen.

"Yes, I noticed," Hannah whispered back.

"They're leaving," Betty said with horror in her voice, "for a liberal church."

"I was afraid of that," Hannah said.

"Are they being excommunicated?" Betty's voice was still a whisper.

Hannah knew this was dangerous territory, especially for a minister's wife. If she had information, she shouldn't share it before a public announcement was made. "Bishop will decide that," she finally said, thankful they were approaching other women and the conversation would have to end.

"I would think so," Betty said with finality.

"Hello," Elizabeth said to the two women.

Amos's wife, Mandy, placed butter on plates and said to Hannah, "You can help with these."

Hannah knew what that meant. She picked up two plates in each hand and headed back toward the living room. When she arrived, the men had already scooted the benches together, two or three wide, and set them on risers to form tables, and two women had covered them with vinyl tablecloths.

With a glance behind her, Hannah saw Betty following with bowls of peanut butter. Together they set out the items with even spaces between them. By the time they came to the end of the table, other women had placed the forks and knives on the tables. The first round of food was ready five minutes later.

Hannah stood in the doorway of the kitchen as prayer was announced and the meal began. Because Jake was now a minister and thus climbing the ladder of seniority, he got to be at the head of the line. The same would, no doubt, be true for her eventually, she figured. But for now, the other women didn't insist on her going first but allowed her to stay in the regular line of women. This suited Hannah just fine because any rhythm from her old life was a comfort and made her less aware of the changes in her life.

She ate during the second round and then helped with a few stragglers in the third round. The last round consisted of only one table, which was set up in the master bedroom. Hannah was certain there was a purpose to Elizabeth helping her serve, and she didn't have long to wait to find out what it was.

"I hope you weren't too disturbed the other night," Elizabeth said more than asked.

Hannah shook her head.

Elizabeth smiled. "I told John he shouldn't conduct church business in front of everyone. He just thought it might help to have the meeting at your place—that it might make Ben and Sylvia more comfortable."

"I hope it did," Hannah said truthfully.

"I see they didn't show up today." Elizabeth glanced around. "John will be disappointed."

"Jake too," Hannah said.

"John is hoping it won't spread," Elizabeth said with a worried look. "I think he's changed his mind about Jake."

"Oh." Hannah glanced around to see if anyone was listening. No other women were close, and the few children at the table were intent on their peanut butter sandwiches.

"Yes," Elizabeth continued and nodded. "I think he's right for the position, especially after today. John will be happy."

Hannah's face showed her question.

"Jake's kind of preaching might be just what is needed for our young couples. You heard what Sylvia and Ben said—about the spiritual part.

This might help. John thinks God might be helping us out through Jake."

"Are there more people thinking of leaving?"

"John thinks so. Seems there's some sort of a movement going on in Kalispell. There's a lot of temptation."

"And here too?" Hannah asked, surprised.

"Well, not so much just yet, but John's afraid it might be coming our way."

"So Sylvia and Ben are gone for good?"

"We don't know for sure," Elizabeth said. "I suppose they went to church over there today—had someone drive them. It does sound like they're serious, though."

"Do you think there's anything can we do," Hannah asked, "to keep them here?"

"That's what I really wanted to talk to you about," Elizabeth said with a quick glance around to make sure she was free to speak.

Hannah waited, wondering what more could possibly come her way.

"At the ministers' meeting this morning," Elizabeth said, "John told me he was going to ask Jake to talk with Will and Rebecca Troyer."

"Will and Rebecca?" A picture of the couple flashed into Hannah's mind. They were already married when she first came from Indiana to help with Betty's riding stable. As she remembered it, Will had moved in from a community in Bonners Ferry, but Rebecca was local.

"They weren't here today either," Elizabeth said.

"Are they leaving too?"

"Well, it's something else...kind of," Elizabeth said, leaving Hannah more puzzled than ever.

Betty bustled up behind them. "Oh, *here* you are. Have you enough help with this table?"

"Yes, I think so," Hannah said.

"Oh," Betty said, glancing at Elizabeth, "did I interrupt something?"

"Not really," Elizabeth said with a smile. "I was done."

"Well..." Betty replied.

Hannah could see Betty was curious. Once again, the burden of kept confidences would weigh heavy on her shoulders.

"I'll go get the water pitchers," Elizabeth said.

"Church things," Hannah said when Elizabeth moved out of sight. Any more than that, she didn't want to say.

"Oh," Betty said, obviously disappointed not to be told more.

Elizabeth returned with the water pitchers and smiled knowingly at Hannah. *Apparently she trusts me*, Hannah thought, not sure she enjoyed the feeling.

"Hannah, why don't you stop by this week?" Betty asked. "On Thursday afternoon we're having the youth over. We're making Christmas packages for a ministry in Libby. There'll be games and such afterward. You could help me get ready. Jake could stop by on his way home."

"Oh," Hannah answered, taking an immediate interest, "I'd like that."

"You'll ask Jake, then?"

"He shouldn't object," Hannah said. She liked the idea of some activity that wasn't associated with Jake being a minister.

"The young people will enjoy it. I think a lot of them like Jake as a minister," Betty said, spoiling the moment. "You'll come, then?"

"If Jake doesn't object," Hannah said.

"Good. Oh, there's Steve," Betty said with a glance out the living room window and toward the barn.

"Jake's not far behind," Hannah replied. She didn't see Jake at the moment but figured he must be about ready to go home. True to her words, the next man to come out of the barn was Jake, his horse following behind him.

Betty left to retrieve her shawl from the table by the back door. She found it just about the time Hannah stepped up to the table. "There it is!" Betty said. "Thought I'd never find it." And with that she disappeared out the door.

Hannah took a minute to find her shawl and bonnet, and by the time she stepped outside, Betty was already in the buggy with Steve. Jake had their buggy pulled up right behind them. Hannah tightly wrapped the ends of her shawl around herself as she walked down the sidewalk and climbed into the buggy.

"Chilly," Jake said, pulling his black suit coat tighter around himself and shaking the lines to get Mosey moving.

"You should have brought your winter coat," Hannah said. Next Sunday she would see that he wore it.

Hannah glanced at Jake out of the corner of her eye. He looked the same as always, yet this was the minister who said all those things this morning in his sermon. She struggled to connect the two images and then gave up. They were simply too far apart. One stood beyond her grasp, the other sat right beside her and talked like the Jake she had always known. Were the two really the same man?

"Bishop wants us to go talk with Will and Rebecca," Jake said just like that.

"Elizabeth told me he might," Hannah replied.

"Oh, she did?" Jake sounded surprised. "Did she say why?"

"No, not for sure." Hannah looked at Jake. "I hope they aren't leaving."

"Like Sylvia and Ben?"

"Yes," Hannah said.

"No, it's something else,"

"Why are *we* going?" Hannah asked. "Why doesn't John go himself?"

"He thinks this might work better."

"Why do you have to do this kind of work so soon?" Hannah asked.

"Bishop wants it."

"I know why," Hannah said. "Elizabeth told me."

Jake looked at her. "What did she say?"

"Bishop likes you now and thinks you might do Will and Rebecca good. He's changed his mind about you, I guess. People like your preaching, and so you are being put to work."

"Maybe that's what we're here for," Jake said, turning his eyes back to the road ahead. "It's the work of the church. I didn't choose it."

"But you enjoy it."

"Maybe," he allowed. "It makes it easier that way."

"It's not easier for me," she said with a catch in her voice.

She looked at Jake, expecting his new preacher look, the one he had worn earlier in the day. She thought he might even say things about duty and how she needed to learn to be a good minister's wife. But instead he brought his arm around her and pulled her close.

"I'm sorry," he said. "I wish it wasn't so hard."

That brought a sob she couldn't hold back.

"You're a wonderful wife," Jake said.

"I lost your child," she said between sobs.

"No," he said. "Heaven gained him. God allows only what works for the best."

"It's still too awful," she said, her head on his shoulder.

"For my thoughts are not your thoughts, neither are your ways my ways, saith the Lord. For as the heavens are higher than the earth, so are my ways higher than your ways, and my thoughts than your thoughts," Jake said.

Hannah looked out at the Cabinet Mountains towering in the sky. As the wind pushed against the trees on the slopes, the sound of Jake's voice and the words he chose soothed her spirit.

Thirty-five

Jake insisted they visit Will and Rebecca that evening, even when Hannah suggested they might be at the hymn sing.

"Hardly," Jake said. "Besides, this is important."

"So what is going on?" Hannah asked once they were on the way. "What aren't you telling me about this?"

"Did you know Will wasn't originally Amish?" Jake asked.

"No," Hannah said. "I never heard that, but I didn't grow up around here. He seems Amish—his brother too."

Jake slapped the reins as Mosey hesitated. "Their parents came from the Baptists and later joined a Mennonite church or a version of it in Bonners Ferry. That was when Will and his brother were young. Will, though, wanted something even more conservative than that. His brother followed his lead, and so they both joined the Amish."

Hannah waited.

"Now it seems Will thinks it was all a mistake and wants to go back."

"To the Mennonites?" Hannah asked.

"No—to the Baptists."

"The Baptists?" Hannah gasped. "And what about Rebecca? Does she want to go back too?"

"No, I don't think so. And that's part of the problem."

"They have two children."

"That's even more of a problem."

"Jake, this is too big for you."

218

"That's what I said," Jake offered, "but I'm just doing what I was told to do."

"Oh, my," was all Hannah could think to say.

They drove in silence, each lost in thought. Hannah was thinking of Rebecca, remembering the faces of her two children, and wondering at the choice that must now be heavy on her heart.

"It's so terrible," she said, finally breaking the silence. "We are so young. This is just too much."

"I know," Jake said, his voice strained.

"What are you going to tell them, Jake? What *can* you tell them? What if you say the wrong thing? Rebecca could lose her husband. You know that, Jake. I know she doesn't want to leave. I know Rebecca. Mennonite, maybe—but never Baptist." She grabbed Jake's arm. "Jake, we have to go back! Bishop must go himself. He really must. You have to tell him. You can't do this. It's too dangerous, Jake. It really is."

"We can't go back," Jake said simply. "The way may be hard, but I have to do this. It wasn't for me to decide."

"What about me?" she asked, looking at Jake desperately.

"You're stronger than you think," he said gently. "Much stronger. We can both do this."

"Can we?" she asked doubtfully, though Jake's confidence touched her. "You really think so?"

"I know so," Jake said, his voice low. "You're my wife."

Hannah looked skeptically at him. She then took a deep breath and calmed herself. "You're going to need a lot of wisdom."

"God will give me the wisdom I need," Jake said.

As Jake pulled the buggy into the driveway of Will and Rebecca's home, Hannah caught sight of their two children disappearing into the house. Jake stopped Mosey at the hitching post, climbed down from the buggy, and tied the reins to the post.

"The children," Hannah said to no one in particular. "What will happen to them?"

Jake led the way to the house. The place seemed wrapped in stillness, perhaps expressing the sorrow the occupants must be feeling.

Jake knocked gently and then stepped back from the door to wait.

For a long moment, Hannah believed no one would open the door. *We are being ignored on purpose,* she thought, *rejected before our errand has even begun. Surely Bishop would understand if Jake failed for this reason. No one could fault Jake if he at least tried.*

But then Will opened the door rather abruptly in front of them. At least he was smiling, Hannah noticed. A little sad around the edges, but it was a smile.

"Good afternoon," Jake said. "Is it okay if we come in?"

"I guess," Will said, opening the door wider.

Hannah went in first, and Jake followed, taking off his hat and winter coat.

"You can put those on the chair." Will said, pointing to the kitchen. "Rebecca will be right out. She's in the bedroom."

The two children—a boy, the older, and a girl, only three or so—squirmed on the couch. Hannah went over to sit beside them and said softly, "Hi."

Andrew only smiled and ducked his head, but Edith said "Hi" very quietly, her lips barely moving.

"Oh, you surprised me." Rebecca's voice came from the bedroom door. "I'm still in my work clothing."

"That's perfectly okay," Jake said from where he sat. "We don't want to disturb your evening."

"I'm so glad to see you," Rebecca said, offering to shake hands with Hannah and then Jake. Hannah was certain she saw tears forming in Rebecca's eyes.

Will brought two chairs from the kitchen. He set one down and indicated it was for Rebecca. He took the other.

Rebecca sat down slowly. "I'm so sorry we couldn't be in church today. I missed it so."

Will nodded soberly.

"There will be other times," Jake said.

Hannah noticed that Jake looked comfortable enough and was glad for that.

"I hope so," Rebecca said, and the tears came freely now.

Will looked embarrassed and glanced at the children, who were still sitting beside Hannah.

"I'm sorry," Rebecca choked. "Maybe the children can play upstairs."

"Do you want to?" Will asked them, now on his feet. "Upstairs in the bedroom with your toys?"

"We want to go outside," Andrew said.

Will seemed uncertain as he glanced out the living room window at the gathering darkness.

"It's okay," Rebecca said. "We can call them in when it gets too dark."

"Go, then," Will said, watching as Andrew and Edith scampered for the front door. "But put on your coats first."

"You have such nice children," Hannah whispered.

"They have a good father," Rebecca said, and again tears sprang to her eyes.

"I suppose you have come to talk?" Will asked as the front door closed. "John sent you?"

Jake nodded.

"Are we being excommunicated?" Rebecca asked with alarm.

"Surely not—" Will said, "at least not yet."

Rebecca looked unconvinced.

"You are not being excommunicated," Jake said firmly. "We are interested in helping. That's all."

"You know what the problem is?" Will glanced sharply at Jake.

"You want to return to the Baptists," Jake said.

"Amish don't approve of that," Will said.

Jake nodded.

"You'd excommunicate me, then," Will stated flatly.

"Don't say that," Rebecca said, alarm again in her voice. "That's terrible. To even think it is terrible."

"You would, wouldn't you?" Will didn't plan to drop the subject.

Jake pondered the point and finally said, "I suppose the church would. I'm not the bishop though."

"That's what I thought," Will said with satisfaction in his voice. "Do you think it's right to do that just for joining the Baptists—the church I came from?"

"Your parents were Baptists," Rebecca said through her tears. "You're Amish now. We're Amish. Don't even think such things. Please."

"You don't have to go back," Jake said. "I always thought you were happy here."

"I thought so too," Will grunted, squirming on his chair. "Maybe my brother and I overreacted, though. That's what bothers me now. Sure, my parents saw things they knew to be wrong—problems with the Baptists. I just went too far the other way. Now I'm seeing that the Baptists don't have a monopoly on problems."

"There are problems everywhere," Jake agreed, "even with the Amish."

Hannah caught her breath. Surely that was the wrong thing to say if he wanted Will to stay Amish.

Will, though, seemed to like the answer.

"See," Rebecca said, "it wouldn't be any better among the Baptists. Besides, I'm not going Baptist. I just can't."

With a glance toward Rebecca, Will asked Jake, "You think Rebecca ought to submit to me? Isn't that what the Amish believe—where the husband goes, the wife goes?"

There was silence in the room. Jake cleared his throat. "I'm just a young fellow. How would I know the answer to that?"

Hannah almost sighed out loud, so great was her relief at Jake's answer.

"You do know the answer, though," Will said, "and I'd like to hear it."

"I don't think she should," Jake said just like that, the suddenness of it jarring the room.

"That's a mouthful," Will laughed. "You think John will back that up? Maybe it's just because you want Rebecca to stay Amish."

"No, I don't think so," Jake said firmly. "I'd say so regardless. The answer would be the same coming the other way. If one of the couple objects, the move shouldn't be made. You decide these things together—as a couple."

"Even if the couple was English and one wanted to join the Amish and the other didn't? You'd risk losing that one member who wanted to join?" Will asked, his eyes intense.

"Yes," Jake said firmly. "That's what I would say. I think it's Amish policy, although I don't know for sure."

"So what about the church's teaching about submission?" Will pressed.

"Submission is a woman pleasing her husband. It's not a woman changing her honestly held beliefs," Jake said. "If the woman has to change who she is, then it's not submission. It's a perversion of submission. God never asks for that."

"Then what am I supposed to do?" Will asked. "I don't want to be Amish."

"I'd tell you to love your wife," Jake said, "and your children. That's probably as good a work as you'll do being a Baptist."

"And I can do it being Baptist," Will said.

"You can do it better being Amish," Jake replied.

Will thought about this for a moment. "I'd have to think on that some. I'm not sure that's so." Then after a moment, he added, "I guess my brother was right."

"Right?" Jake asked. "About what?"

"He stopped by before you came," Rebecca said weakly.

"He said you can really preach. Said you preached really well today," Will said.

"You shouldn't say things like that," Jake said.

"No, I suppose not," Will allowed. "Well, Jake, I'll need to think on this for a while. Some of what you say makes sense. But I can't say one way or another just now." Then he turned to Rebecca and said, "Don't look so white, dear." He gently rubbed her shoulder.

"I can't help it," Rebecca replied, the tears still flowing.

"You've had supper already?" Will asked.

Both Jake and Hannah shook their heads.

"Then you're staying," Will pronounced. "We haven't eaten either."

"I don't have anything," Rebecca gasped. She wiped the tears from her face with her hand. "I wasn't expecting anyone."

"I'll help you," Hannah spoke up, willing to help in any way she could.

"See," Will said, "you'll think of something."

Rebecca hesitated but then got up. The two women left to go to the kitchen.

"I'll see what the children are doing," Will said, getting up and moving toward the door.

"I'll come along," Jake said, joining Will.

At the front door, Will called sharply, "Andrew! Edith!" Soon little feet pattered across the porch.

"Time to come inside," Will said.

"We were tired anyway," a little voice replied.

"Then come in here. Play in the living room," Will said as he ushered the two inside. They crept past the kitchen doorway with Jake and Will behind them.

"They are so dear," Hannah said again.

"I heard you lost yours," Rebecca said softly. "I'm so sorry."

Hannah couldn't find her voice at the moment.

"Maybe God will bless you again," Rebecca offered, "like you are blessing others."

How she was blessing others, Hannah couldn't imagine, but she nodded anyway.

With the two working together, they soon had the soup and salad prepared. Rebecca remembered half a cream pie in the refrigerator, and the two families settled in for supper.

The evening passed quickly enough. Even with the chatter of their voices, the house still seemed quiet, although peaceful now.

"I hope we did some good," Hannah said on the way home.

"I hope so too," Jake agreed. "Bishop will probably want to talk to them himself, though."

"It would be terrible if they left," Hannah said. "Rebecca so doesn't want to go."

"I know," Jake said in his preacher voice, and Hannah was surprised it didn't bother her. She leaned against his shoulder as a yawn overcame her. How she could be so relaxed after this day was a mystery, like a lot of other things in her life right now.

Thirty-six

With the intense activity on Sunday, Hannah nearly forgot the young people's gathering at Betty's. On Thursday morning she mentioned it to Jake, and he had no objections. In fact a little grin spread over his face. "It makes me feel young to be invited to a youth gathering," he said. "It's been a while."

"It sure seems to be lifting your spirits some. You've been so sober-faced lately. You know you shouldn't think about church troubles all the time."

"No," he agreed, "I shouldn't. But I do wish I could talk to John before Sunday."

Not wanting to be involved in a weekday visit with the bishop, Hannah thought quickly. "Betty's going to pick me up after lunch. She suggested you drop by on the way home. Instead, why not swing past the bishop's house? You'd have plenty of time before the gathering starts."

"Yes, I could do that," Jake said, "and I'd still be there early."

Jake left for work, and Hannah spent the morning cleaning the cabin.

After lunch Betty picked her up, and the two women spent the afternoon preparing for the evening ahead. They finished just before the first of the youth arrived. By seven thirty the gathering was in full swing, buggies parked all over the yard and horses packed tightly in the barn. These were not all the same youth Hannah knew from a few years ago, but Hannah easily lost herself in the spirit of the night, as if she were young again. It was as if time had rolled away. For that evening, she no longer was a mother who had lost her baby, a preacher's wife, or even a woman with a cabin to keep.

With a jolt she suddenly realized Jake hadn't arrived. "I wonder why Jake's still not here yet," she whispered to Betty.

"I can't imagine," her aunt said. "You don't think something happened to him? Wasn't he stopping at the bishop's home?"

The two women made their way to the kitchen to check on the cider heating on the stove.

"Yes."

"That could take some time."

"This much?"

Betty smirked. "Church things? Of course."

Hannah could only nod in agreement. It could well be church things. She had learned that already.

"I'm going outside for a minute," Hannah said as she went to get her coat.

Betty nodded in sympathy and went back to the living room to be with the young people.

Hannah stepped out the kitchen door where the chilly night air enveloped her immediately. Overhead a brilliant swath of stars stretched almost from horizon to horizon, slightly offset to the south. Over her shoulder, just above the ridge of the house, the moon hung with one bright star to its upper right.

Hannah gazed at the star. The line of light seemed to come from the depths of immeasurable space and pierced her soul. She shivered with the feeling.

Surely Jake was just talking long with Bishop. She stepped out into the yard and listened for a horse's hooves on the pavement. Jake should be coming from the south. When no sound came, she walked out to the road to listen. There was only the great stillness of the sky above her. Even the voices from the house had faded away.

So this is to be my life, she thought, and the loneliness almost overwhelmed her. Jake was being taken away from her slowly but surely. *This is how it will always be, church work and demands taking up ever more of our time—Jake's time and my time—until none is left.*

The chill penetrated her coat even as her thoughts pierced her heart. Hannah pulled her arms tightly around herself. It helped keep out the cold air but not the unwanted thoughts. Only the sound of hoofbeats on the pavement would comfort her at this moment, but no sound came.

As she walked slowly back toward the house, she was struck with the horrible thought, *What if something has happened to Jake? An accident?* So real was her fear that she walked back out to the road to listen again, shivering in the cold.

There was no sound of sirens in the distance. But then she told herself, *Maybe I can't hear them from here. The accident could have happened anywhere, somewhere far from here—maybe just outside Libby before Jake had even gotten out of town.*

Jake could have been taken to the hospital. How would she be notified? Jake carried no identification. He would just be a nameless Amish person lost in some numbered room at the hospital.

That is *if* he made it to the hospital. A worse fear ran through her. Had not Bishop Amos died in a wreck just after ordaining Jake? Was this something that could be passed on? At the moment, anything seemed possible.

When Hannah, her body chilled from the cold, went back inside, her face must have shown the distress she felt.

"Nothing?" Betty both asked and answered the question. "Oh, they're probably just talking long. That's to be expected."

Hannah nodded numbly, forcing herself to move to the living room. It wouldn't help to stay in the kitchen, away from the others. That might only draw attention to herself. With a pasted-on smile, she joined the group.

As they had for the past two years, the youth were busy assisting Helping Hands, a ministry in Libby, with their Christmas package preparations. They were wrapping up the clothing and toys, supplied by the Goodwill in Libby and its sister store in Kalispell, so that the packages could then be distributed to the area's needy children.

Hannah offered to take her turn at one of the six ironing boards set up to press the clothes before they were placed in the packages.

"Over here," Emily Nisley, Bishop John's oldest daughter, said cheerfully. "My arm's about ready to drop off."

Hannah gripped the handle of the iron and leaned against it for support, her emotions still swirling because of Jake's absence. The iron's angry sizzle at being pressed into the cloth caused her to jerk the iron upward.

"Oh," she said at Emily's puzzled look, "I'm not always that clumsy."

"The iron gets hot a little quickly," Emily said in a helpful tone.

Hannah smiled her thanks.

She slid the iron across the dress, and Emily left, finding a seat beside Enos Chupp, who was busy folding clothes for the packages.

Enos was Mose Chupp's second boy and a little older than Emily. Not too long ago, Hannah would have known every boy's age pretty close to the month, but how things had changed. She was definitely no longer one of the youth. Even less so now that she was a minister's wife.

Hannah had to smile at the way Emily looked shyly at Enos as she helped him fold the clothing. From time to time, she would drop her gaze to the floor and then raise it back to Enos, who seemed to enjoy the attention. His lips moved easily as the two engaged in conversation.

Oh, to be young again, Hannah thought, turning her mind back to her ironing before she burned something else. *Young love and where it leads, I ought to know,* she told herself.

As soon as all the packages were finished, Betty and Hannah served the refreshments. The young people took their plates into the living room, the hum of conversation filling the room.

Hannah tried to keep busy and not focus on the fact that Jake had still not arrived.

"Maybe Steve should go look for him," Betty whispered when she noticed Hannah's drawn face.

"No," Hannah said. She simply wouldn't allow her mind to entertain the thought of something wrong. Whatever was keeping Jake—no doubt just a long conversation with Bishop Nisley about church business—was easier to handle than any other option.

"But what if?" Betty asked, apparently having no qualms with troublesome thoughts of possible danger. "Surely he would have let you know."

"He's just talking long." Hannah pressed her lips together firmly, struggling to control her fears.

"You have more courage than I do," Betty said with admiration. "It's getting pretty late."

"I know," Hannah said, dreading the moments ahead when the young people would leave and there would possibly be no Jake.

Thirty minutes later, as the boys began to drift out to the barn to hitch their horses to the buggies, Jake still had not arrived. Hannah watched the horses snort white steam and jerk their heads into the air as the boys drove their buggies near to pick up sisters or cousins and take them out into the night.

Hannah went back to a chair at the kitchen table to calm herself. When the last young person had left, she knew she had to consider the worst. Someone would have to go look for Jake, and she knew what he would be looking for—a mangled body along the road or an equally torn body in the hospital. It would be just another of the frequent buggy and automobile accidents the Amish had come to accept as their lot. She folded her arms across her chest and willed herself to continue to breathe.

She would not go along. Betty would see to that. Steve would go on his own, and the tense, drawn-out wait would begin. Already her knuckles were white under the kitchen table. She pushed the unthinkable away, gathering herself together.

The noise of the departing buggy wheels crunching in the snow outside must have kept Hannah from hearing the sound of Jake's buggy arriving. Jake tied Mosey to the hitching post and briefly greeted the last of the youth on their way out.

He feared what awaited him inside and said as much to Steve, who had been helping the last of the boys hitch up.

"I know I'm really late," he said, his breath coming in long white streams.

"Hannah's been worried," Steve admitted, "but Betty's kept her busy."

You missed out on a good youth gathering. We had quite a nice group here."

"Always did," Jake agreed. "We were part of the group ourselves not that long ago."

The two men made their way to the house, and Jake waited while Steve opened the kitchen door.

The suddenness of Jake's appearance brought Hannah to her feet.

"I'm so sorry," Jake said as he walked over to Hannah. "I would have let you know, but there was no way. It just took so long."

Hannah couldn't find words but knew her face showed her distress far more than her words could anyway.

"Did Bishop keep you?" Betty asked from the living room door.

Jake ignored Betty as he sat down. He took Hannah's hands and drew her back down to her chair. He said nothing, allowing his eyes to express his regret over the pain his lateness had caused. Hannah resisted being drawn in by his gaze but then let go as the tears came.

"I didn't know what kept you," she said. "It could have been—"

Jake squeezed her hands. "But it wasn't. I'm here now."

Hannah relaxed and smiled.

When he saw that Hannah was fine again, he turned to Betty and asked, "Is there any food left?"

"Isn't that just like a man!" Betty said. "He comes in late and thinks of nothing but food."

"There's plenty left," Steve said with a chuckle. "Help yourself."

Jake did help himself, and Hannah, now feeling relieved and finding that her own appetite had returned, fixed herself a healthy plate. Betty, of course, fussed over them as if they both needed attention.

Hannah leaned against Jake on the way home. They rode in silence. *It is better this way*, Hannah thought. Apparently neither Jake nor she could change what they had become—two puppets pulled along by the strings of life. She yearned to stop everything and just hold on to Jake until the two of them were left alone, letting life and all its troubles pass them by.

"Bishop said Will and Rebecca are staying," Jake said sleepily as they pulled into the driveway.

"Really!" Hannah sat up straight upon hearing this good news. "That's wonderful."

"Yes," Jake said, "it is. It will be best for them and for all of us."

Thirty-seven

On the Friday before Christmas, a fierce snowstorm blew in from Idaho. Mr. Howard had insisted Jake leave work at the hardware store early and get home while he could. By the time Jake pulled into the driveway, the storm was gathering its full strength.

Hannah watched Jake unhitch Mosey as snow swirled furiously around them. Jake pulled on Mosey's reins, trying to get him to move inside more quickly. Apparently the horse, after his hurried drive from town, was too tired to care. Finally Mosey relented. Jake quickly got him settled in his stall and then rushed to the house. Reaching the porch, he shook the snow from his coat and hat before entering with a sigh.

"Quite some storm," he said. Then he quickly added, "Look what I have!"

"What?" she asked.

"A bonus check!" Jake drew a piece of paper from his coat pocket and waved it around. "Mr. Howard sold all the furniture we've made so far. It's partly due to Christmas sales, but it doesn't matter. Sales are sales. He kept his promise and paid me my share of the profits." Jake grinned broadly with satisfaction.

"That's wonderful!" Hannah let relief flow through her freely, though she felt a little ashamed that money should mean so much to her. In their situation that was just the way it was.

"Two mortgage payments," Jake pronounced. "Two! That will put us past January."

"We might need it," Hannah said, her mind on the snow outside.

She could just see them snowed in for weeks on end and Jake unable to work.

"I think the worst is over, moneywise," Jake said, still wearing his broad grin. "The furniture shop seems to be a winner."

"I hope so," Hannah said. "I'll get supper going. I didn't expect you home early." She started toward the kitchen.

"Wait," Jake said. "I bought us something. I thought it was time."

"What?" she asked, puzzled.

"It's still out in the buggy. I wanted to tell you first."

Hannah waited, letting Jake take his time.

"Meat," Jake said. "Hamburger from the store. I want us to have some for supper."

"Can we afford it?" It was all Hannah could think to say.

"With this check, yes, we can," he said, his grin returning. He lifted up the check again. "I'll cash it Monday. We'll have money left over after we pay the bank for the cabin."

"Meat," she said. "I've forgotten how much I missed it. Have you thought of it?"

"First thing," Jake said. "I know you've been missing it."

"I wasn't complaining," she made sure to say.

"I know you weren't. You're too good a wife to complain."

"And *you* have a silver tongue!" she said.

"I thought maybe golden?" he teased.

"Silver is good enough. Now, you go bring in the meat. I need to start frying it if you want some for supper."

"I'll be right back," Jake said, reaching for his coat again. As he opened the front door, the snow and wind blasted into the cabin.

"The storm's getting worse," Hannah said.

"We are snug as two bugs in a rug," Jake said as he disappeared out the door, the latch firmly clinking in place behind him.

Hannah stoked the fire in the stove. When Jake came in, she thawed the hamburger over the stove. Soon the rich aroma of freshly fried hamburger filled the cabin.

They sat down to eat, Jake prayed aloud, and the two served themselves healthy-sized portions of the meat. Jake, to Hannah's teasing, squeezed ketchup liberally onto his plate and dipped each piece of meat before he brought it to his mouth.

As she watched him, Hannah felt her own pleasure grow. *Is this not how things are supposed to be—life with my husband, the two of us gathered around the dinner table with snow blasting outside? Closed in together?* It made the moment feel as though all the outside problems they could ever face were far away. Perhaps if life was changing for them—if things were really getting better—she might have an answer to her silent wish.

The snow continued to fall as they went to bed. Drifts were now up to the top of the front porch, but Hannah didn't care. Jake's check had brought them a measure of security that set aside worries about the weather. Let it snow. Let it do its worst. They were safe inside.

When they awoke in the morning, the snow was still falling, and it continued throughout the day. Jake stayed inside, studying his German lesson book and not seeming to mind the forced imprisonment.

By evening the outside world seemed completely shut down, and still the snow fell. Jake raised the question that had just occurred to Hannah at nearly the same time.

"Do you think there will be church tomorrow?"

"I don't know," she said. She walked to the front window and looked out. It was hard for her to imagine how a buggy could get through the drifts piled in the yard, let alone those on the road.

"I wonder how we will know?" Jake thought out loud.

"Do people ever stay home from church here?" Hannah wondered aloud. Rarely in Indiana did such a thing happen. The roads were usually plowed before a person had time to decide to stay home. Montana, though, was strange country, Hannah reminded herself. This was definitely not Indiana.

"I guess it depends," Jake said. "I'm going over to Steve and Betty's to find out."

"No, Jake, don't," she said firmly. "It's too late in the day. You could get stuck in those drifts, and it will be dark before long."

"Well, maybe you're right," he said, bending to her logic. "I guess we'll just have to wait until morning."

Hannah thought the problem was solved and rose to prepare supper.

"I'm going to see Mr. Brunson," Jake said suddenly a few minutes later.

"Now?" she asked from the kitchen.

"He might be having trouble," Jake said. "Someone should check up on him."

"You just have the itch to get out of the house, that's all."

"I suppose that's part of it," Jake said with a grin, but Hannah could tell it was more than that. And since she too was concerned about Mr. Brunson, she made no further objection.

"Just don't get stuck," she said as Jake bundled up. "I'll have supper ready by the time you get back."

Watching Jake struggle through the snow troubled Hannah, but she comforted herself with the knowledge that it would take a lot to stop Jake or even slow him down. He took huge strides up the slope, tracking back and forth to avoid the worse drifts, but made good time.

When he got back almost an hour later, he looked happier than when he left. The time outside of the cabin in the elements had done him good.

"No problems," Jake said. "The old man seems well settled in. He has plenty of wood and food. He said he doesn't need to get out till spring, if necessary." Jake laughed at the thought.

"Did he say anything about his son?" Hannah asked. "Has he heard from him?"

"No...at least he didn't say anything to me about him," Jake said and then turned to another subject. "While I still have my coat on, I'm going out to the end of the driveway for the mail."

"For the mail?" Hannah asked in astonishment. "Surely no mailman went out today. Besides, supper's almost ready."

"They probably plowed the main road. We have all night for supper. There's not much daylight left. If there *is* mail, I want to get it before dark."

"You'll get stuck. Really, you will."

"I also want to see the main road—see if it's as bad as it is at Mr. Brunson's. Maybe the roads aren't plowed after all."

"The mailman hasn't come. You're just wasting your time."

"I've got it to waste," he said, already partway out the cabin door.

This time Hannah didn't watch him go. If he could make it up the mountain, he surely could make it down to the main road. But then as darkness fell and Jake hadn't come back yet, she began to worry a little. This time there was no church business that could be keeping him away. Instead, visions of Jake stuck in a snow bank flashed through her mind.

With supper ready and spread on the table, she looked out the window for some sign of Jake. Surely he ought to be back by now. His tracks were still visible in the snow, blown over a little but there. What were not there were any return tracks.

Hannah sighed and went back to the kitchen, where she tried to occupy herself. When she realized the supper would soon be cold, she began to worry more about Jake. He knew supper was nearly ready. What on earth could happen on a walk to the end of the road?

She stuck her face out the cabin door and was startled by the sharp chill in the air. Apparently the temperature had fallen rapidly. Her emotions swung from irritation with Jake to genuine concern that something might have happened.

Finally she knew she had to do something. There was no phone to call out with and the thought of a trek to call on Mr. Brunson for help was abandoned when she realized that the hike up there would be as arduous as the hike out to the road. Besides, it might accomplish nothing—Mr. Brunson was old and could hardly be expected to traipse through such large snowdrifts.

There was only one thing to do, and that was go herself. Resolved, Hannah bundled up in her thickest coat and pulled on a pair of Jake's pants under her dress. She wrapped two scarves around her neck, but when she opened the cabin door, the wind still cut through them like a knife. It then occurred to her that she needed light and perhaps a blanket for when she found Jake. Obviously something was wrong by now, and she might as well go prepared.

In the bedroom, she pulled Jake's torch out from under the bed, draped a blanket over her arm, and set off once again.

The first snowdrift was worse than expected, and she almost floundered, tempted to turn back. In her imagination, she could see Jake pass her in the dark, beat her home, and laugh heartily when she got there herself.

But it was not possible, she told herself. Jake would see the light if he walked past her. He had to be out here somewhere.

"Jake," she yelled, and the wind took her words away.

Hannah pressed on, following Jake's tracks around a snow bank. With the depth of snow here, she sank in above her boots even when she stayed in his tracks.

"Jake," she tried again but soon gave up. She needed all her energy just to move forward.

It seemed like forever, her eyes glued to the tracks in the snow, before the main road came into sight. It appeared plowed with some snow drifting back.

"Jake," she hollered with what strength she had left.

"Here!"

She heard the distinct voice, but it wasn't a voice of alarm. Surely Jake wasn't playing games with her. "*Where?*" she yelled back, finding new energy come into her body.

"Over here—beside the post," the answer came back.

Hannah walked past the next drift, and there he was, seated on the ground, the snow scraped away from where he sat.

"What happened?" she asked.

"I twisted my ankle," Jake said, rubbing his leg. "I got the mail and made it this far back. I knew you'd come. There's a letter from your mom," he said, pulling it out of his pocket as a fresh blast of wind rushed at them.

"Are you really hurt?" she asked.

"Of course," he said. "I wouldn't make you come out in this weather just for a joke."

"How'd you know I'd come?"

"Because you're a good wife," he said. "Now help me up."

"I can help you up, but I can't carry you," she said, stating the obvious.

"You can't get Mr. Brunson either," Jake said, having reached the same conclusion Hannah had arrived at earlier.

"Now what?" Her teeth began to chatter from the cold.

"First, I'll take the blanket." Jake held out his hand. "Thanks." He wrapped it tightly around himself.

"I only brought one," she said.

"It's enough," he said. "Go back to the barn and harness Mosey. Tie one of the traces on the little sled. There's a rope on the wall. I'll get both traces on when you come back. Ride the horse, though—don't walk back."

"You'll be okay?"

"Yes," Jake nodded. He shifted his weight on the ground and said with a laugh, "I'm not going anywhere."

Thirty-eight

Hannah struggled back up the driveway toward the barn, pushing hard through the snow, her breath coming in gasps. Twice she had to stop and take shelter behind a snowbank to rest for a moment.

Finally she reached the barn, tugged open the door, and barged in. Mosey looked up, seemingly curious as to why she was there. Hannah quickly moved the horse from his stall, threw on the harness, found the sled, and tied on the rope.

She almost got tangled up in the awkward contraption as she led Mosey outside. The horse objected to the wind, shaking his head in protest. She talked quietly to him, telling him that Jake needed them and he had to be a good horse and behave.

Her voice seemed to calm him down. He even stood still while she clambered up onto him by standing on a leather strap. She shook the lines draped across Mosey's neck to get the horse to move—if only at a dull plod. Even so, the trip went considerably faster than it had on foot.

When she got close, Jake called out to remind her where he was. When she reached the spot, she started to get down but thought better of it. She deftly maneuvered Mosey into place, close enough to Jake so he could tie the other tug on. Jake managed to pull himself up on one leg and soon had the sled rigged so that he could lie on it. When he was ready, he had to yell to Hannah to be heard over the wind. She urged Mosey forward and glanced back occasionally to see Jake hanging on and bouncing through the snow.

Hannah ignored Jake's requests to take him to the barn so he could help her unhitch. Instead she pulled as close to the front porch as the horse could go.

"Thanks, big man," she told him through frozen lips, "but tonight you listen. Get inside."

"Okay," he grumbled, hopping off the sled and releasing the tugs before he went inside, half crawling toward the front door.

When Hannah came in from the barn, Jake had his leg up on a chair and his sock off. His ankle was visibly red and swollen.

"Is it broken?" she asked.

"I don't think so," he said, wincing as she felt his ankle for a sign of a break.

"Some pain pills," she said, heading for the bathroom cabinet. She came back with three Advil tablets and a glass of water. Jake gulped them down without complaint.

"You should see a doctor," she said.

"On a night like this? No. Besides, it's just a sprain."

"How do you know that?"

"I just do. Besides, we can't get out anyway."

That Jake was right was obvious, so she relented and instead brought him his dinner on a tray.

"Your letter," he groaned, pulling the now wet envelope out of his pocket.

"I'll look at it later," she answered, waving it off.

"I'm okay. Read it now," Jake said as he handed it to her.

Hannah seated herself on the couch and opened the letter carefully.

"Read it out loud," Jake said. "After this, I need some entertainment."

Hannah rolled her eyes in a tease, but read the letter aloud.

Dear loved ones,

I hope this finds you all well. Our first snow came last week, just a light dusting, but we loved it. Dad seems well recovered from the accident, for which we are thankful.

Christmas will be at Aunt Esther's—a big affair. It would
be nice to have both of you here, but we understand.

"It's boring," Jake said and groaned. "I wanted entertainment."

"Don't be complaining already," Hannah said. "Betty was right. You
men are not very good patients."

"I'll be a better patient when those pain pills take hold."

"Give them time," Hannah said, realizing she was sounding just like
a mother. *Now isn't that something new? Mothering Jake,* she thought
with a secret smile.

"Finish your letter," Jake said wearily, "in quiet, though. On second
thought, I'm not up to hearing it. Now if it was from my mother…"

"That would be nice, but it wasn't that long ago that you wrote her,
and you haven't heard back from her. Maybe she's busy. Mothers can
be, you know. Perhaps if you write her again, she'll write back."

"My leg hurts too much now."

"Not now, silly. I didn't mean that. Later."

"Looks like I'll be here for a while," Jake muttered, glaring at his leg.
"How clumsy can one be?"

"You didn't have to go get the mail," Hannah reminded him. "Just
be thankful we could get you back to the house on a night like
this."

Jake just groaned again.

"Do you want to go to bed?"

"Not till this pain lets up."

As it turned out, the pain didn't allow Jake to sleep until after midnight. Hannah stayed up with him until he finally wanted to get up
from the couch and try to get in bed. Gingerly they made their way
into the bedroom with Jake using a broom for a crutch.

In the morning the snow had stopped, and the sun came up in a
blaze of white glory. Hannah let Jake sleep late. He couldn't go to church
with his swollen foot even if there had been no drifts on their road.

Hannah expected a snowplow to come up from the main road any-time, but none showed by the time Jake finally awoke. He looked so rumpled and sleepy-eyed Hannah laughed out loud.

"You certainly don't look like a preacher now," she teased.

"I suppose not," he said. "You think anyone from church will come looking for us?"

"They'll just think we're snowbound," Hannah said, actually enjoy-ing the chance to stay home on a Sunday. The feeling was delicious—just she and Jake and no place to go. "They probably didn't have church anyway."

Jake laughed. "No, during winter in Montana, the snow doesn't stop. They probably did have church."

Hannah thought about it and considered that he was probably right. "Well, maybe so, but they can have church without you. Now, I seem to remember something about a letter to your mother…"

"Okay, okay," Jake said. He got out his letter pad and began a letter to his mother. Hannah playfully tried to read it over his shoulder, but he covered it up every time she got close.

"I'll mail it tomorrow," he said, "when we go in to have this ankle looked at."

"Tomorrow is Christmas," she reminded him.

"Oh, right. I guess I forgot." Jake shook his head as if trying to clear it.

Hannah watched him and said, "You sure you didn't hurt your head last night?"

"I don't think so," he said

Just then they both heard the noise of the snowplow on the main road. Hannah looked out the window to see the plow as it passed below their driveway. Then, behind the plow, as if waiting to get through, was Mr. Brunson's truck. But instead of following the plow along the main road, the pickup turned into the driveway.

Hannah went out to the porch to let Mr. Brunson know they were home in case he wanted something.

"Are you folks okay?" Mr. Brunson called from his truck.

"Jake sprained his ankle last night," Hannah called back.

That produced an "Oh" from Mr. Brunson. He drove into the

driveway, parked his truck, and stepped onto the porch where Hannah was waiting to invite him in.

"Hello," Jake said from the couch, his foot propped up on a chair.

"So what have you done, young man?" Mr. Brunson demanded.

"Oh, I insisted on walking to the mailbox and got careless, I guess," Jake said.

"You've seen a doctor?" Mr. Brunson asked.

Jake shook his head. "Not with the roads like they've been. And now it's the holiday weekend."

"You can go to Urgent Care in Libby," Mr. Brunson said. "Now, let me take a look at that ankle."

"We heard the plow. I guess that means the roads are open now," Jake said, pulling up his pant leg to reveal his swollen ankle.

"Wiggle your toes," Mr. Brunson said.

Jake wiggled them as much as he could.

"Turn your foot." Mr. Brunson gently felt the ankle as Jake pivoted his foot from side to side.

"So what do you think?" Jake asked, hoping for a positive answer.

"Well, it's not broken," Mr. Brunson said. "I'm not a doctor, though. You should have it X-rayed."

"After Christmas," Jake said, "if it's not better."

"Sure you don't want me to take you in?" Mr. Brunson asked. "I'm going that way."

Jake shook his head. "No, not if it's not broken."

Mr. Brunson shrugged. "Suit yourself. Tuesday's a long way off."

"We'll make it," Jake assured him.

"All right, then. My advice is to stay off that foot as much as possible… and go see a doctor on Tuesday." With that, Mr. Brunson left.

"I can't have this lay me up very long," Jake said. "Mr. Howard has quite a few orders lined up."

"I'm sure you'll mend just fine," Hannah said hopefully.

During the rest of the afternoon, she thought of several ways to cheer Jake up but couldn't settle on anything. Popping up a batch of popcorn didn't really suit the occasion, and besides, she had no apple cider to serve with it. She wished someone would visit, but no one knew about Jake's injury. People likely figured they were simply snowed in.

Jake finished his letter and sealed it with a lick and then said, "My ankle is starting to throb. Can you give me some more pills?"

"Every four hours—" she told him firmly, "no more than that."

Jake groaned and lay back down on the couch.

The lonely Christmas holiday came and went in much the same way. Betty and Steve were hosting Steve's family for the holidays, so there was really no other place to go, even if Jake hadn't injured his ankle.

Hannah made snow cream by scooping up a large bowl of snow from the drift near their front porch. To her delight, Jake clearly enjoyed the treat. She then suggested they play some games, but Jake didn't want to.

Instead he wanted to sing a song and read the Christmas story from the Bible. She agreed and sat beside him on the couch. They sang a Christmas song, but because it was just the two of them, it didn't sound quite right to Hannah. Jake read the first two chapters of Luke with great tenderness and then offered a prayer.

"Those were some times back then," he said as he set the Bible down. "Angels…I wonder why we don't see angels anymore."

"Maybe we have to live out in the hills," Hannah said with an image of the shepherds tending their flocks flitting through her mind.

"That must have been a glorious sight," Jake said with awe in his voice. "A sky full of angels. What must that have been like? Such singing."

"Better than ours!" Hannah said.

Jake laughed. "I suppose so."

"What must it have been like to be with child and without a husband?" Hannah asked, shivering at the thought. "Do you think anyone believed her?"

"Some did," Jake said. "Elizabeth believed her."

"Just think, Jake. Mary talked to an angel, just like that—face-to-face." Hannah drew closer to Jake on the couch.

"He shall be great," Jake quoted, "and shall be called the Son of the Highest."

Outside, the wind was blowing across the drifts, swirling the snow around the living room window.

"Yes, those were the days," Jake said as Hannah nestled even closer.

They sat there comfortably, lost in their thoughts until finally Hannah got up and fixed their Christmas supper. It was a simple meal, and they ate it early. Almost immediately after the meal, Jake said he was ready for bed even at this early hour.

Hannah stayed up for another hour, rereading her mother's letter and then the two chapters from the Bible Jake had read. In the peace and sleepiness that followed, she joined Jake in bed.

Thirty-nine

Having gone to bed early the night before, Jake woke up early Monday morning and got up right away. He wanted to stop in at Betty and Steve's house on the way into Libby. He seemed to think it necessary to make contact with someone because they hadn't been to church.

Hannah went out to the barn, readied Mosey, and then pushed the buggy into the driveway. The snow was still abundant, covering a quarter of the wheels in places. Jake hobbled out with his broomstick crutch, stuck it under the backseat, and climbed in. Hannah had Jake hold the lines as she went back inside for an extra blanket.

The snow had stopped falling in the night, and the morning sky dawned clear blue. Jake took care not to bump his foot against the buggy dash by holding it with one hand when they turned and drove out onto the main road.

Betty raced out the kitchen door when they pulled up, the straps of her boots still loose. "Where *were* you two?" she exclaimed before Hannah got the buggy door open. "I had to stay around the house all day yesterday. Steve's relatives stayed much later than planned."

"We survived, but that's about all," Hannah said grimly.

"Were you snowed in?" Betty asked. "That's what everyone thought on Sunday."

"Kind of," Hannah grinned. "Jake sprained his ankle Saturday night. We're on our way to the doctor now."

"Sprained it?" Betty asked, her voice full of concern. "Is it broken? How do you know it's just sprained?"

"So you *did* have church?" Jake asked. "There's no way I could have gotten out until the plow opened our road."

"That's what we figured," Betty said. "The foot, though, how bad is it?"

"Mr. Brunson looked at it," Hannah said. "He thought it probably wasn't broken."

"What does Mr. Brunson know," Betty said. "The foot needs to be seen by a doctor."

"Yes, we know," Hannah agreed. "We're on our way. Dr. Lisa will probably see him. Think we should call her office ahead of time?"

"I'd just go in," Betty said. "You might have to wait a little. You should have tried to go in right away."

"Jake didn't want to," Hannah said. "Besides, the snow and the holiday—"

"So like a man," Betty huffed.

Jake urged Mosey to go faster as they drove into Libby and finally arrived at Dr. Lisa's office. Hannah tied the horse while Jake hopped toward the door without his broom. She caught up with him in time to hold the door open.

Inside, Jake told the receptionist what had happened and was soon taken back for an X-ray. When he came out, he told Hannah the doctor hadn't seen him yet and that he was supposed to wait.

A short time later, Dr. Lisa invited Jake and Hannah to come back to the examining room. She showed them the X-ray, confirmed that it was just a sprain, and instructed Jake to keep his ankle wrapped and take a pair of crutches home with him. He would be good to go in a week or so.

"And how about you, Hannah?" Dr. Lisa asked when she was done with Jake's instructions. "Are you doing okay?"

"I think so," she replied, not really sure if she was or not.

"That's a good girl. Take care of yourself." Then she was gone.

Hannah stayed in the buggy while Jake went into the hardware store, looking quite capable with his new crutches.

When a good twenty minutes passed and Jake failed to come out, Hannah was almost ready to tie up the horse and go see what was keeping him. Surely Mr. Howard hadn't persuaded him to do any work today.

Just then the hardware door opened, and she saw first the crutches and then Jake move out of the building. He swung smoothly across the parking lot and used his good foot to hop onto the buggy step. Hannah handed him the reins, and they were off.

On the edge of town she glanced over at Jake who had said nothing since he got in the buggy.

"Does the ankle hurt?" she asked.

"Mr. Howard let me go," he said simply.

"What?" A feeling of alarm surged through her.

Jake just nodded, his eyes on the road.

"Why?" she demanded. "I thought you were doing so well."

"Too well, I guess," Jake said grimly. "His nephew is taking over the furniture making."

"How can he do that?"

"There's no reason why he can't. I worked for him."

"But it was you who made the furniture."

"Mr. Howard says anyone can make furniture." Jake's face was glum. "I don't believe that, but that's just what he said. He said I can't possibly keep up with the demand while I'm hobbling around like this. He figures his nephew can work faster than I can—and probably cheaper—although he didn't say that."

"But he gave you a bonus for being so good."

"Maybe he was already planning on this and was trying to make it easier."

"So what are you going to do?"

"I don't know." Jake shook the reins as if to emphasize some point. What point, Hannah wasn't sure.

When they got home, Jake hopped through the doorway while Hannah took the horse to the barn and tried to think of something for lunch, her mind still in a spin. Jake was in the kitchen when she came in, his crutches under his arm.

"What are you doing?" she asked him.

"Maybe I can do something in the kitchen," he said, and his voice nearly broke.

She took him by the arm into the living room and made him sit on the couch.

"We'll make it somehow," she said, putting her arm on his shoulder.

"I suppose so," he said, his eyes dull.

"You'll think of something," she said, desperately wondering what that could be.

Her thoughts were interrupted by Jake's kiss on her cheek. "You're too good for me," he said, his voice catching again.

"No," she said, blushing and allowing herself to be pulled into Jake's embrace.

They held each other for a long moment and looked out the cabin window at the snow. The barn stood out in sharp relief against the blue sky.

The snow didn't melt all week because the temperature rarely rose above freezing, and then on Saturday another storm moved in. Thankfully, the snowplow came up their road sometime after midnight, which allowed them to attend church. Jake didn't have to preach, for which Hannah was glad. All week, his troubled face had conveyed the stress they both felt. She couldn't imagine what kind of sermon he would preach had it been his turn.

To pass his time, Jake read most of the daylight hours away and said little about what they would do about their future. What *could* he say? It might take till spring to find more work—if even by then. At least for now, their mortgage was paid up, and they had a little food stored.

They could eke out an existence for a while, she supposed. But tomato soup was sure going to become boring, that was for sure.

Hannah soon found out she was wrong about Jake's lack of a plan. He started to exercise his ankle the following week, testing it carefully before he placed weight on it. That was his plan number one—getting better.

Three days later, he limped out to the barn. When he stayed out there for a good hour, Hannah thought she had better check on him. She found him measuring the back side of the lean-to, which was attached to the barn, and scratching figures with paper and pencil.

"I'm turning this into a shop," he announced when she walked in. That was apparently plan number two.

"But money? It takes money to start up something like this," she reminded him.

He nodded. "Yes, I know. But maybe only a little if I'm willing to start small. I can borrow a few tools from John and Steve until I sell some pieces."

"You're not serious?"

When he turned, she knew by the set of his jaw that he was.

In the days ahead, Jake constructed a makeshift workshop by nailing backboard to a few simple stud walls with tools borrowed from Steve. He then installed a wood stove to heat the small shop. Jake's only investments were in the wood and parts he needed.

Hannah started to take his lunch to him in the *shop room*, as Jake called it. His breakfast and supper, he ate in the house.

A few days into the construction, Mr. Brunson stopped by for a visit. Hannah directed him out to the shop room and then went back to the laundry. She watched, though, as the two men spoke. Mr. Brunson must have asked Jake something because she saw him shake his head.

A few days later, Mr. Brunson visited again. What he and Jake talked about was unknown to Hannah, although she thought she saw Jake shake his head a little less vigorously this time.

When yet another hard blizzard blew in, Betty said this was the hardest winter she had been through. Toward the end of January, another blizzard arrived, this time from Canada. All this and the Christmas snow hadn't even begun to melt.

Even on the coldest days, Jake worked like a man on a mission, mostly by hand because he had no power tools. He told Hannah if Jesus could work with hand tools, he could too. But when the blisters appeared, Hannah told him to quit—they could live on tomato soup and potatoes until spring.

When he refused to let up, Hannah drove Mosey down to Betty's to ask for salve. Betty started to ask questions immediately, and Hannah spilled the whole story through her tears.

"There's nothing you can do," Betty said, "except help him."

"But he works from dawn to dusk." Hannah said, wiping her tears with the back of her hand.

"A man must work," Betty said. "That's his nature. What's he making?"

"I haven't seen it," Hannah admitted.

"Then go look," Betty said, her arm around her shoulder. "Just remember you have a good man. Don't ever forget that."

When she got home, Hannah took the salve and bandages out to Jake. He quit willingly enough, so she could wrap his hands.

"It's really nothing," he said with a grin. "You shouldn't make such a fuss."

"I'm not making a fuss," she said. And then she remembered Betty's advice. "Will you tell me what you're making?" She glanced around but saw only pieces of wood and small logs on the floor.

Jake hesitated, then grinned, and pulled a small rocker from behind his work table, still unvarnished but done.

"My third try," Jake said. "This one is good enough. Can I varnish it indoors?"

Hannah didn't have to think twice. She just nodded. The rocker was beautiful, and it was obvious how hard he had labored over it.

Jake carried the rocker inside and carefully set it on sheets of paper from the *The Budget* Hannah had placed on the floor. Later, when he came in for supper, he explained how she could varnish it the next day. In the morning, she applied the first coat right after breakfast.

During the next several weeks, they worked out a system for finishing the pieces, including a large log desk, which took both Mr. Brunson and Hannah's help to move into the house. After Hannah had given it three coats of varnish, it fairly glowed in the light of the gas lantern.

"Good job," Jake said approvingly.

"Now to sell it," Hannah replied.

"I know. We'll think of something."

Forty

One Sunday morning Hannah sat in silent amazement watching Jake preach. *How does he do it?* She knew that last night he was worried about his message. He had even tossed and turned in his sleep, but all that was gone now.

Jake was quoting what sounded like Scripture. He said the words slowly and reverently. When he had memorized them, Hannah had no idea. His eyes swept over the congregation, his chin was firm, and his beard had already grown down to the second button on his shirt.

Hannah didn't quite know what to do with the deep and various emotions she felt. Sorrow still lingered around the edges, but in the center something was growing. It was a feeling she didn't quite know how to describe—a swelling of admiration and awe for this man.

Of course, to show her emotion in church was completely out of the question; she simply beheld in her heart the wonder of what Jake had become. That they now faced the next mortgage payment on their cabin seemed insignificant at the moment. Though fear and uncertainty would surely return, for now it seemed enough to know that Jake was hers and would be with her no matter what happened.

Jake concluded his sermon and then asked for testimonies. After four men had spoken, Jake closed the service. He did that also, Hannah thought, almost without effort. Afterward she saw Bishop Nisley speak with Jake, and from Jake's expression, she was sure it had nothing to do with his sermon.

"He wanted to know how we're doing," Jake said on the way home, "because I have no job."

She waited and then turned to look at him. "And?"

"I told him I was building furniture on my own with Steve's tools."

"And?" Hannah asked again.

"He said he was glad to hear that, and if I needed help to let him know."

"Did you tell him you haven't sold anything?"

"No," Jake said. "It's not the time yet. We have to try first. Maybe in town on Monday?"

"Where?"

"Maybe Mac's Market?"

Hannah envisioned them standing inside some corner of the market, embarrassed and trying to sell log furniture to people who simply rushed on by. She had a hard time imagining it.

"It's not really a good time, I guess," Jake said, pulling on the reins to turn Mosey onto their road. "People spent their money at Christmas. Still, we have to try."

Hannah shuddered. "I suppose so," she managed.

"I'll do it," Jake said, picking up on her reaction. "I'm not expecting you to."

"But you need to be making more furniture. You can't do that and sell at the same time."

"I know that, but there's no sense in making more if we can't sell it."

The words hung in the air, an awful finality about them. Hannah remembered the hours Jake had labored and the cold he had endured while working in the barn. Was this then to be the end? The risk, was it all for nothing?

Behind them came the sound of an automobile, and Jake pulled over to let it pass. The dark blue jeep drove around them slowly. Hannah caught a good look at the driver, a young man in his late twenties or so. He seemed to be unsure of himself and kept to a slow pace even after he had passed their buggy.

"Not someone we know," Jake commented.

"Maybe someone to see Mr. Brunson?"

"I've never seen him have any visitors."

The thought went through Hannah's mind like fire. "It's his son!" she said, grabbing Jake's arm.

"Surely not," Jake said.

"Wouldn't that be something?" Hannah breathed in deeply. "What if it is?" She could see it as clear as day—the man getting out of his car, Mr. Brunson coming to his door, and the astonished look on his face. But what would the reaction be? Was the son angry? Would he confront his father? Or would there be tears and embraces? Oh, surely the latter, she hoped.

"You are dreaming again," Jake said with a smile.

"It's still a sweet dream," she said. "I hope it comes true."

"He's probably just a hunter who has lost his way or maybe scouting for next season."

"I like my version better," Hannah said as Jake turned Mosey into their driveway.

"Mr. Brunson hasn't even talked about his family lately."

"Why doesn't he just go visit and get it over with, no matter if it's rejection. At least then he'd know."

"I guess he can't handle it if it is a rejection. I suppose he'd rather not know at all than risk the anger of a loved one."

"But it's his son," Hannah said firmly, stepping out of the buggy. She waited on the porch while Jake took Mosey to the barn, and then walked into the cabin with him.

"I think I should make something extra for supper—something special," she said.

"What for? Are Betty and Steve coming over?"

"No, I'm thinking Mr. Brunson might bring his son down. I'd like them to stay for supper."

Jake raised his eyebrows but didn't comment.

"I might even make a cherry pie."

"On a Sunday?"

"It's a special occasion."

Jake laughed. "I guess we'll just have cherry pie, then. That will make it a special occasion in any event."

"They will come," Hannah said. "I know they will."

When the afternoon was drawing to a close, they were both sitting on the couch, lost in their own thoughts. Hannah was still thinking of Mr. Brunson. Jake was considering how he could sell his furniture the next day.

As Hannah gave up her idea of a cherry pie, the evening began to look long and dreary. Eventually she suggested they go somewhere—perhaps a visit to Betty or the young folks' hymn sing that evening. But before Jake could answer, they heard the sound of Mr. Brunson's pickup in the driveway. When they looked out the window, they saw the young man from the jeep sitting in the passenger seat.

"It's Mr. Brunson," Jake said.

"And look who's with him," Hannah said smugly, wishing now she had baked that cherry pie.

Jake opened the cabin door and waited. Hannah couldn't resist and stood behind him, looking over his shoulder. Mr. Brunson came up the walk with the young man close behind.

When Mr. Brunson got closer and looked up at her, she knew her dream would be coming true. There were tears in his eyes.

"My son, Eldon," he said. "This is Jake and Hannah Byler. I just had to stop in and let you know."

Mr. Brunson's eyes shone brighter than Jake or Hannah had ever seen before.

"I'm glad to meet you," Eldon said, stepping forward and extending his hand. "Dad said you two look after him real good."

"No," Jake said, "it's more like he looks after us."

"Just don't let him shoot any more bears," Eldon said with a laugh. "One was all we needed."

"So you did notice?" Jake asked.

Eldon glanced at Mr. Brunson. "Dad said he told you. We did notice—it was the first clue we had since Dad left. I've been looking hard. After all, I lost two members of my family—my mother and my sister—and I couldn't stand to lose my dad too."

"I guess I just let my grief get the best of me," Mr. Brunson said, making no attempt to hide his tears.

"I would have told him all that," Eldon said. "It wasn't his fault. No one ever said it was. He just disappeared on us. I never blamed him."

"What will you do now?" Jake asked. "Will you move back East?"

"I don't think so," Mr. Brunson said, "at least not just now. I like it here too much. I'll visit—often, I guess. Eldon drives back to Missoula tonight and flies out in the morning."

"Well, won't you come in?" Jake asked, as if he suddenly remembered Hannah's prediction. "Hannah was going to make a cherry pie. When we saw the jeep pass us on the way home from church, she was sure the driver was your son."

"We really do have to be on our way, Dad," Eldon said, glancing at his watch. "Maybe on some other visit?"

"Of course," Hannah said. "Let us know when you're coming again. We'll plan a real nice dinner."

The men shook hands with Jake again and turned to leave. Then Mr. Brunson turned back and said, "Oh, one more thing. I know it's kind of sudden. I'd like to send a piece of your furniture along with Eldon. I'm sure he can find someone who will want to buy handcrafted Amish furniture."

Eldon chimed in, "I sure can. Most of the *Englishers* are charmed by your good work. We pay good money for it too."

Mr. Brunson continued, "As a matter of fact, I've been giving this some thought, and I think Eldon just showed me the last piece of the puzzle. Jake, perhaps this spring I could help you out with a better place to work—maybe in town. Maybe I can get you set up right so you can produce a lot of this stuff. You do real good work."

"That's awfully nice of you, Mr. Brunson," Jake said, "but..."

"It's not charity, Jake. I'd be investing in you. In a sense you'd be working for me in the same way you worked for your Mr. Howard. Now, do you have a piece Eldon can take with him to the airport?"

"I have a small rocker that might work," Jake said, still in a sort of daze over this unexpected attention.

"Good!" Mr. Brunson said. "Can you get it ready so Eldon can take it with him and ship it from Missoula?" Mr. Brunson paused. "You *do* like the idea, don't you?"

"Like it?" Jake asked, but the relief and joy on his face gave the best answer.

"Dad, we really have to be going," Eldon said.

"Jake, go get your rocker," Mr. Brunson said.

In just a few minutes, Jake had the rocker in the back of Mr. Brunson's pickup truck, and after words of thanks from Jake, father and son left.

"Do you really think he can sell your furniture?" Hannah asked.

"It does seem too good to be true. I guess we have to wait and see."

"Jake, you deserve to succeed in this. You really do. I hope it happens."

"God doesn't decide things that way," Jake said.

"Maybe He will this time," Hannah said. Then she added, "Isn't it wonderful about Eldon? Now he and his father are reunited. That's the best part of the whole thing."

"That it is," Jake agreed.

"Jake, I'd love to tell Betty the news. Do you think it's too late?"

"Not if we go now," Jake said, sounding just as eager as Hannah to share their news. "Let's go," Jake said, grabbing his coat.

When they pulled into Betty's driveway minutes later, they were warmly welcomed in. From the living room, Steve hollered, "The starving and the poor are welcome. We have food."

"Steve," Betty said, "that's not nice."

Jake just grinned as Hannah said, "Tell them our news, Jake."

Betty and Steve both perked up as Jake said, "Well, it looks like the clouds could be breaking up for us…and sunny days could be just ahead."

"Mr. Brunson may be able to sell Jake's furniture," Hannah said, too excited to wait for Jake to say it.

"How's that?" Steve asked.

"His son came to visit from the East and thinks he can sell my work back there for a good profit. I think it might actually work out," Jake said.

"That is good news!" Betty exclaimed. "I was so worried about you two."

"Good news indeed," Steve agreed.

"It's God's doing," Jake said, "and we're very thankful."

Hannah just nodded.

Betty and Hannah then went to the kitchen to prepare a fruit plate. In the middle of slicing apples, Hannah told Betty about Eldon and Mr. Brunson's happy reunion.

"That is so wonderful," Betty said, her eyes edged with tears. "He could have ended up old and lonely and never reunited with his son."

Hannah smiled her agreement.

Betty stopped in mid slice and said, "Oh, Hannah! I just thought of something. You really owe all this to that troublesome bear."

Hannah thought for a second and said, "I don't understand."

"Don't you see? If that bear hadn't shown up, Mr. Brunson never would have shot it. If he hadn't shot it, he wouldn't have been fined. And if he hadn't been fined, his son wouldn't have found him. Why, if Mr. Brunson's interest in Jake's furniture proves out, then that too is a result of all this trouble with the bear, at least as far as having Mr. Brunson's son sell it for him back East."

"I never thought of it that way," Hannah said, "but I suppose you're right."

Hannah finished the apples and added the grapes and oranges Betty handed to her. She carried the plate back to the men while Betty followed with water glasses. They ate and chatted till after nine when Jake said they had to get home. He had work to do tomorrow.

When they went to bed that night, Hannah told Jake what Betty had said about the bear.

Jake thought for a moment and said, "I think she's right. God does work in mysterious ways sometimes. That bear did bring about some good for us…and even more for Mr. Brunson."

On the following Tuesday afternoon, Mr. Brunson stopped by with the news that Eldon wanted more pieces of Jake's handiwork. He also left a check, representing Jake's share of the rocking chair sale. He said Eldon wanted the pieces—large or small—shipped as soon as Jake could have them ready.

Two weeks later Mr. Brunson found a place to rent in Libby and set Jake up as the owner of his own furniture shop. Mr. Brunson told Jake he was investing in the shop and knew that both he and Jake would profit from the enterprise.

Within a week, Jake had things up and rolling; building baby rockers, log desks, and the specialty items Eldon ordered for his upscale clients. Jake also made a trip to Dr. Lisa's office with a baby rocker in hand as payment for her services after Hannah's miscarriage.

Spring broke early that year—according to Betty—and arrived with a warm breeze from the south. Hannah stood on the porch, watching Jake drive the buggy out of the driveway and onto the main road to go to his shop in Libby. The dawn had just broken, and the peaks of the Cabinet Mountains were splashed with reds, yellows, and bright oranges. The sight filled Hannah's soul to overflowing. She suddenly remembered her old desire to move to Indiana and then realized the thought had not crossed her mind in weeks.

"*This* is our home." She said the words softly, surprised that they were true.

"Yours too," she added a moment later. The awareness had come last night while Jake slept. Life had awakened inside her once again.

Discussion Questions

1. Do you believe Hannah had valid reasons to want to leave Montana? If so, what were the reasons and why do you think they were reasonable?

2. What responses does Mr. Brunson give to make Hannah believe he is hiding from past problems?

3. Do you think the game warden and other officials responded properly to Jake and Hannah's grizzly problem?

4. Have you or a family member ever experienced a pressure cooker malfunction? If so, describe the experience and the damage.

5. Regarding Jake's appointment to the Amish ministry, how does his experience differ from what is typically experienced in Protestant churches?

6. Why do you think Mr. Brunson so enjoyed the dinner and time spent with Hannah's parents?

7. Were Bishop John Nisley's fears for his new minister's future well-being groundless?

8. How well does Hannah handle her miscarriage?

9. As Jake's wife, describe Hannah's ability to fully accept her new responsibilities and handle the strains of marriage and ministry.

10. How has Hannah's faith in God's goodness grown? Do you believe it will continue to grow and become stronger? Why or why not?

About Jerry Eicher...

As a boy, **Jerry Eicher** spent eight years in Honduras, where his grandfather helped found an Amish community outreach. As an adult, Jerry taught for two terms in parochial Amish and Mennonite schools in Ohio and Illinois. He has been involved in church renewal for 14 years and has preached in churches and conducted weekend meetings of in-depth Bible teaching. Jerry lives with his wife, Tina, and their four children in Virginia.

The Adams County Triology
by Jerry Eicher

Rebecca's Promise

Rebecca Keim has just declared her love to John Miller and agreed to become his wife. But she's haunted by her schoolgirl memories of a long ago love—and a promise made and a ring given. Is that memory just a fantasy come back to destroy the beautiful present...or was it real?

When Rebecca's mother sends her back to the old home community in Milroy to be with her aunt during and after her childbirth, Rebecca determines to find answers that will resolve her conflicted feelings. Faith, love, and tradition all play a part in Rebecca's divine destiny.

Rebecca's Return

Rebecca Keim returns to Wheat Ridge full of resolve to make her relationship with John Miller work. But in her absence, John has become suspicious of the woman he loves. Before their conflict can be resolved, John is badly injured and Rebecca is sent back to Milroy to aid her seriously ill Aunt Leona.

In Milroy, Rebecca once again visits the old covered bridge over the Flatrock River, the source of her past memories and of her promise made so long ago.

Where will Rebecca find happiness? In Wheat Ridge with John, the man she has agreed to marry, or should she stake her future on the memory that persists...and the ring she has never forgotten? Does God have a perfect will for Rebecca—and if so how can she know that will?

Rebecca's Choice

Popular Amish fiction author Jerry Eicher finishes the Adam's County Trilogy with an intriguing story of a young couple's love, a community of faith, and devotion to truth. Rebecca Keim is now engaged to John Miller, and they are looking forward to life together. When Rebecca goes to Milroy to attend her beloved teacher's funeral, John receives a mysterious letter accusing Rebecca of scheming to marry him for money.

Determined to forsake his past jealousies and suspicions, John tries hard to push the accusations from his mind. Upon Rebecca's return, disturbing news quickly follows. She is named as the sole heir to her teacher's three farms. But there's a condition—she must marry an Amish man. When John confronts Rebecca, she claims to know nothing. Soon Rachel Byler, the vengeful but rightful heir to the property, arrives and reveals secrets from the past. Now the whole community is reeling!

Rachel's Secret
BJ Hoff

Bestselling author BJ Hoff promises to delight you with her compelling new series, The Riverhaven Years. With the first book, *Rachel's Secret*, Hoff introduces a new community of unforgettable characters and adds the elements you have come to expect from her novels: a tender love story, the faith journeys of people we grow to know and love, and enough suspense to keep the pages turning quickly.

When the wounded Irish-American riverboat captain, Jeremiah Gant, bursts into the rural Amish setting of Riverhaven, he brings chaos and conflict to the community—especially for young widow Rachel Brenneman. The unwelcome "outsider" needs a safe place to recuperate before continuing his secret role as an Underground Railroad conductor. Neither he nor Rachel is prepared for the forbidden love that threatens to endanger a man's mission, a woman's heart, and a way of life for an entire people.

Where Grace Abides
BJ Hoff

In the compelling second book in the series, Hoff offers you an even closer look at the Amish community of Riverhaven and the people who live and love and work there. Secrets, treachery, and persecution are only a few of the challenges that test Rachel's faith and her love for the forbidden "outsider," while Gant's own hopes and dreams are dealt a life-changing blow, rendering the vow he made to Rachel seemingly impossible to honor.

Many of the other characters first introduced in *Rachel's Secret* now find their gentle, unassuming lives of faith jeopardized by a malicious outside influence. At the same time, those striving to help runaway slaves escape to freedom through the Underground Railroad face deception and the danger of discovery.

All the elements you have come to expect from author BJ Hoff (romance, drama, great characters) join together in *Where Grace Abides* to fill the pages with a tender, endearing love story and a bold, inspiring journey of faith.

Shadows of Lancaster County
Mindy Starns Clark

Following up on her extremely popular Gothic thriller, *Whispers of the Bayou,* Mindy Starns Clark offers another suspenseful stand-alone mystery full of Amish simplicity, dark shadows, and the light of God's amazing grace.

Anna thought she left the tragedies of the past behind when she moved from Pennsylvania to California, but when her brother vanishes from the genetics lab where he works, Anna has no choice but to head back home. Using skills well-honed in Silicon Valley, she follows the high-tech trail her brother left behind, a trail that leads from the simple world of Amish farming to the cutting edge of DNA research and gene mapping.

Anna knows she must depend on her instincts, her faith in God, and the help of the Amish community to find her brother. She also must finally face her own shadows—and pray that she's stronger than the grief that threatens to overwhelm them all.

**The Homestyle Amish Kitchen Cookbook:
Plainly Delicious Recipes from the Simple Life**
by Georgia Varozza

Straight from the heart of Amish country, this celebration of hearth and home will delight you with the pleasures of the family table as you take a peek at the Amish way of life—a life filled with the self-reliance and peace of mind that many long for.

You will appreciate the tasty, easy-to-prepare recipes such as Scrapple, Graham "Nuts" Cereal, Potato Rivvel Soup, Amish Dressing, and Snitz Pie. At the same time you'll learn a bit about the Amish, savor interesting tidbits from the "Amish Kitchen Wisdom" sections, find out just how much food it takes to feed the large number of folks attending preaching services, barn raisings, weddings, work frolics, and much more.

Shoo-Fly Pie

2 8-inch unbaked pie crusts

SYRUP:	CRUMB TOPPING:
1 cup molasses	2 cups flour
½ cup brown sugar	¾ cup brown sugar
2 eggs, beaten	⅓ cup butter
1 cup hot water	½ tsp. cinnamon
1 tsp. baking soda, dissolved in hot water	

Mix syrup ingredients thoroughly together. Divide mixture in half and pour into the two unbaked pie shells. Thoroughly mix together the ingredients for the crumb topping. Divide and sprinkle crumb topping onto the two pies.

Bake at 450° for 10 minutes and then reduce heat to 350° and continue baking until done, about another 30 minutes. Enjoy!

CPSIA information can be obtained
at www.ICGtesting.com
Printed in the USA
LVOW01s2310260317
528557LV00007B/98/P